ALL FLASH BALDWIN'S FATHER LEFT HIM WAS A SIX-GUN—WITH ORDERS TO USE IT TO AVENGE HIS DEATH!

When Flash Baldwin's father is murdered, his only legacy to Flash is a six-gun. To Flash, this inheritance means only one thing—find the killer!

Avenging his father's death takes Flash Baldwin on the most dangerous search of his life—a search which becomes the most desperate manhunt the West has ever known.

COMING NEXT MONTH

THE BORDER BANDIT by Max Brand writing as Evan Evans (52-443, 50¢)

GUNMAN'S LEGACY

by Max Brand

writing as Evan Evans

PAPERBACK LIBRARY, Inc.
New York

CHAPTER 1

Old Tom Baldwin came home between the daylight and the dark, and when his mustang scuffed the deep sand outside the corral gate, he dismounted, sliding slowly out of the saddle, putting his feet gingerly, one at a time, upon the ground.

He stood, then, for a moment, resting his forehead against the rank, sweating shoulder of the horse, while his dulled eyes looked to the side toward the Rio Grande. No one would have thought it to be a wretched, muddy trickle; for now it was glorified with the last light from the west and ran golden and crimson, dull gold and dull crimson, between its banks. The banks themselves were disguised by a heaped dignity of purple shadows and blue.

When he had seen this, Old Tom undid the cinch knot. His fingers stumbled. To loosen the strap and let it run, he had to heave three separate times, crouching, using a log-lift as though to spare his stomach and back muscles. At last the cinch was loosened. He pulled the saddle off, and let it flop to the ground, where it sank and was half lost in the depth of the loosened soil. He paid no attention to this. He dragged off the bridle, pushed open the corral gate, and let the mustang go into the corral with a lurch, a snort, and a flourish of tail and heels.

"Damn her," said Old Tom. "She had plenty left. She was only dogging it home!"

He turned, and went past the saddle, which he allowed to lie where it fell, though usually he was a careful man about such things. He went on toward the house.

At the windmill he stopped. It was running with a well-oiled hum and a steady clanking. He listened to the gush of the water with pleasure and said to himself: "Skinny, he's a steady boy. He minds things pretty good."

Then he unhooked the dipper from the nail and held it under the water vent, where the stream burst out and fell with a heavy plump into the first of the long water troughs. The next pulse of the current almost knocked the dipper from his hand, then filled it, overflowed it, and he carried it dripping to his lips. His hand was shaking a little, and as he looked down into the face of the dipper he saw again a faint reflection from the sunset, like a thin stain of blood in the water.

He drank that dipper to the bottom. He drank another.

5

Then he leaned for a moment against the fence, breathing irregularly, gathering his strength, resting after the effort.

He let the dipper fall as he had let the saddle fall, and went on into the house, bent over, his feet dragging and scuffing the sand like one afflicted with a pain in the stomach, or nausea.

He leaned his shoulder against the kitchen door and walked into a swirl of steam and smoke. The face of the Negro cook appeared through this mist, shining with sweat. To add to the fog, he had a cigarette between his lips. He puffed at it. Little showers of ashes and burned paper fell off from time to time as he stirred a pot of frijoles, scraping well the bottom of the kettle.

"Where's the boys?" said Old Tom.

"They're out. They ain't rode in. They're coming pretty soon. You look sort of set back, Mistah Baldwin."

"Shut yer mouth," said Old Tom, and went out of the kitchen toward his own room.

It was at the back of the house, beside the store room, so that it was always fouled with the odors that seeped through the thin partition—the smell of spoiling potatoes, old onions, bacon sides picked for power to stay, not delicacy of flavor. But the room was fairly cool; it was on the north side of the house.

As he went down the hall, he hoped that the door was not locked. It would save him trouble if it were not locked. He hoped that it might be ajar; that would save him most of all.

He was in luck, for the door gave to the first push of his hand, and he went in. However, crossing the threshold his heel caught against the wash molding so that he stumbled, and this made him fall against the wall. He kept himself from falling by spreading his hands against the wall. A sick sweat ran down his face. The back of his head was moist with it, and his hands trembled against the wall. Suddenly he remembered how he had built that wall—the very look and the hot breath of the day.

There was hardly a ghost of light in the room, only dark drippings from the walls, and heaps of deeper shadows here and there, but nearly forty years of familiarity guided his feet to the bed. He lowered himself carefully upon it, turned on his back, pulled a blanket across his stomach, closed his eyes, and waited.

After a time, he heard the beat of hoofs, shouting and loud laughter from the corrals, and he knew that his sons had come in from their day's work. He thought of their brown faces, lean and hard, their flannel shirts with salty incrustations across the back. All of his boys were hard workers—all save one. They had helped him make the ranch—all save one.

Next, he heard them at the windmill and knew that they were

6

washing up for supper. They were laughing and joking. Other men might have been beat after a day's riding under such a scalding heaven, but the Baldwins were not the stuff that pegs out.

Then they came in; he heard the heavy tramp of their boots, making the whole floor of the house vibrate; he heard the jingling of their spurs, that passed through the cheap partitions of the house as if through paper walls. It seemed to be chiming in his own room, and he wondered how much blood had been drawn by those spurs on this day, for they were hard riders, all the Baldwins.

Next he heard the loud scraping of chairs as they sat down around the table, and the high, whining voice of the cook, asking about the day's work.

He closed his eyes again, and waited. He pulled another fold of the blanket across his stomach, and waited.

They were talking about the day's work. Shorty wanted to make a new tank on the ground that had been bought from Sol Myers. Two days' work with a plow and a scraper would heap up sufficient dam to hold a large body of water, he was saying. Well, Shorty always was the brains of the lot—save one.

At last he heard Skinny say: "Where's the old man? He oughta be back."

"He's back," said the cook.

"Where is he, then? He don't miss no meals."

"I dunno," said the cook. "Maybe he's in his room."

"What the hell does that mean?" said Trot. "I'm gunna go look."

"Finish your coffee," said another.

"No, I'm gunna look now," said Trot.

"The oldest kid, he's always got the love for you," said Old Tom. "And he's always got the smallest brain."

The rapid step of Trot came down the hallway; the heavy hand of Trot banged the door open.

"Hey, pa!" he called. "He ain't here," he added.

"Yeah. I'm here," said Old Tom.

"Hey, what're you doin' here in the dark? Nappin'?" said Trot.

"Nope. Dyin'," said Old Tom.

CHAPTER II

Trot lighted the lamp that stood on the table near the bed. It stood there because Old Tom used to sit up in bed and do accounts. Accounts had to be done, now that the ranch had grown to such a size. In the old days—which he often regretted—one could carry the sums in the memory, from month to month.

Trot looked down on him.

"What's the joke?" he asked. "You ain't gunna die, you old shoe leather, you!"

"Shut yer mouth," said Old Tom, "and fetch the rest of 'em."

Trot went and brought in the others. Old Tom watched their faces as they came through the doorway: Peter, young Tom, Joe, Dick, Hank, Bill. But they had other names. To the community—some twenty or thirty thousand square miles of range land and desert—they were known as Trot Peter, Single-jack Tom, Rabbit Joe, Blondy Dick, Shorty Hank, Skinny Bill. It saved time, to hitch on nicknames in this manner.

Blondy came last, still eating. Old Tom had numbered their faces, coming in. All there, save one.

"Where's Flash?" he asked. "Where's Flash David?"

For he had seven sons, and Flash David was the seventh and last.

"I dunno," said Trot Peter. "Nobody never knows where Flash is, except when he comes in for chow."

He spoke darkly. Darkly the other sons glanced at one another.

"I'm sick," said Old Tom. "I'm gunna die. I gotta have Flash here, too. Go look for him."

"You ain't gunna die!" said Trot. "Why, old Doc Forbes—"

"Where might he be?" asked Trot anxiously.

And the others stirred, with a harsh jangling of their spurs.

"I'll tell you where," said Old Tom. "Trot, you go down to Pazo, and you look through the tramp jungle under the bridge; if he ain't there, they may know where he is. Single-jack, you go out to Beckwith's saloon. He's likely there, I guess. Rabbit, where they're makin' up the big outfit for the drive north, he's pretty sure to be out there shakin' craps or playin' poker with the punchers there. They got a month's pay in their pants. Blondy, they's three new greaser horse breakers on the Tully place. Flash ain't likely to be nowhere but there. Short Hank, you slide down to the jail, and more'n likely you find him there, restin'. He's used to it, and he likes the cool of the place. Skinny, they's a gypsy outfit down by the river, and the best bet is that he's down there; he likes something new. Now, get your best hosses and scatter. I ain't got much time to wait."

They went hastily from the house.

"It's gotta be Flash," said Skinny, bitterly. "He's gotta have Flash. He can't do nothin', without that loafer."

"He's gunna die, and he's gunna leave about half of everything to Flash," said Blondy. "The rest of us, we can work our hide off for him, and he'll keep us on his payroll, maybe."

But they went out to the corrals and they wrangled their best horses out of the herd. Then each departed in his bidden direction.

Trot Peter Baldwin rode furiously down to Pazo, and through the town, and he came on the farther side of it to the great arch of the railway bridge. A thin moon was rising like a golden sword in the east, and beneath him, in the hollow, he saw among the shadows of the brush something like a flickering, golden star. It was like looking into water and seeing in it the reflection of a monstrous new planet. That was the tramp fire; cookery and boiling-up must be in progress there.

So Trot rode his mustang down the slope through the brush, finding a winding, precarious trail, until he came to a thick brake, and pushing through the brake he found five men seated around the fire. The excellent savors of a chicken mulligan steamed out of a wash boiler which was blackened and stewing over the fire.

"Get down, puncher, and rest your feet," said one of the tramps.

He looked them over. They were a wild lot. He despised them, but he feared them a little, as the law-abiding always fear the lawless.

"Any you boys seen Flash David?" he asked.

They all turned their heads and looked at him, silently.

"Who are you?" asked one of them.

"I'm his brother," said Trot. "I'm his older brother."

"Sure you are," said the first speaker. "And your middle brother is the man in the moon, ain't he?"

They all laughed, all the five. The laughed and stared at Trot, as though asking what he would do next.

"I'm his older brother, Trot Peter," said he, steadily. "His pa is dyin'. He's askin' for Flash. Have you seen him?"

"I ain't seen him today," said one of them. "Is Flash's old man really dyin'?"

"I'm gunna take Flash on the road with me," said another. "I always said that I'd get him to Chi with me, one day."

"You lie," said another. "South is the place for him. New Orleans, is what I say, and he goes with me."

"Who's this Flash?" asked a third of the group.

"One that ain't named wrong," came the answer, as Trot turned the head of his mustang and forced his way through the brush again, and then up the wooded bank of the draw.

Single-jack Tom went to Beckwith's saloon. There were other saloons in Pazo, but Beckwith's was half Mexican cantina and half American bar. He kept Mexican wine, and tequila, and there was even pulque here, now and then. Men of all nations crossed his threshold.

When Single-jack entered the place he made sure of the gun on his hip, then he walked up to the bar and faced Beckwith. Single-jack was a man among men. He had done his fighting, he had drawn his blood; but facing Beckwith was enough to trouble anyone. He looked up at the lofty figure, the lazy, hazel eyes, the untidy fall of mustaches on either side of his mouth.

"Beckwith," he said, "have you seen Flash David?"

Beckwith parted his moist mustaches with a thumb and forefinger. He finished an odd, milky-looking drink, took a napkin from under the bar, and dried the mustaches again. He wore a thoughtful look, this while. He seemed to be considering deeply.

"Juanna!" he called.

A pretty little soft-eyed Mexican woman came hastily through the rear doorway.

"Juanna, you seen Flash?"

Her face lighted. Then the light went out.

"He was here this morning. He was playing his guitar and singing with me."

"He was singing with you, was he?"

"Si, senor."

"You leave him sing by himself. You can listen better," said Beckwith.

A tall man with a fierce, hollow-cheeked face and yellow-stained eyes arose from the dark of a cool corner and strode to the bar.

"Who might be askin' for the Flash?" he demanded, staring grimly at Single-jack.

"Aw, it's only his brother," said Beckwith.

"Do *you* know where Flash might be?" asked Single-jack.

But the other turned his back without a word and walked off.

Single-jack was very angry. He muttered an oath and made a lurch to go after the tall stranger, but Beckwith reached across the bar and grabbed him by the shoulder. He shook his finger at Single-jack.

"Muy diablo!" said he.

So Single-jack left the saloon and rode home.

Rabbit Joe was as small as a jockey and rode as well as one. He went down by the river to the big holding corrals and pens where the herd was gathering for the long drive north. He found the red glare of the campfire and went to it.

And, around the campfire, he found a number of punchers gathered. Some of them were drinking night-black coffee which they dipped out of a great pot that simmered by the fire.

"Any you boys seen Flash David?" asked Rabbit.

The question struck the group to a blank silence.

Then up started a fellow with a bulldog look.

"Look at here," he said, "is that a joke, you damn little viper, you?"

"Whatcha mean?" asked Rabbit. "I'm askin' you, you seen my brother Flash around abouts here?"

The bulldog growled. So did the other men. And one of them, a wild-eyed youth, leaped up and said: "Your brother's a damn crook. The next time he comes out here with a crooked set of dice he's gunna get—"

"Shut up, kid," said another. "He licked us all, didn't he?"

"Who says my brother's a crook?" demanded Rabbit hotly. "I'll let light into you, you——!"

The camp boss strode between. His authority like a wall of shadow shut the two ready combatants away from one another.

"There ain't gunna be no more language," he said calmly. "But you tell your brother that he'd best keep off from this outfit if he don't want trouble."

"He wants trouble. He loves it. He lives on trouble," said Rabbit furiously, for all the Baldwins were a fighting lot.

"He don't want the kind of trouble that he'll find down here," said the boss, with undisturbed calm. "Now either set down and rest your tongue and feed your face, or else slope, brother, slope!"

So Rabbit sloped. "I'll have to fight for him, one day," he said to himself. "One day I'll get blowed to pieces on account of that worthless, lazy, no-account kid!"

Blondy went out to the Tully ranch which lies where the

Devil Mountains throw their shadow at prime. He went out to the bunkhouse and there he found a game of poker in progress. Three of the regular hands sat in on it, and three were Mexicans. By their eyes and their reckless faces; by the gleam of the ornamental clothes, and the conchos that ran in a chain of silver pools down their trouser legs, he knew that these were the horsebreakers with whom his father was so sure that he would find Flash.

" 'Lo," said Blondy from the doorway. "Any you boys seen Flash around here?"

One of the punchers looked at the Mexicans with a broad grin.

"Did you see Senor Baldwin, Don Flash, this morning?" he asked.

The three Mexicans rose like three rockets. Like three rockets they exploded.

"Here's his brother," said the malicious puncher.

They rushed at Blondy. He thought he was about to be knifed but, being a Baldwin, he put his back against the wall and gripped the butt of a gun. He delayed the draw to the last moment, as any good fighting man will, after he has seen blood a few times, his own or another's.

The Mexicans did not draw weapons. They merely clustered around Blondy and talked vociferously, with many gestures. There was such a babble of voices that Blondy, at first, could not untangle the meaning of so many remarks.

But gradually the thing cleared. It appeared that his youngest brother had appeared that morning with a rusty-looking, down-headed mustang under his saddle, that he had paused by the corral, that he had smiled at the operations of the Mexicans, that at last, when their tempers were hot, which meant that their minds were ductile to his handling, he had declared that even the children, in his part of the world, knew more about horses than these gentlemen did, and he bet them fifty dollars that his old mare would throw all three in turn.

They took the bet, they were bounced from the back of the old mare, and the boy went off with the money. But now the Mexicans were very wroth, for they had learned that the mare was a famous outlaw, subdued only to the cunning wiles of Flash David. They would not forget. There were other ways of paying debts than with money!

Curling their mustaches fiercely, they said their say.

And then Blondy rode home, chuckling to himself, and watching the moon sail like the Egyptian ship of the dead through the black waters of the east.

Shorty Baldwin rode into Pazo and stopped before the jail. There he heaved his squat, powerful, bowlegged body out of the saddle, threw his reins, walked up the front steps, and knocked at a door where few willingly presented themselves.

"Hullo?" said a gloomy voice inside.

"Hullo," said Shorty. "Hey, is Flash David inside of here?"

"Flash David?" answered an eager voice.

Then the door was pulled open. The jailor appeared there. He was grinning broadly.

"What's the kid done now?" he asked, with an air of pleasant anticipation.

"Plenty," said Shorty.

"Yeah, he's done plenty, always," said the jailor. "Rode any more hosses into any more saloons?"

"Not as I know of."

"A funny thing," said the jailor, "Beckwith drawin' his complaint after he'd jailed the kid! A kind of funny thing, that!"

"Yeah," said Shorty. "That was kind of funny. But you ain't had the kid or seen him today?"

"I ain't had that pleasure," said the jailor. "D'you ever hear that story he told me about the three greasers that had the knife, the string, and the—"

"Oh, damn his stories," said Shorty, and returned to his horse.

CHAPTER III

Skinny Baldwin had secured that name while he was still very young. He was not very old now. In age he was next to the youngest, the Flash himself. But he had grown out of the appropriateness of that nickname. He was tallest of the sons of Old Tom. He had the widest shoulders, and though there was no spare flesh on his body he was the toughest bundle of sinews and iron-hard muscle on the entire range. It was said of Skinny Baldwin that he could ride for three days without stopping, sleep three turns of the clock without waking thereafter, and thrive and grow fat on three meals a week. But what meals! He was a man who feared neither other men nor the wilderness. He had jumped off a bridge on a bet; he had ridden Tower, the famous outlawed gelding of the rodeos; he could shoot the cigarette out of your mouth or the eye out of your head.

Skinny mounted his best horse, according to his father's

order. It was a lofty black, with hipbones that stuck out like elbows, a head as long as a man's arm, and an eye as small as a dime and as red as blood. He got that horse on the Baldwin place not by priority, not because other people failed to know its good qualities of bone and blood, but simply because, outside of the Flash, he alone could ride it. And when had the Flash sufficient interest in anything on the ranch even to put in a claim?

He preferred to drift until he snagged, and then he waited for the current of life to float him away again. Home was to him less than the Bedouin's tent; he used it only now and then. And the sting in the souls of his brothers was they knew he loved the Flash better than all the rest.

On his bony black gelding, Skinny undertook the longest ride of all, clear down to the flats beside the river, where the scrub of willows made a dank tangle in winter, a thin shade in summer. Although it was the longest ride, he got to his goal before the rest, for he went on wings, like a great dark spirit scorning the ground he had to cover.

When he came to the willows, he saw no fire, but he smelled the smoke of one and followed it as accurately upwind as ever a red Indian could have done. As he jogged through the soft of the ground beneath the willows, he saw the moon skid through the branches high in the east, sailing like a bright shadow among ghostly boughs.

At last he saw the small wink of the fire.

As he came up to it, he dismounted, saw that both his guns were in working order—for he had the ambidextrous skill which permitted him to be a two-gun man—and then went forward. He knew that those who ventured alone, especially at night, among the children of Egypt, were taking their lives in their hands.

He saw them spilled in a loose encampment. It was only the first fire which he had seen. There were half a dozen others, with high-wheeled wagons beside them, and clutters and piles of nondescript household goods. The children were herding the livestock in the near-by clearings, where the grass was strong and thick. The adults and the infants sat about the fires or sprawled on the ground, and by the high lights that fell upon their faces Skinny Baldwin saw the dusk of the skin and the gleam of the slant eye.

They were the readiest thieves, knife men, and liars in the world. Skinny Baldwin felt like one who explored a new continent of humanity.

He stared over them, bewildered, and passed several of the fireside groups, searching each one of them. No one paid the slightest attention to him, though he could feel eyes

14

probing the small of his back as he passed on. But he saw no trace of the Flash.

At last a youth stood up and approached him with a step like a cat's.

"I speak pretty good English," he said. "You tell me what you want. Had a horse stolen?"

"Horse?" echoed Skinny, rather amazed by this frank inquiry.

"You wouldn't find it here," said the youth. "The horse we steal, we pass 'em along quick. We get 'em out of sight, into another county—or from here, it's an easy road into the Land of No Questions!"

He waved toward old Mexico.

He grinned as he spoke, and Skinny grinned back.

"Where'd you learn that kind of good English?" asked Skinny.

"Me? I learned it in jail. I done a stretch."

"You done a stretch and a yawn, I reckon," said Skinny. "You seen Flash David, down here tonight?"

"Flash David? Flash David?" said the other, emptily.

He might be lying, he might be really ignorant, Skinny knew.

So he said: "A young kid with an eye like a baby's and a skin like a girl's and a step like yours. Like a cat, I mean."

The other smiled again, his eyes turning into glittering slits.

"No," he said. "I would like to see him. I haven't seen him."

"Yeah," said Skinny, "sometimes he goes invisible, like a fairy tale. He could steal the cream off a cat's lips and it wouldn't know it had been robbed till it tried to lick 'em. He could pick diamonds out of a pawnbroker's hand while the man was blinkin' of his eyes. Sometimes he goes invisible, like I said, and you might of missed him."

"I might have missed him. I'm sorry I did," said the other.

"Lead me to the richest gambler that you got in your tribe," suggested Skinny, passing half a dollar to the other.

The boy spun the coin in the air and made it drop into a coat pocket. Then he took Skinny Bill to a place where an old man sat by a fire with a bit of red silk tied around his head, and a beard sloping from his chin, and the muzzle of a long-stemmed pipe lost in the curls of the beard.

Skinny Bill looked around him.

"No, he ain't here," said he.

He thought a moment and added: "Show me the best spinner of stories and lies in the whole outfit, will you?"

15

"Sure," said the other, and took the stranger to a place where a fat woman with vast spangles in her ears was talking in a deep, masculine rumble that changed to the high pipings of a girl's voice, and then to the nasal twanging of a Yankee. She had an audience of half a dozen before her, and they followed the course of the narrative with swayings of the body and with nods, and with smiles that flashed in and out, and laughter swallowed lest it should interrupt.

Skinny Bill searched the group and sighed.

"He ain't here," he said. "I guess that I've lost my bet."

He turned to the guide.

"Where's the prettiest girl in the outfit?" he asked. "And I might have started there in the first place."

"The prettiest girl?" said the guide. "Ay, *that* is a way that I know!"

He led toward the outermost rim of the wagon circle, and to a wagon rather apart from the rest. The brush closely hemmed it in. There was no campfire near by. And when the guide paused at the verge of the willows all that Skinny had to show him the picture was the light of the rising moon. But this was brightening, changing to a paler gold, and by it he was able to make out two figures who sat on a pile of blankets at the side of the wagon.

His eyes growing accustomed to the light, he was further guided by a soft flutter of laughter, and now he could make out that one form was a man, and one was a woman who, as she moved, showed a bright cloth tied around her hair, a cloth that flowed down to a tassel at the small of her back. Further, as she stirred he heard the tinkling of bells, small as voices in a dream. Her throat, her wrists, her ears were dimly marked with light from her ornaments.

"There is the prettiest girl of the tribe," said the guide, "and —there is a man with her!"

His voice had fallen and grown indistinct. It seemed to come from behind locked teeth.

But Skinny paid little heed to this. He was staring fixedly, striving to make out the features of the man. As he waited, the girl picked up a guitar and, plucking with muted fingers at muted strings, she raised the mere ghost of an accompaniment to a voice no stronger than some charming memory. Skinny Bill found himself leaning forward and canting his head, the better to catch all its sweetness; and a peculiar giddiness mounted to his brain.

"I'm a damn fool!" said Skinny Bill.

The girl's song ended. He had been able to hear the tune, not the words. Then her companion took the guitar from her, and he also played with an equal skill, and with fingers as dainty, and strings as delicately quiet. But his voice was just a shade louder, and as he sang, Skinny Bill could make out most of the words. They told of gardens drenched in moonlight, of the breath of unseen roses, of the fountain whispering and showing its heart to the moon; wherefore, then, should you not show your heart to me, beloved!

Skinny Bill grinned.

"It's him, the night thief!" said he to himself.

"It's him," he said, and turned to find his companion. "I'd know that lingo, even if I didn't know his voice and—"

He stopped; the companion had disappeared from his side and was nowhere within eye reach.

But, before Skinny could act, he saw a form slither like a silent snake from under the wagon. It leaped at the singer just as the song was ending, and something gleamed in its hand.

This was so quickly done that Skinny could neither cry out nor stir a hand. He gripped his revolver; his eyes widened; but before he could draw the weapon he saw the singer slip to one side. The shadowy form shot past him, and Flash David instantly pinned him to the ground.

Skinny Bill strode forward. As he came, he heard the voice of his brother saying gently: "Listen to me, you son of an owl and a rat, what are you to have a canary in your nest? Now, mind you. If you lay a hand on her, if you so much as drift an eye over her, I'll hear of it and I'll come after you, and I'll cut the lids off your eyes and stake you out on your back and let you look at the sun. That's the word of Flash David, and it's a good word, and it never was broken. Look at her for the last time, now."

He seemed to lift the prostrate body by the hair of the head. And somehow, even through the dimness, Skinny Bill was able to make out his recent guide.

"Look at her, little mouse," said Flash David. "And you, sweetheart, look at him. You had your eyes half closed when you saw him before. Open them and see what the truth of him is. You see, now, that there's a knife in his belt? But the knife stays there. Pah!"

He threw the gypsy from him and the latter went, reeling a little, with a sound of choked sobbing. As for the girl, she laughed!

Then Skinny Bill spoke suddenly, loudly: "Flash, pa's dyin', and he asks for you!"

CHAPTER IV

They came back together through the night. The long-legged black went well, with the spurs of Skinny Bill buried in its flanks, but the lithe animal which carried the Flash went far more easily. It stirred the heart of the larger man to see the speed and the grace of that bounding creature. It was to other horses like a deer.

"Where did you get it?" he could not help asking, as they went more slowly up the slope toward the bridge.

"The gypsies. I found it there, and I made a trade."

"You traded in that rusty old mare? Ay, and how much boot?"

"They had to give the boot," said the Flash.

He spoke no more. His voice was quiet and grim, and his eyes held straight before him.

Was it possible, wondered Skinny Bill, that after all the boy loved his father, wild and careless as he had always seemed?

At the door of the house they sprang down and went inside. In their father's room they found his other five sons standing in a silent semicircle.

He did not open his eyes. He merely muttered:

"Is that Flash?"

The Flash dropped on his knees beside the bed.

"It is I, father," he said.

"Now, listen at him," said Old Tom. "To say, 'It's me,' ain't good enough for him, 'It's me, pa,' that wouldn't be good enough. It was that same damned school ma'am that spoiled him. He growed straight and he started right, but book learning up and spoiled him. It kind of molded him, is what it done! It give him dry rot inside. Where you been, Flash?"

"Singin' to a gypsy," said Skinny Bill. "Pa, how you feel?"

"Shut yer mouth," said Old Tom. "You're a good boy, Skinny. You found him, eh?"

"I asked for the prettiest girl in the tribe. That's how I found him."

"Nothing but the best, it wouldn't never do for our Flash," said Old Tom. "That's the way he was set up, and that's the way that he carried on. Nothin' but the best. Now that I come to lie here dyin'—"

"Not dying," said the Flash. "Not dying, father!"

"Shut yer mouth," said Old Tom. "Hush, lad. Hush, will ye?"

For the Flash had buried his face in the bedclothes and groaned deeply.

The six other sons looked to one another with stern glances. This lamentation was not put on to gain a larger share of the estate; they were at least above that. Men they had been all their lives, and men they would remain to the end, through death scenes and all. But they saw the property slipping through their calloused fingers into the soft hands of this boy.

"Now that I lie here dyin'," said Old Tom, "I'm thinkin' what it is that's best on the ranch. All that's best on the ranch has gotta go to him."

There was a stir, but no voices from the other sons.

"Skinny, you know hosses," said the father. "Tell me what's the best hoss on the place?"

"My gelding, I reckon," said Skinny. "And he's mine, too, I reckon."

"Mine till I take him from you," said Old Tom, sternly. "But they's something better than the gelding, ain't there?"

"There's the thoroughbred stallion that we got to improve the saddle stock. There ain't anything else."

"And ain't my boy a thoroughbred?" said Old Tom, lifting his head a little. "He is, and he gets the stallion. Yes, sir, that's my last will and testament and my wishes."

A faint muttering passed among the sons, but no outright word.

"And what else?" said the father. "Well, there's my pearl-handled Colt. There ain't no truer shootin' gun ever wore by man than that there Colt is. And account of its pearl handles and its slick look, it goes to my boy, my Flash. You can file the sights off, you scalawag, and the trigger, too, and fix the spring for your doggone fine-fangled fannin', as they call it. I never could handle no six shooter that way."

He made a pause.

Then he said through the dark of the heavy silence: "That's the share that goes to my Flash. Outside of that stallion and that gun, there ain't anything here that's fitting for him to have. Nothin' but a shack of a house, and some raggety cows, and such stuff as barns and hay stacks, and such. He never had no interest in 'em. I wouldn't be weighin' down his hands with 'em. Not me. I know that nothin' but the best will do for him. He's got the two best things on the ranch, and that's all he gets."

The other six sons gaped upon one another with wide

19

eyes, and with slowly dawning grins of joy, and bewilderment.

Then said Old Tom: "All the rest that I've got in the world goes to you, Shorty—and to your brothers. But you run things. You run things right, or they can vote you out and put another man in your place. But you got the business brains. They ain't gunna be such fools, I reckon. And the system will be this. When one of you wants to pull out and go elsewhere, the ones that remain they gotta buy him out. They gotta have his share appraised fair and square, and give him his sixth, and let him go. And they got no more'n six months to do the buyin'. You all hear me?"

"We hear you pretty good, sir," said Skinny.

"It's 'sir,' now that I've beat Flash out of his share," said Old Tom. "Five minutes back, it was only 'pa.'"

They shifted, all those men, and looked down, guiltily.

"Now," said Old Tom, "them's my last sentiments. I ain't gunna see you no more. I'm gunna be dead when you look at me agin. Bury me quick. I don't want no church. I never used none. I don't want no incense and I don't want no song. Now, so long, boys, and good luck to you all."

"Pa," said Shorty, "I would only be askin'—"

"Shut yer mouth," said the father, "and get out of here, or am I gunna spend my last breath arguin' with a pile of brats?"

They turned. In single file they trooped for the door, stepping lightly, putting down the outside rim of the sole first and following gradually with the rest of the foot and weight.

Skinny closed the door behind himself and all the rest. Softly he closed it, and softly he followed the rest outside, where the night wind came with a sudden chill against their wet faces. They could breathe there. A vast and unexpected thing had happened.

"He can wangle and pray and beg," said Shorty, "but the old man has give his word, and he won't go back on it. A hoss and a gun! Well, what else does he deserve to get?"

The others said nothing. They had a guilty feeling, and would not speak.

But back in the bedroom, the Flash was saying: "How long have you lain here? How long? Do you hear me? I'll have a doctor here inside of—"

"Time and doctors couldn't help me," said Old Tom. "Pull the blanket off me. And pull off my coat."

The blanket was drawn away, the coat unbuttoned. And then a red patch appeared over the breast of Old Tom.

"It's straight, clean through," said he, calmly. "I seen where it went in, in front. I felt where it come out behind,

20

and I knew that I was done for. So I come home; and I sent for you. But a good deal of time is used up, and I been bleedin' steady. This bedding, it won't be good for much, after."

The Flash, raising the lamp, shone the light of it straight into the eyes of his father. His hand trembled, and he put the lamp back.

"You seen it," said Old Tom, calmly. "I've seen it, too— the fog that comes up in the eyes of a dead man. I got only a minute or two left, and I need it for talkin'."

The Flash did not stir. His dark and handsome face remained intent; his eyes never left the dying eyes of his father.

"They'll do smart and well," said Old Tom, nodding his head at the distance. "They'll raise the cows. They'll make the ranch grow. Makin' it grow, they make me grow, because I done the plantin'. But I knowed them. They worked all their lives, straight and hard, while you was idlin', and loafin' around, and never raisin' a hand."

The Flash said nothing. His hungry eyes devoured the pain, the weariness, the end of life in his father's face. His lips pinched as he watched, but he offered no excuses.

"I ain't abusin' you," said the father. "I got seven sons. Six of 'em will carry on my work. And one of 'em will kill him that killed me. So I'll rest mighty easy in my grave. I'll sleep like nobody ever slept before."

He closed his eyes, and smiled, and the boy thought that it might be the smile of death.

"Hark at me," said the father softly. "I can't give you no name, because names is nothin' to him. One name this week, and another the next. That's the way with him, all the time. But I'll give you his picture. A fine head of curling brown hair, and a fine brown eye, and a fine brown skin, with apple red in the cheeks of it, and an upstandin' look in his eye, and a fine straight walk, and a fine straight look. Oh, that's the man for you to find, Flash."

"Can you tell me where I would likely find him?"

"Wherever there's meanness and hell-fire. Because that's what he deals in."

"How old is he?"

"Maybe thirty-five. Maybe forty-five."

"Gamble? Drink?"

"He does the handy thing."

"Father, for God's sake," said the boy, "you're failing fast, now. Give me some clue to him. Try to help me find him."

"Women," said the old man. "If one of 'em is pretty enough, you might find him near."

"And why did he kill you?"

"Because of one woman that I told what he was, ten years back, or so."

"Is that all?"

"Nothin' else I could tell you would do."

"Here," said the boy, "is my hand."

Old Tom took it. His grasp remained on it, pulsing and failing as his strength went out of him.

"If I don't find him," said the Flash, "I'll stay on his trail forever. I'll stay with it till I die on it."

"Hush," said Old Tom. "Hush, lad. D'ye think that I want promises from you? Lemme tell you what happened the day that you were born. I looked at you, and I says to your ma: 'None of the rest was ever so small!'

" 'Ay,' says she, 'and this one may be worth them all, if only—' "

Here he paused.

The Flash grasped both his hands.

"If only what?" he cried.

But the life went out of the eyes of Old Tom, and his head sank back more deeply into the pillow. He was dead, with the lamplight shining into the fog of his eyes.

CHAPTER V

As a matter of fact, the whole range came to the funeral. Or, since there was no service, perhaps it would be more accurate to call it a mere burial. But they came with an equal gusto, as though an archbishop had presided in a cathedral filled with incense and with music. There was no incense saving the smell of the alkali dust that blew in the wind, and there was no music other than the stamping and neighing of the half-wild horses, and the mutterings of the human voices.

Shorty, as a matter of course, took charge of everything. Since he was the head of the household, by special and last appointment, he took it for granted that he would have the management of the burial, and none of his brothers disputed this arrangement. Therefore, he sent the hired punchers around the countryside. They spread the news, and those who received word passed it on to those who were farther outlying. So the ripple crossed the desert and washed up the sides of the mountains, and brought a strange gathering to the burial the next day.

Young Flash David, lying in bed late that morning (as usual) saw them come trooping in, old trappers for coyotes and bounty hunters of the wolves, and squatters from odd corners, and grizzled prospectors, still alight with the fire of hope, and small farmers, out of the irrigated bottom land, and ranchers, big and little, like the dead man; but the great majority of the guests were the ordinary punchers of the range. The father of Flash had been one of them. He had blown in his savings like the others, for a few years, and he had never saved a penny until his marriage. He learned to sacrifice some of his pleasures in order to provide for his wife; and in learning to provide for her he learned to save, to work day and night, to avoid all chances, to fight the battle of life with hands of iron. So he had made this ranch.

The Flash, looking out from the window, allowed his eyes to wander carelessly around the rolling acres of it. Even the morning sun, slant as it was, was reflected blinding bright from the sands. There was hardly an acre of really rich soil on the entire place. It made up in size, to a certain extent, for wealth in detail. And it was true that the cows did well enough through the winter so that they could be driven north the next year and fattened for the great Eastern market.

There was a great deal of money in that business. The East, it might be said, rediscovered its taste for meat now that it could get it cheaply from the unharvested herds of the West. And the West, which had been slaughtering cattle for the value of their hides and horns, began to fatten its meat, increase its poundage, and send them trailing overland to the Middle-Western railroad lines. So the East put fat around the belt, and the West put fat around the wallet, and both sections of the country were proud of one another.

To work those cattle required a host of brave, hardy, enduring, skillful workers. The dangers were great, the life was apt to be short, and the pay was comparatively small. But still there were plenty of applicants for jobs, as a rule. They came not so much because they loved to sit in saddles or work beef as because they were following the call of the frontier, and here they found it.

Young Flash David, staring out over the faces of the crowd, paid little attention to the successful ranchers who had driven up with their families in stanch buckboard, and ridden in on fine horses. He preferred to look at the rank and file, the free-swinging, red-necked, grinning punchers. They were of the kind he liked, although it could be fairly said that he never had swung a rope or branded a calf in his life.

For work went against the grain of the Flash. He did not like it. He would not do it. His mother had tried persuasion and tears; his father had tried threats and the lash. But neither one of them could affect the iron resistance of the Flash.

He would not work. In laziness was his creed, and he was perfect in it. He knew every chapter and verse. He was a prophet among his kind. Perhaps that was why he liked to look down at those hard laborers, those cowpunchers. It was the very sense of difference that made them attractive to him.

He knew that they referred to him as "that loafer, that Flash," and as "a tramp," or "no good," or a "dead beat." He knew of these things, but they did not disturb him. If his skin was not thick, then it might fairly be said to be oiled, and language was a water that rolled unheeded off his skin. So, knowing what they said of him, he comforted himself with two facts—that they liked his company, and that they dared not repeat their remarks to his face.

Now, as he lay there in the window of his attic room, the sun falling about his head and shoulders—lying there, basking, sleepy—he relished that heat of the sun like a delicious wine, and turned his thoughts lazily back to the day before.

Where all thinking stopped was at that point where his mother's words had been repeated to him: "He may be worth them all, if only—"

What had she left unsaid?

"If only—he would work!"

That was the phrase which she had left out.

The Flash sighed. A faint frown wrinkled his smooth forehead for an instant, and then went out again, leaving his face as clear as the water of a pool.

Well, if that was the solution, his poor mother's spirit would be disappointed forever. He would not work. He never had worked. And he felt neither shame nor regret.

When he had well marked the crowd, the growing numbers of it, and the tables loaded with simple refreshments which Shorty had placed under the shade of the trees near the house, the Flash—turned over and went to sleep again! For he felt that although the crowd amused him sleep would content him still more. So he slept, and without a dream.

When he wakened, he found that the shadow no longer slanted in through his window, but fell perpendicularly down outside of it. The attic room was an oven, and he was drenched with sweat.

He got up, stripped, and went down to the kitchen pump. There he pumped three buckets of water, and in turn held them over his head and allowed the cold of the water to trickle over him, little by little.

It would have sent another man to bed with chills and fever, that gradual, icy dousing; but to the Flash it simply meant that he would be cool all through the rest of the day.

No matter how the sun burned, it would not burn him, more than surface deep.

Then he went upstairs and dressed.

He had seen his brothers dressed in their soberest and best attire. Perhaps that was the stimulus which urged him on to dress in his gaudiest. He liked to defy public opinion. It was one of his most profound pleasures. If public opinion condemned him, he condemned the public, and that was sufficient.

He put on a blue silk shirt, and a red silk handkerchief, and trousers with silver conchos along the outside seams and fanning out, Mexican style, at the ground. He wore delicately made boots, spoon-handled spurs of gold, and a great sombrero, the crown of which was a thin plate of gold and the band of which was golden Mexican wheel work, incredibly brilliant. It looked like a coronet fit for a duke. Then he buckled on a belt of snowy white goatskin, with an even more brilliant holster, and out of the open flap of the holster appeared the milky gleam of the handles of the revolver which his father had given him.

Most of the men at the funeral, he had noticed, were not wearing arms—at least, they were not wearing them openly, though he did not doubt that their respect for the dead did not keep them from bearing a weapon or so inside of their coats. Their hypocrisy made his lip curl a little.

At the door of his room he hesitated. Then he nodded, made up his mind, and went back to don a gaudy Mexican jacket—such a thing as costs two years of the life of a skilled needlewoman, a network of dainty design, all glistening with silver and with gold work.

He then surveyed himself, deliberately, in the mirror, and he smiled. He looked the Mexican from head to foot. He had the same swarthy skin. He had the black hair. Only his blue eyes said no to the first suggestion.

Well, he would shock the soberness of that assemblage.

So he sauntered down the stairs and went out the front door, past the parlor where his father's body lay, with a sheet draped over the coffin.

That must have been Shorty's idea of a fitting decoration!

Through the doorway, he caught a glimpse of half a dozen figures in the death room, and one of them, old Mrs. Martin, was leaning over the coffin, sniffling. She turned away, stifling sobs, as he went by.

Well, he thought, old Mrs. Martin had lost a friend, after all; perhaps she was not pretending. But as for the rest—?

He stood at the front door and surveyed the groups which were half lost under the shade of the trees. They stood stiffly about. They kept their voices low.

Why, he told himself, there were a hundred fellows there who, for the sake of a good horse race, would forget all about the most beloved relative in the world, to say nothing about a mere friend or simple acquaintance. They were there only for the show. They were there only because they would want to talk about it, afterward. It was an event, a public event, and therefore they wanted to make the most of it.

As he walked outside, he could feel heads turning toward him. He could hear the murmur go buzzing around. So he stopped in the full flare of the sun, which would make his costume gleam like a star. There he calmly rolled a cigarette, lighted it, and then continued on his aimless way.

The men, as he approached, stopped their muttering, and smoothed their faces long enough to nod and grunt at him. The women did not have to fear anything; they did not need to be so polite. And he could hear the words of their anger and their disgust.

He was utterly shameless, it appeared. He had no decent and natural feeling. But there had to be one black sheep in every family.

Well, that was all right. Let them talk. They were only women! In the meantime, he would give them all something a little more exciting for gossip. If the neighborhood wanted gossip, he would give them all they wanted for a subject!

Shorty hove at his side, sweating and panting with anger.

"Whatcha mean?" demanded Shorty, in a half-throttled undertone. "Whatcha mean by them clothes? You're a disgrace to us. You're makin' a sight and a show of us. Why, a low drunk would have more sense!"

He turned to Shorty, drew in a breath of smoke and, with a smile, blew it into his brother's face.

Through the mist, he saw Shorty's brow contract, his face flush with rage; but the elder brother controlled himself.

The Flash laughed, and walked on.

CHAPTER VI

As a blue jay flutters among the tops of the trees, hunting for mischief of any sort—eggs to eat, nestlings to murder—so the Flash went through the crowd, regardless of its murmurs. He saw big Skinny Bill actually turn his back and go striding off. He could guess that Skinny's face was crimson with shame, because he possessed such a brother.

Well, let Skinny grow hot, and then grow hotter. It mattered not to Flash.

Like the blue jay, he was a single gleam of color in that darkness of sober costumes. Like the jay, he had no care for the opinion of the other birds. He had not even, like the jay, a hawk to fear!

Very gaily he walked, smiling to himself, and presently he swerved to the side. He had found mischief ready for the working! For there stood young Hal Morgan, from the big Morgan ranch, Hal Morgan, the hardest rider of them all, the wildest spirit. Handsome, gay, alert, what kept Hal from being the most popular lad on the range was something of over-eagerness to his spirit. He was too headlong. He wearied all companions.

The Flash paused by him.

" 'Lo, Hal," said he.

Hal Morgan looked him over, and bit his lip to keep it from sneering.

"All dressed up, ain't you, Flash?" said he.

"No. This is just regular," said the Flash, yawning. "There's usually a lot of color at a regular funeral. I'm the color."

"Yeah, you're a lot of color," said Hal Morgan, ironically.

"I hear that you've got a new horse, Hal," said the boy.

"You just heard that?" asked Hal, sharply.

"Why, maybe a little while ago I heard it. Three thousand they say you paid."

"I paid enough, all right."

"A regular racer, Hal, I guess."

"He can move."

"Three thousand for a gelding. That's a lot," said the Flash. "You'll never get that out of him."

"You know, do you?" asked Hal Morgan, aggressively.

"I can guess," said the boy.

"Well, take a look, and guess again. That's the gray, down there at the rack."

It was a grand horse. It stood like a king, a head above its neighbors. And the head was enough to see. No horse with such a head, all bone and fire, could be other than a fast mover.

"He's a picture horse. You've been sold," said the Flash. "A picture horse like that is never any good, Hal. They've sold you!"

If Hal Morgan knew anything, he knew horseflesh. He grew calm.

"I'll let you try her, some day," he said.

"Why," said the Flash, "I don't want to hurt your feelings. Let's change the subject."

"Why should I?" asked Hal. "Why should I change the subject, I'd like to know?"

"You pay three thousand and you're stung," said the Flash. "I turn a card down in the gypsy camp, yesterday, and I get more than you paid three thousand of your dad's money for. That's hard luck, old man."

"It makes me feel pretty good to get your sympathy, like this," said young Morgan. "One of these days we might try the two together."

"Look," said the Flash. "There's a half-mile straightaway leading up to the house. I'll race you from the turn up to the house. And there's no time like now."

"Like now!" cried Hal Morgan. "It ain't what you mean, Flash. When your father—"

He stopped, to allow a sense of shame to work properly in the other.

"Look!" said David Baldwin.

He lifted his foot as he spoke.

"I'll bet you these spurs against—well, twenty dollars!"

Hal Morgan looked and looked again. They were beautiful spurs.

"You're crazy, man," he muttered.

"Against twenty dollars. That's giving you plenty of odds, Hal. What do you say?"

Nothing but riding equipment could have tempted Hal Morgan. But these were beautiful spurs, and suddenly he thought how they would set off his heels, and how they would flash against the side of the gray.

"Well, it's your picnic," he said, grimly. "I'll race you, if you want. It's your picnic, Flash!"

And he went striding down to the rack to get his high-priced gelding.

The Flash sauntered to the corral and roped and saddled his mare, which he had got for the turn of a card, as he truly said. He did not say how much money he had backed against that same card; he did not describe the murder that had been in the face of the gypsy when the luck went against him.

With the mare saddled, he rode her from the corral. She was not a great deal to look at. She was long and low. Her forelegs looked too short. Her quarters seemed too heavy, her hips too sloping, and she went at a job with her head down and her hoofs scuffing up the sand.

In this wise, the Flash went winding among the guests.

"This mare against Hal Morgan's gelding," he announced as he went. "What are you betting, boys? From the far turn back to the house. I'll take a few bets myself. Anybody offering odds?"

He saw many tempted hands reach for wallets. But then they remembered the cause for which they had come to the Baldwin house, on this day, and they snatched their hands away again.

At last he saw Dick Murphy.

There never was a time when Dick Murphy could resist a bet. Men said that once he had bet everything down to his shirt with a pair of Mexican shepherds, and actually had walked in naked, fifty miles to the nearest ranchhouse. His feet were cut to shreds on the way.

That might have been merest talk, but when he tempted Dick Murphy today, Dick's purse was out like a gun.

"I'll put a hundred against—thirty!" said Dick.

"Here, Joe Slocum," said the Flash. "You hold stakes. What about a bet yourself, Joe?"

"Flash, are you drunk? Don't you remember that—"

Then Slocum finished looking over the mare, and down in the road he saw the gray prancing.

"Well, it's your picnic, Flash," he said, unconsciously quoting. "I'll bet you fifty to twenty."

"Here, Bud," said the Flash, "you hold the stakes. Unless you want to get down a bet yourself—"

There were four hundred dollars in the pockets of the Flash. He bet every penny, before he was through, at fat odds, and when he jogged the brown mare down to the roadway, he had what he wanted. Every eye was turned from the funeral. Even the women were climbing onto the fence to get a better view of the race!

"That's their sorrow!" said the Flash, to himself. That's their friendship, too. Why should I give a rap about their opinion, I'd like to know? I don't. I never will!"

He joined Hal Morgan at the far turn.

They lined up their horses.

Sam Daniels came in by a buckboard, his wife and freckle-faced daughter with him. They halted Sam, and made him give the word, and at the word the Flash sent the brown mare bounding down the road.

She was made for action, not for a picture, standing still. When she began to move, she was what Skinny Bill had seen the night before, galloping through the darkness—she was a wild deer!

And she jerked the good gelding thirty feet behind her at the very start!

Ay, but it came again, nobly. Not for nothing had Hal Morgan spent his three thousand dollars. There was bone and blood and quality in the good gray, and two hundred yards from the finish it caught the low brown mare and galloped nose to nose with her.

"Well done!" said the Flash. "You've looked her in the eye, Hal. But now how do you like the looks of her going away?"

So he laughed as he spoke, and bending a little forward he took a short grip on the reins. It seemed to Hal Morgan that the legs of the mare lengthened a foot. It seemed to him that she hardly touched the road with her hoofs, but flicked it lightly, and took to invisible wings.

With a cruel horsemanship, with spur and whip, Hal Morgan scourged his beauty to the finish, but the switching, ragged tail of the brown mare was three lengths before him at the end.

And all along the hillside they shouted, and they whooped, and they danced—all those who had not bet their good money. The others, with sour faces, tried to smile and could not.

"She's a ringer. We're sold," they told one another.

And the Flash went up the hill to collect his money. He went with a smile, but there was bitterness in his heart. They had smiled and sneered at him because he would not observe a holy and a dismal day in his family's history. But this was all that their smiling, their friendship, their kindness amounted to. The first call of easy money was a call too loud for them to resist.

He took the solid weight of the money—there was little paper money in those days, in the West, at least. And when his pockets were heavy and jingling with it he took the mare back to the corral and unsaddled and unbridled her. He waited a moment, rubbing her nose, and she closed her eyes and leaned her weight a little against his hand.

He had watched the gypsy and learned the secret of that caress.

"She's worth all the rest," said the boy. "The rest, they're only shamming and mumming. She's real. She's real!"

He let her go and, pausing a moment as he shut the corral gate, he gripped the top rail with all his might until his arm trembled.

He felt better after that. Some of the savagery was out of him, and he was smoking another cigarette and smiling once more as he sauntered back among the groups beneath the trees.

He felt them staring, and he felt the cruel bigotry of their criticism; so he forcibly maintained his smile, in order to avoid sneering back at them.

Only one stern, set face of condemnation troubled him

at all. He turned toward it, absently, drawn by the power of the eyes, and he saw Jacqueline Moore under a tree, with a big brown-faced, rosy-cheeked man beside her.

CHAPTER VII

When he saw her staring at him, he went straight toward her, and she did not wait for him. It was plain that she excused herself to the big fellow who was with her, and now she came to meet him and left the other behind. He was stroking his fine, silky brown mustache and smiling a little to himself, this other, as though from the distant heights of middle age he looked down upon youth, its concerns, its conduct, its hopes. For he had lived through them, understood them perfectly, and found them diminished in importance, as objects are diminished by distance.

It seemed to the Flash that he had seen this man before, but he had no time to think where. When Jacqueline Moore was about, it was hard to find room in one's mind for other things.

She walked to him. Her step was as straight as her eye, and her eye went through him like a sword.

"Do you know what you've done, David?" said she.

She was the only person on the range who called him David. But she was always original, in one way or another.

"You tell me what I've done," said the Flash.

She frowned on him.

"You know perfectly well," she said. "You've disgraced the day of your own father's funeral. There's not a man or a woman or a child here who isn't ashamed of you. You've made a joke of everything. I'd like to know why you did it."

"Listen, Jack," said he. "You're all right. You're fine. But you're like the rest. You wouldn't understand."

"Look here, David," said she, "don't you go making yourself into a mystery. That's no business."

"I'm not making myself into a mystery. I'm just taking some of the mystery out of other people," he assured her.

She nodded at him, compressing her lips a little.

"Well, I might have known it before," said she. "You'd have some sort of a queer explanation. You always have. Nobody ever catches you out, David. You are taking the mystery out of other people, are you? Out of me, for instance?"

He regarded her with care.

31

"Well, there's not much bunk in you," he said. "But there's some."

"Go on and tell me," said the girl, angrily, "what's the bunk in me?"

"Being a doggone Moore, that's part of it," said the boy. "That's a part of your mystery. You're proud as the deuce of it. You'll admit that?"

"I'm proud of my father," said she, "if that's what you mean."

"So was I proud of mine, if that's what you mean," he countered.

"You show it a lot!" said the girl.

"You think that Moores are better than other people," said the Flash. "They're not. Nobody's better than anybody else. You ought to know that."

"I see," said she. "You're getting democratic."

"I always was."

"Do you know what people will say about you?"

"We're talking about you just now."

"Go on and finish, then. Tell me the rest of my mysteries."

"I'll tell 'em to you. I could tell you a list," said the Flash.

"I won't run away," she assured him, scornfully. "Go right ahead with the list, then."

"I won't give you a list. You start in and look at one thing, though. You like to go around through the crowd smiling at everybody. You're extra nice to the half-breeds and the colored folks too. You pretend to be a regular democrat. You know why."

"*You* tell me that!" said she.

"Yeah. I'll tell you, Jack. It's because you want them to say: 'Look at Jacqueline Rosemary Olivia Moore—'"

She interrupted: "Nobody on the range calls me by my full name!"

"Yeah. But you'd like 'em to," the Flash told her. "'There goes Jacqueline Rosemary Olivia Moore! Isn't she sweet? I think she's a darling. Blood will tell, mind you. The old Moore blood—but there's nothing aristocratic about her, the darling. I'll tell you what she did. She baked a cake with her own sweet hands and took it around to poor old Sam Jenkins' wife when she was—'"

"Stop this instant!" exclaimed Jacqueline Moore, stamping.

He continued, singsonging his words, and canting his head from side to side: "'Lucky the man that gets her, I say. No pride in her. Just a naturally sweet nature. A lamb, is what she is. You take at a dance, she dances with everybody. She'd never show a common puncher that *she* preferred dancing with somebody else in the room. No, sir, not her! And if—'"

"David, be still," said the girl. "I just about hate you!"

"I'm just about glad that you do," said he. "I'm glad, so long as you climb down out of the pulpit that you were going to preach to me out of. You quit your preaching, Jack. Don't preach to me, anyway. I don't want to hear it."

"You think that you're bright and incisive," said the girl. "You're just plain rude, if you want to know it, David Baldwin!"

"All right," said the Flash. "It's your innings. Don't talk like the third grade, though. That doesn't mean anything to me."

She was so angry at this that she could say nothing at all for a moment, but stood there breathing and looking fire, so to speak, her face flaming, her head high.

"Keep like that, Jack," said he, dryly. "They're all looking at you. They're all telling one another—the old hens—that you're giving me the dressing down that I deserve. Why, you look fine right now. You look good enough to paint, pretty near. Go on, Jack, and just hold that pose."

"You've made up your mind to be contemptible," said the girl. "There's no good in me talking to you. And I won't."

"Don't, then," said he.

She had half turned. Now she turned back.

"I just want to tell you one thing, David," said she.

"Yeah," said he. "I knew you wouldn't quit before you'd had a slam at me."

"I wish you'd stop pretending to read my mind," said she, quivering with anger and with dignity that had been offended.

"Well, I'll read your mind for you," said the Flash. "You want to say: 'David, you're a disgrace to your father, your family, and the whole range. You've never done a day's work in your life. You're a gambler, a jockey, a card player and a dice shaker. Some people say that you're a thief. I'd hardly put it beyond you. Now comes the death of your father, and you turn the sorrow of the whole range into a mock and a shame. You actually ride in a horse race. You drag poor, impulsive, hotheaded Hal Morgan—the darling!—into the race with you—' "

"Yes," broke in the girl. "Every word you say is true. You don't subtract any of the truth by admitting it!"

"And," said he, "I wound up by getting this whole crowd of mourners dancing, and climbing fences so that they could see the finish of that same race!"

"You ought to be proud of that," said the girl. "Human nature of course is—"

"It's in Jacqueline Rosemary Olivia Moore, too," said the Flash. "She climbed a fence as well as the rest."

"I didn't," said she.

"You did," said he.

"I didn't," she answered hotly. "At least, I only stepped on the bottom rail because those stupid Dennis boys got right in my way and—"

She stopped. She began to blush.

Then, in the face of his grin, she broke out: "Who could have thought that your wretched rag-tail gypsy mare would beat that race horse of Hal Morgan's? Who could help wanting to see?"

"Yeah. You wanted to see," he said, bitterly. "You were like all the rest. And yet I'll bet that you were in there with the rest of 'em, boo-hooing over dad's coffin and the sheet that fool of a Shorty draped over it. It's a wonder that he didn't put an American flag or something in place of the sheet. I'll bet he would, if he'd been able to get one big enough."

"David," she said, with a sudden change of tone to one of anxious curiosity, "what is the matter with you?"

"Nothing's the matter with me," he said. "Whatever I am, I don't change. There's not enough of me to be worth changing, you may say."

She watched him, steadily.

"What's happened?" she said. "Something's happened. You're changed. Is it the responsibility, David? Because I suppose that your father left you about half the ranch? You were always his favorite!"

"God knows why?" he suggested.

"Stop it," said she.

"I'll tell you," he answered. "I got the best part of the ranch."

"And so you're happy," said she. "Of course your spirits are overflowing a little!"

"I got the best *things* on the ranch," he corrected. "A horse and a gun."

She gasped.

"Oh, poor David!" said she. "I don't wonder that you're full of thorns, then! What a day to cross you! Only, I didn't know—"

He took her by one arm, at the elbow, so hard that her arm was stiffened by the pressure into a rod.

"I pretty nearly despise you, Jack," said he, "when I hear you talk like this. I don't expect you to really know me. But I thought you'd guess that I'm a fairly good sport about things."

"You are, David," she told him. "I know that, at least."

"Then," he said savagely, "do you think that I'll whine because I get what I've worked for? I've loafed and lazied around the place. If my father had given me a full share, I would have thought him a fool. No, we understood each other. And I'll tell you what—there's nobody in the world who gives a damn about his death—except old Mrs. Martin and me!"

He stepped back from her, shrugged his shoulders, seemed trying to relax.

"I'm sorry, Jack," he said. "That was like something out of the third act of a melodrama, I know."

She did not answer. She was still looking at him on account of the deadly earnestness which she had seen in his face for the first time in his life.

"Talk about something else," said he. "They'll march out with the body in a minute. Talk about something else. Who's that big boy that looks like a sailor. A captain, I mean. The one you were with?"

"That's Uncle Tom Winter," she said.

"Uncle, my foot," said the Flash. "Who is he?"

CHAPTER VIII

They had known each other from infancy.

And every year they had met and played together. And every day of their acquaintance they had fought. He had pulled her hair. She had scratched his face. She had hit him with a fence board; he had punched her lily-white chin, as the good old ballads would put it. When he fell into the Blackstone Draw, while the spring water was raging through it, she had ridden her pony belly deep, until it staggered in the current, and snatched young Baldwin away from death. When a top branch of the oak they were climbing broke under her feet, he caught her, was dragged from his own bough, and hung by the toes—and by the grace of God!—until he swung her to safety. For three months his shoulders were black and blue from the frightful strain.

He was six months older than Jacqueline, but, until they were both thirteen, she was tall, as nimble, very nearly as strong, and fully as daring as he. She could ride fully as well, jump nearly as far, run almost as fast, hit very nearly as hard a blow. She was an excellent wrestler, too, in their younger days, and out of the infinity of her cunning tricks she had fairly put him down, more than once. Furthermore, when it came to scaling heights, or to walking a wind-bent bough or the eaves of a house, or upright on the rooftree, she was incomparably his master. She had more power over animals, too, in those early days and, if he was better with a revolver, she could shoot rings around him with a rifle.

Their friendship ran a rougher course than that of true love. They became notorious. People rarely asked them to the same parties; otherwise the good time of all was dissolved by the violent wrangles between Jacqueline Moore and David Baldwin.

Then came the time when she was forbidden ever to see him again.

They had had a diving contest at the deepest pool in that same Blackstone Draw. They dived in all their clothes, because the idea had occurred to them impromptu, as it were. And when the Flash dived from the top of the steep, overhanging rock, she climbed up and did likewise, and struck her head on the bottom, and came floating to the surface half drowned. Wholly drowned she would have been had she not been stunned.

He pulled her ashore, and managed to drag her limp body onto a horse, and carried her so all the way home.

The next day she got her senses back, but she kept a sore neck and a stiff back for a month; and her parents naturally blamed everything on young Flash Baldwin, whose reputation already was none too savory. He generally wore a rich, ripe black eye, while the other center of vision was mourning in milder greens and purples. A few scratches usually decorated his face in a freehand pattern. His trousers hung by one strap. His elbows were apt to be through the sleeves of his shirt; and mud cakes, dust, tar and oil stains were everywhere visible on clothes and skin. For the Flash loved nature at first hand. He liked to be literally in touch with her.

If this was the sort of a playmate that the heir to the Moore estate picked out—and almost broke her neck playing with—it was high time that her mind should be changed for her. So they forbade her to see the boy again and sent her away to school when the next term began.

She was different when she returned. So was David. She had become feminine and dainty; he had become—the Flash!

But as she looked at him now some of those older days drifted across her mind, and she sighed.

"Well," she said, "it's almost like the old days—wrangling like this. We never got along very well, Dave. But we had fun."

"Yeah," he said. "We had our share."

"I don't know what happened," she said. "We haven't seen so much of one another lately!"

"Of course we haven't," said he.

"I don't know why," said the girl.

"I do," said he.

"Well, tell me, then."

"Well, you got proper and I got improper," said the Flash.

"You've been pretty wild," said she, nodding, "but I never got so proper."

"Oh, didn't you?"

"Well, you tell me when?" said she, frowning.

"I remember the first time you came home from school," he declared. "It made me sick, the way you'd changed."

"It made me sick the way *you'd* changed," said she. "You were dressed like a dandy. A Mexican dandy," she added, with contempt.

"You were dressed," said he, "like a lady—Boston, or something. You were all slimpsy. You turned down your eyes. You blushed pretty easily, too. You never used to blush in the old days."

"Well, maybe not," said the girl.

She was still thoughtful as she looked at him.

Then she said: "They'll never come back, but the old days were the best days, David."

"Well, I'll tell you something," said he. "They were the only days when I was really happy."

"Oh, come, David," said she. "That's not right. All you've done these years is just to amuse yourself."

"Yes," said he, "and that's a pretty dull job."

"Is it?"

"Yes," he assured her.

"What do you want?" she asked.

"Some job that will fill my hands," he told her. "That's what I want! And maybe I've found it."

"What is it?" she asked him.

"Oh, nothing. I was asking about that fellow you called Uncle Tom. Who is he?"

"Oh, he's just an old friend of dad's. He's come out to see us. That's all. Why are you looking at me like that?"

"I thought *he* had a way of looking at you," said the boy.

"Stuff!" said she. "What in the world do you mean? He's fifty or so!"

"He's not a day more than forty."

"David, you're simply idiotic," she told him.

"You look me in the eye," said he.

She did so.

"Now tell me again that I'm an idiot about it," he urged.

37

She felt the blush burning about her cheeks, on her forehead, down her throat. She wanted to turn away, but she endured the torment and kept staring at him.

"It's easy enough to make me blush," said she.

"Yeah, I see that," said he. "I wish you luck, Jack. I see how it is. You're all right. You're fine. But you're like the rest of 'em."

He turned and left her abruptly, as abruptly as he would have left her in the old days of their childhood, when they fell out.

"David!" she called after him.

He paused and only half turned.

"You're rude," she said, "self-centered, mean, and suspicious!"

"All right," said the Flash, and walked on again.

A moment later, the funeral cortege left the door of the ranch house and went up the hill, eight chosen old friends carrying the coffin.

Behind it walked six of the sons of the dead man. All were there, saving one!

The rest of the crowd fell in behind, and the whole procession moved on until they came to the nest of tall cottonwood trees that grew beyond the hill, in the hollow. There they paused. A dozen men, with shovels, already had dug a profound pit for the burial of the coffin. They lowered the coffin down on the ropes. There was no priest to read a service. Lawrence Moore, the father of Jacqueline, stood up with his hat in his hand.

He was a fine, big fellow. The clothes he wore were tailor made, and looked it. There was nothing to connect him with the range except his sombrero. As he talked, he perspired. His bald, lofty forehead shone with the sweat.

But he merely said:

"Friends and neighbors, we are putting Old Tom Baldwin in the ground without any rites of the church. But for a man like him, rites are unnecessary. His whole life was the fulfillment of a rite, in the proper sense of the word. He was the stuff that has made the West.

"He was a good friend and a hard enemy. He never forgot, though he could forgive. He never refused a stake to a fellow who was down. He never refused a meal to any man who came to his door. He worked hard. He raised a big family. And he raised them well, according to our standards.

"He was the best neighbor I ever had. I'll never have as good a one again.

"It's a sad thing that a man as familiar with weapons as

38

Tom Baldwin should have been carried off by an accident like this. But his luck was good while it lasted.

"Friends, I have nothing more to say. I'm not a priest. But even if I were, the most I could do would be to say 'God bless him,' and I think God will."

When he had finished, he picked up the first handful of earth, crumbled it in his fingers, and let it fall into the grave. And then the shovelers laid to with a will. As the first heavy clods thumped down, hollowly, upon the coffin, old Mrs. Martin burst into shrill, hysterical sobbing. Some women led her away through the dusk of the gathering evening.

The grave was filled, the mound was raised; the guests finished off the edibles on the long tables beneath the trees nearer to the house, and then they departed, leaving the family alone.

All departed except Jacqueline and her father, and her father's friend, Thomas Winter. They were impatient to go, but the girl held them. They had driven their buckboard past the grave and up the next hill beyond. There, lost in the shadow of the lofty brush, they waited ten minutes, fifteen, half an hour.

"I want to see something. You've got to wait," was all Jacqueline would say to her father, and like a well-trained father he endured and groaned, but did not drive on.

At length, when the shadows were very deep, she said: "Do you see anything there in the hollow?"

"No," said her father.

"Yes," said Thomas Winter. "There's a fellow who has walked out from the trees. He's gone to the grave. There he's standing."

"Yes!" said the girl, in an excited whisper.

"He's kneeling down, now," said Thomas Winter. "Yes, by Jove, he's thrown himself flat on the grave! One of the boys, I suppose!"

"Yes," said the girl. "It's one of the boys. Let's go on, now. Let's go fast!"

"Hold on, Jacqueline," said her father. "What's the matter with you? You're crying, I think!"

"Rot," said she. "It's just the alkali dust in the wind."

CHAPTER IX

When the day had ended, and when the dusk had gathered into the dark of the night, still young David Baldwin had not appeared. His brothers, gathered closely together, talked of him. They talked without bitterness, to be sure, but they talked with deep emotion.

Shorty guided the talk; the main dissenter was Skinny. But when, out of the darkness, the form of David appeared, the brothers had reached at least an outward semblance of agreement in all things, and Shorty acted as the spokesman.

The Flash, entering the house, found the family meeting held as usual in the dining room, where the six brothers were seated around the long table, with Shorty at the head of it.

There was no one at the foot of the table. So the Flash sat himself down on the edge of it. In this manner he faced some of them, his back was toward others. And he had to turn his head to see Shorty. He seemed to prefer not to turn his head, but to look straight forward.

On this side of the table sat Blondy and Trot Baldwin. They were not at ease under the careless touch of the eye of their youngest brother.

"Well," said the Flash, "you fellows seem to have started a regular congress here. The first bill you've passed is about me, I suppose. So let's have it. But first I'd like to ask a question of you."

"Well, let's have your question," said Shorty, at the head of the table.

The Flash paid no attention to him.

"Skinny," said he, "you have a pair of eyes. Did you take a look at the fellow with Jack Moore today?"

Big Skinny Baldwin sat just behind the Flash, and, since the latter did not turn as he asked the question, but continued to look calmly, genially, unseeingly upon Blondy and Trot, Skinny was forced to speak to the slender back of the boy.

The insult implied in this Skinny felt so keenly that he flushed to his high, prominent cheekbones. He stirred from one side of his chair to the other and glanced aside, as though to make sure that the rest of the family had noticed the way in which he was being treated.

He discovered that no one was looking at him, however. All eyes were fastened upon young David. They watched him with a curious intensity, and a sort of fear. As though he were playing the master hand and knew the cards they held in their hands. Of course, the opposite was the truth, and yet the boy dominated them all.

"I saw him, of course," said Skinny Baldwin.

"What did he look like?" asked the Flash.

"You seen him yourself," growled Skinny. "I guess you got the sharpest pair of eyes in the family."

"But I want to hear what you saw," said David. "You know, Skinny, that a man is apt to see what he expects, and miss what he doesn't expect."

"I dunno what you're talkin' about," said Skinny

"Just describe the fellow who was with Jack, will you?" asked the Flash, still without turning.

Skinny glared at the back which was turned toward him.

"How old was he, would you say?" asked the Flash.

"Around about between thirty-five and forty-five," said Skinny. "When he smiled, he looked tolerably young. When he frowned, he looked more oldish."

"What kind of complexion did he have?" asked the Flash.

"Mighty brown," said Skinny. "As brown as I ever seen, and reddish in the cheeks."

"Ay?" said the Flash, dreamily. "And what sort of an eye did he have?"

"It's a hard thing to talk about a man's eye," said Skinny. "I'd say, though, that he had an eye like a fighter. He wouldn't back down none in a pinch."

The Flash nodded, his eyes half closed in thought.

"Thanks," said he. "That's all that I wanted to hear. Thanks a lot, Skinny."

"You interested in him?" asked Skinny. "Jealous, maybe?"

"Jealous?" repeated the Flash carelessly. "Well, I'm more interested in him, just now, than I am in anything else in the world, and that gets us back to this meeting you fellows are having. What's the decision?"

Shorty spoke in answer.

"We wanta do what's right by you, Flash," said he.

"Of course you do. Of course you do," said the Flash. "Go on, Shorty."

"What it looks like to us," said Shorty, heavily, beginning to sweat about the face, "is that you and us ain't gunna get along none too well. Today you sort of busted things loose, I'd say. You kind of made a show of the old man's funeral, Flash. That's the way it seemed to us."

"All right," said the Flash. "You fellows are all right.

41

You're decent and straight, all of you. I don't suppose that I belong in the same corral with all of you."

"Hold on, Flash," said Skinny. "That don't go for me, no matter what the others may think."

"Wait a minute, Skinny," said Shorty. "Are you with us in this, or ain't you with us?"

With the question put to him thus bluntly, Skinny rubbed his knuckles across his forehead and groaned.

"Well," he said, "I guess it's all right. Go ahead and have your say, Shorty."

But Skinny was miserable. His color had heightened, and he looked sullenly down at the edge of the table and his big, bony, powerful hands.

Shorty continued, now that this objection had been overruled: "You see how it is, Flash. We wanta do what's right. We know what the old man's will was. But we ain't sticking by that, only. We wanta do more than that for you, of course. Question is, whatcha want? You know that there ain't so much cash on the place. It's mostly cows. But we'd give you something every month, and that'd leave you free."

"Free to get out?" asked the Flash, smiling down at Blondy and Trot.

"Say," said Trot, the eldest son, "it ain't me that's done the deciding, Flash. You needn't look down at me!"

"I'm not looking at you," said the Flash. "I'll tell you how it is, boys. You're generous. You want to give me more than the will calls for. But that's not what I want. Father gave me the stallion. But he's not for me. He's fine to look at, but he's only a picture. A day's hard riding would melt a hundred pounds off those fat sides of his, and two days' riding would break him down. He might do pretty well on a track, but he wouldn't be so much use across country. So I give him back to you."

Shorty sighed with relief.

"We could use him," he admitted. "And we'll buy him back from you. I mean, we'll pay what's fair for him. He ain't worth quite the price that the old man gave for him, but he's worth something. How would twelve hundred dollars suit you?"

He squinted sharply at his youngest brother.

Said the Flash: "I didn't say I would sell him to you. I said that I'd give him to you. I mean what I say. He's yours. Now, there's one more thing that my father gave me."

He took the pearl-handled revolver from its holster and laid it on the table.

"It's a pretty good gun," he said. "It fits a hand, well,

and it shoots hard and pretty straight. But it's not exactly what I'm used to."

From somewhere in his clothes, with an easy gesture, too swift for the eye to follow in detail, he produced two blue-black Colts, big ponderous weapons that appeared to overweight his slender fingers.

"This is what I've been raised on," he told his brothers, still looking only at Blondy and Trot, "and the others are likely to be too slick for my grip. So," he continued, making the guns vanish as smoothly as they had been conjured forth, "I'm going to leave the pearl-handled gun with you, also. I keep my own, and you keep your own, and so we part fair and square!"

He stood up from the edge of the table, and gave his cold smile to them all.

And the six brothers stared at one another—all saving Skinny, whose sullen eyes were still fixed downward.

"As for the money," said the Flash, "I don't want it. You don't have to hire me to go away. I go away willingly."

He made a small bow to them.

"Good-by," said the Flash, and turned to the door, putting his hat on his head.

Not a move was made by five of the brothers. Only Skinny, as he saw young David go through the door into the black face of the night, leaped up with a cry.

"Hold on, and mind what you're doing!" called Shorty, fiercely.

"Damn you and all your ideas!" called Skinny, in return, and dashed on through the doorway, slamming the door behind him.

He overtook the Flash at the gate of the corral.

There he laid his great, resistless hands on the boy and turned him about.

"Davie," said he, "I'm not with the rest. I'm with you. I've always been with you. I've damned you now and then, a little. Yes, pretty hard sometimes! But I've always been with you. You're more to me than the rest. If you go, I'm gunna go with you!"

The Flash looked up at the face of the taller man, and presently he sighed.

"This is a mighty big surprise, Skinny," said he. "But I always knew that you were worth all the rest. Only—you can't go with me."

"Why?" asked Skinny.

"Because of the place I'm bound for," said the boy.

"You mean hard riding? You're a devil with a horse,

Flash, but I'll stick with you somehow. I'll keep in sight of your dust. I'm not gunna let you down."

"I don't mean only riding, though there'll be riding, too," said the Flash. "I mean the whole country that I'm bound for. You wouldn't be at home there."

"You mean Mexico?" said Skinny. "Well, I can't speak the lingo as good as you can, and I don't know 'em or like 'em as well as you do. But I can get on down there too, if that's where you're bound for."

"No," said the boy. "It may be Mexico; it may be Canada. It may be above timber line in the Devil Mountains, yonder. It may be in the towns along the river. It may be in some big city. But the country that I'm bound for is the land where people go that live outside the law. Go back to the rest of 'em, Skinny. You're too straight and honest to go where I'm going. You'd feel mighty cold and lonely, out there beyond the law. God bless you for coming out here after me, but don't follow me one step beyond the corral gate, or you'll never be able to turn back home again!"

CHAPTER X

Beyond the corral, Skinny did not follow.

The Flash, looking back at him, saw him standing like a great, rudely carved statue of black stone, half lost in the night shadows, and the bars of the corral fence crossed him and held him away like the bars of a prison.

"That's what it is," said the Flash to his own strange young heart. "That's the life which these brothers of mine are leading. They're inside of the prison. And I'm outside of it. Society is a ball and chain hanging onto a man's feet; and law and order make the prison walls and the cells where they live."

But as he rode off he kept his head turned, looking back, and he saw the light from the dining-room window dwindle and dwindle until it drew together to a point, from which starry beams struck out.

He was not happy, entirely. He felt very much as he had told Skinny *he* would feel. But he went on.

The description which Skinny had applied to the stranger at the funeral was too close to his own ideas of the tall, brown-faced man. And he felt more than reasonably sure that the man his dying father had named to him was the same fellow who had come with the girl to his father's burial.

There he was, in all respects. A man between thirty-five and forty, upstanding, big, erect, an air of command, a brown and red-stained complexion, like a sailor's, and an eye that would be hard to endure at close range.

It was the murderer of old Tom Baldwn who had come there to see the burial of his murdered man. And the heart of the boy went as hard and as cold as chilled steel.

So he held his way across the country at an easy pace, because he did not wish to arrive at the rance of Lawrence Moore before bedtime. When the people turned in, that was the time for him to get in his work.

Death was in his mind. The slaying of the big stranger was what he proposed to himself. Not out-of-hand murder, but a fair fight. He nodded to himself in agreement that this was the fair and honorable thing. Perhaps his skill with weapons— he seemed to have been born with a sense for guns—would make the battle a somewhat one-sided one, but what more could he do? What more *should* be done for the slayer of his father? There had been no question of fair play then, so far as he knew. It had been a meeting and a death. So it would be tonight.

Hastily he sketched the familiar picture of the Moore ranch house. He looked up at the stars. Boötes was standing at the zenith, with Arcturus small and dim through the dusty air of the desert. He knew that the picture of this sky would never come out of his mind.

He gave attention to the way the brown mare was traveling. In tribute to her incomplete mane and tail, he called her Rags, a name which appeared to please her as much as the next one. She had little care for names.

She was an interesting animal. She had a developed personality like that of a human being. For instance, her ears were never still but continually lagged back or pricked forward. Sometimes they moved together, sometimes they worked one by one, like the ears of a mule. And it was plain that she was listening to all the sounds of the desert and recognizing and registering them with much expertness. Every time the lobo howled from the northern mists of night, she lifted her head a little; but the yipping of the coyotes in the southern draws—the scoundrelly chicken thieves!— only made her wise little ears quiver a bit.

She shuffled her feet through the sand so that one would have sworn that here was a born stumbler, and yet she never made a mistake. When he reached the rocky patch that crowned the second range of hills, she picked her way through them as neat footed as a mountain sheep, and the boy knew that he had a treasure, indeed.

45

He loosed the reins, going down the farther slope, and she went at a soft, rocking lope. A man could sit the saddle all day without fatigue, with a pace like that under him. And, perhaps, before long, he would need to sit the saddle through many a weary hour. For when man hunters took the trail in this part of the world, they were not easily tired, they were not easily put off the trail.

What he chiefly felt about Rags was that she was honest. She gave herself no airs. It took an expert eye like his own to read the signs of her, and see her points; and as she was in appearance, so she was in character, casual, careless, with a most undignified carriage. But many a high-headed prancer would eat her dust, he felt, before the tale was ended! She had no waste motions. She never lifted her foot half an inch higher than the obstacle before it. And when she was put at a yawning ditch, she hopped across it without fear and without hesitation, and barely gave herself footing on the farther side.

He tried her at brush, and she went through it, rather than over it. Oh, she was a wise one in every way, beyond a doubt!

And the Flash liked wisdom, it appeared, more than he did virtue.

Presently he was traveling up the last hollow, and he could see above him the jumbled outlines of the roofs of sheds and barns and the more commanding presence of the Moore ranch house itself.

He took a good deal of pains, here.

In the center of the draw there were rocks, washed bare by the spring floods. Over these he sent the mare, and Rags stepped warily, for the surface of the stones was as polished as glass. Yet she went with never a slip!

He wanted no easily legible back trail, when the man hunters went out to find the slayer of the brown-faced Tom Winter. Was it not barely possible that he might do his work and slip away again, and never a man the wiser for what he had done? He was not confident of this. Those who slew others were always discovered. Something in his heart told him that. As for his own forays south of the Rio Grande, it might be true that his deeds were only dimly known north of the river; they were well enough advertised to the south of the same muddy stream. The Mexicans knew him; and more than one of them wanted his blood!

All of these things were thronging through the mind of the boy as he came close to the house of Moore.

There was a run of water from a spring at a little distance from the house. This water made a pool in the winter. In the summer it was generally absorbed by the thirsty, sandy soil. But enough of it percolated underground to support a small grove of aspens. The trees grew small and close together. Every ten years they were thinned out to make firewood, and the new sprouts came up quickly, and became tree sized again. At this time they were of a good height, and within the shelter of the trees he dismounted and threw the reins over the head of Rags.

Then he started for the house.

He went up back of the corrals, and passed through them, knowing that the dogs were less apt to be on this side of the house. As a rule, they crouched or roamed in front of the place, facing toward the direction of the cooling winds or wallowing in the cool of the dust that had been stamped and worked up by the horses in front of the long hitching racks.

He was in luck until he came very close to the house and had cleared the last corral fence. Then a black shadow fairly rose up out of the ground and sprang at him.

It was the lurcher, the silent and savage hunter which poachers use and love. The Flash sidestepped and caught the big hound out of the air by the scruff of the neck. With his other hand, he fastened a firm hold under the jaws of the beast, and so was jerked to his knees in the dust.

He could hear the beast growling deep in its throat, a soft lullaby of hatred. But he knew the dog, and now he spoke to it, gently. Presently he saw the tail begin to wag, and he could loose his hands to caress it.

Animals quickly knew him and rarely forgot him. The lurcher in a moment was fawning on him, and then the Flash stood up and went on.

An air of sweetness came to him, baffling his memory. But then he recalled that three years ago, at the inspiration of Jacqueline, honeysuckle had been planted around the house. Some of it had grown in a scraggly fashion. Other sprigs had quite died. But there were a few vines which flourished wonderfully and clothed the house to the eaves, and above them. This was the sweetness that hung heavily in a windless air.

With a bitter pleasure he thought of Jacqueline, and how her head would rise, and how her lip would curl, and the rage and scorn and detestation in her eyes when she learned that Uncle Tom Winter had been murdered, and by whom!

She would never understand. No one ever would understand. For he would be living out yonder in that land which he had described to Skinny Bill—the land beyond the law.

He began to skirt the house.

Next to the corner of the building there was a lighted

window in the second story. That was a room which was often offered to a guest. So he climbed up the drainage pipe that carried away the rain water from the roof, and peeked into the chamber.

There was no one in it. A carryall, a sort of huge knapsack, lay upon the floor on its back, spread open, with odds and ends of clothing protruding. There was a heavily bitted bridle hanging from a peg beside the head of the bed, and an oversized saddle lay on the floor at the foot of the bed.

He regarded the saddle with interest. He never had seen one with so capacious a seat, he thought. It must have been specially ordered for a very large man, and yet, strange to say, the stirrups were short enough to have accommodated a child!

He slid back to the ground.

At least, Thomas Winter never could have used stirrups as short as this, and therefore it was not Winter's room. It was rather odd that a saddle should have been brought into the house at all, he felt! It might have been left out in the barn with the rest of the outfitting.

He slid back to the ground, cautiously. And there the lurcher welcomed him, licking his hand, and frolicking then about him, but making no more sound than its heavy panting.

For the night was very still, and momentarily it seemed to grow hotter. His hair stuck to his forehead. Breathing was difficult after his climb, which had made his arms ache at the shoulder. He kneaded the muscles until they were relaxed again. For what he had in mind, it would be madness to have a strained arm or a shaking hand.

Another window, just beneath the first, suddenly flared with yellow lamplight. He did not need to climb. He had only to stand on tiptoe and look over the sill, and there he saw Thomas Winter, fitting the lampshade over the lamp which he had just lighted.

CHAPTER XI

The first thing to do was to make sure that Winter was in the room for the night; matters would be much worse if other members of the household should appear suddenly, or if they were expecting his return.

The point was settled to the satisfaction of the Flash

48

when he saw the other throw off his coat, pull off his shoes, and thrust his feet into slippers of a soft, black leather. Some sort of kid or other skin, thought the Flash.

The big man settled back into his chair with a roll and a faint grunt. From his vest pocket he took a case open at one end and filled with two rows of thin cigars. One of these he drew out. It was narrow as a pencil, and as straight, and very dark in color. It had the oily and mottled look of a good Havana, and when the mouth end was cut and the tobacco lighted, the fragrance of the smoke told the watcher that it was of some specially fine leaf.

Mr. Winter, having established himself properly in the chair and shaked out a newspaper, was hidden behind the folds of it. Thin curls of blue-brown smoke began to issue and curl around the edges of the newspaper. The paper itself, from time to time, gave out a crackling like the sound of a fire on an open hearth.

Such a welling of hatred filled the breast and the very throat of young Baldwin that he took out a revolver and aimed it across the window sill. One touch of the trigger, and Winter was a dead man, but two things held the boy back. One was that he could not find it in his nature to take advantage of a blind ambush in this fashion. The other was that he wished to have a taste of his man, so to speak, before destroying him. To meet a stranger and shoot him down, even in equal combat—that was one thing. But to have a sense of the human soul he was destroying would be quite different—to discover through talk the villainy of the other, to guess at the cunning or the dangers in him, to sample the poisons of which such a nature as this must be composed—and then to tread the thing underfoot like a snake—that would be satisfaction, in some small measure, for the destruction of his father.

So thinking, he swung himself lightly up to the sill of the window. A simple thing to mention, but many a circus and stage athlete would have failed to manage the trick, gripping at the thin, narrow moldings with the tips of his fingers.

He took another glance into the room, but he found that Winter was unmoved. At this moment, he merely stretched his legs, crossed one over the other, and in the height of his satisfaction, he wriggled his toes slowly within their encasement of soft leather.

The Flash set his teeth with anger and disgust.

Then, changing his grip, he fairly swung himself through the open window and into the room.

Another simple thing in the mentioning, but which required a body as supple as a well-oiled bow, and muscles like powerful strings.

He landed on a rug before the window with a thud not much lighter, say, than a cat would make, jumping down from a similar height, so delicately did the knees bend to absorb the shock and the impact.

This noise, and its jarring vibration, slight as it was, served to make Winter lower his paper.

Over the still-smoking rim of it, he looked out at the Flash with an eye as bright and as clear as the eye of a boy. It was the youngest eye that the Flash had ever seen. It was an eye that would never grow old. And therefore it had an ageless quality that was older than time itself.

The years that had flowed through the spirit of Thomas Winter had not left behind them any marking upon his nature or upon his mind. Time had been to him an incident. The emotions, the losses, the sorrows, the sufferings, the joys which shadow the eyes of most had been to him no more than an occasional dimness and brightening such as moving clouds make on open water, passing as soon, and affecting him as much.

This unusual eye, then, looked out at the Flash, and then he nodded at the boy.

"You're late," said Winter.

The Flash smiled.

His face was always handsome. It became wonderfully beautiful as he smiled. His glance darkly and tenderly caressed the features and the form of the older man.

"You've been expecting me then?" he said.

"Oh, yes," said Winter.

"I'm glad of that," said the Flash. "I should have gone around to the front door, perhaps."

"It would have been just as well," said Winter, "but now that you're here, you're here. And I'm glad to see you."

"I dare say you are," said the Flash, and smiled again. "When did you get the first notice of my coming?"

"When I saw you come out of the shadows and throw yourself on the grave of your father," said Winter. "That was the time when I knew that you would drop in on me. Through the window, I took it for granted."

"You were there?" said the boy. "You were there by the grave, were you?"

"Tut, tut," said Winter. "I was not by the grave. I was with the Moores, of course, on the next hill, looking back. The girl wanted us to wait there. And she was waiting because she expected, I suppose, exactly what she saw you do. Oh, she covered it up from her father. But I could look under the surface. I could guess that she knew that it was you."

"You're an interesting fellow," said the boy. "I thought you would be. By the look in Jack's face, you saw that it was I, eh? As if in a mirror?"

"Don't sneer, my boy," said Winter, "sneering never becomes the mocker. It's a foolish and a light state of mind that dictates a sneer. Whereas, as a matter of fact, most people are worthy of a good deal of serious attention. Even a Thomas Winter!"

"I'm giving you more attention, per second," said the boy, "than you ever received in your life before."

"Ah," said Winter, "you're watching my hands and even my feet. You're making sure that I don't suddenly conjure a gun or a dynamite bomb, say, out of a vest pocket. But as a matter of fact, my lad, I was not speaking of physical awareness. I mean something of the spirit, which keeps one humble, and that is the attitude which prevents sneers, and such unchristian things."

"You're fine," said the Flash, with enthusiasm. "You're all right. Go right ahead. You were telling me that from an expression in the girl's face, you knew that it was I— off there in the distance—among the shadows?"

"Of course," said Winter, "I didn't leave it to mere guesswork. I had noticed you during the course of the day. I'd noticed the other brothers, too. In a way, I'm quite a student of human nature—perhaps because, as I was saying, I respect it so much. And I saw nothing in the other six that would lead them to throw themselves—so romantically—upon the grave mound of their father, when there was no one by to see what they did. But you, my lad, have a touch of the spark that burns the soul or makes it live. Perhaps a short time, but as it consumes, it casts a light. So I leaned to my dear Jacqueline and said to her: 'Poor David!'"

"The devil you did!" said the Flash.

"Why not? Of course I did. And when she received that much sympathy from me, the tears which she had been hiding overflowed. They ran down her cheek. She was quite blinded, and when she fumbled for a handkerchief and couldn't find one, I gave her mine. I, as you might say, dried her eyes when she was crying over you."

"She cried, did she?" said the boy, looking intently at the other.

"Oh, you can believe me," said Winter. "I never lie about unimportant things."

"You'll hardly believe it," said the boy, "but that's not altogether unimportant to me."

"Oh," said Winter, "you mean it proves that she loves you? But you couldn't be in doubt about that—not with her father fighting against the idea so hard. He's smoothing your way

51

for you. If you could have been present at supper tonight, it would have pleased you—to hear the way he denounced your frivolity in racing the horse. And then to see the fine, starry-eyed way in which she defended you. A girl of spirit. I love a girl of spirit. They are always easily handled. Their emotions make fools of them. Have you noticed that?"

"She defended me?" said the boy.

"Shall I tell you how?"

"No," said the Flash. "We've talked long enough about her. Suppose we change the subject?"

"You're gallant and chivalrous, too," said Winter. "I've never known a young scamp who wasn't—except sneak thieves, and their ilk. I like the gallant and the chivalrous youths, too. They also follow the blind emotions that put them into the hands of the birdcatchers."

"You catch them, do you?" said the boy.

"Oh, yes. I'm an expert. You might call it my profession."

"But granting everything, what made you feel that I would call on you? I don't quite follow that," said the Flash.

"Why," said Winter, opening those strange eyes of his a little. "What else would a lad of spirit do, when he knew the murderer of his father was so close at hand?"

The Flash sighed.

He sat down on the edge of the center table, his back to the door and his face toward his host.

"I like you, Winter," he said. "I've never met anyone I liked so well. I hate to kill you."

"Do you?" smiled Winter.

"Yes. But the time wears on. I could sit here and talk to a fellow like you forever. I could learn about life from you, I know. But I haven't the time. Have you a revolver?"

"Yes. I'm never without one."

"Then if you'll take it and stand at that side of the room, I'll stand on this side, and we'll have the thing out."

"Ah, a duel?" said Winter.

His eyes were laughing joyously. They twinkled and they snapped at the Flash.

"Yes. We'll have it fairly out. I hope you're good with guns," said the Flash.

"Thanks," said Winter, "but I won't use a gun on you tonight."

"No?"

"No, I don't have to."

As he spoke, he raised one forefinger from the half-smoked cigar which he was holding, and the Flash was seized by mighty hands from behind.

CHAPTER XII

The Flash looked over his shoulder—and immediately regretted the glance. For he saw behind him a face that seemed hardly human. He saw a low forehead, with shaggy hair bristling over it, a smoky-yellowish skin and eyes of a smoky yellow, also. The face smiled, its jowls bulging on either side and showing teeth which had a little division between them, like the teeth of an animal which bites not to eat so much as to wound.

"Tie his hands, Sammy," said Winter, "and put him over in this corner. Tie them good and hard, and then take the guns away from him. I'm sorry about the tying," he said, "but I want to have a little chat with you—first."

First—and then what?

The Flash found that his wrists were being held from behind by a single hand. He made a sudden, wrenching effort, with all his might, but long fingers wound about his wrists, and he was helpless. He felt a swift lashing of cord being wound into place, and the grip of the bonds held him securely. Then he was lifted from behind, as a man might lift an infant and hold it out at arm's length. In this manner, he was borne to a chair and placed in it.

Over him leaned the creature who had carried him. He no longer wondered that his wrists had been held by a single hand, for never had he seen or dreamed of such hands as these. They seemed twice the human size; the fingers extraordinarily long and square ended, and the thumb seemed as long as the other digits, which were covered over the first joint with a fur of red hair, close growing, and strangely repulsive to see.

The hands of Sammy and his queer face were not the only attractions he had to offer. His arms and shoulders could have fitted a giant seven feet high, but his own height was a full foot and a half short of this. He had the barrel and the bulk of body necessary, it appeared, but from the hips down, he was wrong. The hips themselves pinched in, very oddly. And the legs were ridiculously bowed, thick, and short. They were so malformed that he seemed to be a cripple, and had to swagger from side to side as he walked.

It would be easy to imagine Sammy aloft on a yard in the midst of a hurricane, working at home when other men were likely to be blown scooting down the wind.

The huge hands of Sammy now investigated the clothes of the Flash and brought forth his two Colts.

"Thank you, Sammy," said Winter. "Just sit over there for a moment, will you? I want you to watch this fellow for me. He looks young and of course he's weak in your hands. But still he's dangerous. Even with his weapons gone, and his hands tied, and you in the room, he's still a little dangerous. Sit over there and keep an eye on him, will you?"

Sammy waddled across the room, turned, and in one movement crossed his legs and sat down on the single step that led to the door of the room.

He began to pick his teeth with a casual, vast, forefinger. One smoky eye he rolled towards the gap of the open window. And a corner of his regard remained continually upon the prisoner.

"How did he get in?" asked the Flash. "Did he rise through a crack in the floor, or did you just materialize him?"

Winter smiled.

"He came through the door," said he.

The Flash shook his head.

"Not that, I think," said he.

"Yes," said Winter. "When Sammy wants to open a door without making a noise, he can do it so that even a wild wolf wouldn't know. He can close it, too, the same way."

"He can even make the wind stop blowing, I suppose?" said the Flash.

"Well, you'd be surprised if you knew all that Sammy can do. Wouldn't he, Sammy?"

Sammy, for answer, merely laughed. It was absurd and rather horrible to hear only a thin, high-pitched, squeaking sound come out of that bull throat and that vastness of chest.

"How did he know that I was here?" asked the Flash.

"Oh, I suppose he heard you say something. He's got extraordinarily good ears. Haven't you, Sammy?"

But Sammy did not appear to have understood the question. He stopped picking at his teeth and began to suck at them in the same meditative manner, with his head turned toward the window. But from the corner of one eye his attention never left the face of the Flash.

The latter returned the glance with interest. He began to center all the power of his will upon the misshapen face of Sammy and the corner of the single eye that was visible. For he felt a desperate desire to confront the man face to face and look straight into his soul, if soul there was in the great body.

In the meantime, Winter was talking.

"You speak rather better than most of them that I meet out

54

here," said Winter. "How does that come, David? Did your father send you away to school?"

"No," said the Flash. "But I had more time to spend on books."

"More time? You mean you were an invalid?"

"No," said Flash David. "I never was sick, to speak of. I had time because I took time. I didn't work. I never worked. I never *will* work. That's why they have no use for me, around here."

"Except Jacqueline," said Winter, his eyes narrowing a little.

But the Flash kept his regard centered upon Sammy, as he talked, still hauling with all the force of his will to make the fellow turn toward him.

"Jacqueline is all right," he said. "You haven't her yet. I suppose you think you'll get her, but you're wrong. She'll see through you. She has a knack of seeing through people and things."

"My dear boy," said Winter, "do you think that I'm seriously interested in little Jacqueline?"

"Yes," said the Flash. "Or her coin. I don't know which. It's all right, anyway. It'll all come out in the wash. I'm not afraid for Jack. I wouldn't be afraid for her, if she were dropped at the North Pole with nothing but bare hands and her wits."

"What would she do?" asked Winter, curiously.

"Why, she'd make harpoons out of icicles and spear a whale, and lay up his meat in storage, and build a house out of his bones, and warm herself with burning his blubber, and cool herself using his tail for a fan. That's the way that she'd carry along, if you want to know!"

"Thanks," said Winter, "because now I know!"

He smiled as he spoke, but just then Sammy rose to his feet. It was an odd thing to see him rise. He did not even uncross his legs, but he gave himself a shove sidewise with one long arm and came at the Flash with a lurch and a swing.

The Flash had what he wanted now—a full-face view of Sammy, and the full view was a thing worth painting. For Sammy was in a frenzy. His long, loose upper lip curled from his teeth. His nostrils flared. His smoky eyes were lights at last with points of fire. And he came with his great hands spread, as though ready to take the Flash and break him in two.

"Hold on, Sammy," said Winter. "What have you been doing to him, Flash? You mustn't bother Sammy. Even I don't bother Sammy. But we respect each other and leave one another alone. Don't touch him, lad. *I'll* do all the touching that is necessary."

Sammy returned to his seat on the step in front of the door. He did not turn around. He simply walked backward, and by instinct seemed to find the right time to sit down again. He lowered himself slowly, and his blazing eyes never deviated from the face of David Baldwin.

An odd chill and tingle worked in the spinal marrow of the Flash. But he answered that furious glare. He looked straight at it, calmly and coldly, and mastered the shudder that started to shake him.

Suddenly the fire died in the eyes of Sammy. His eyes wavered down. Then they rolled askance toward the window's empty blackness. They flashed back at the prisoner but, as though frightened, Sammy looked as suddenly away again. He was not watching the Flash, now, but he was intensely aware of him—as intensely as though touching him with a hand. He shrugged his massive, loose-jointed shoulders and continued to stare out toward the open night.

"And now," said Winter, "that we've had our little chat and built our little house at the North Pole, what am I to do?"

"I can tell you," said the Flash.

"Go right on," said Winter. "*Do* tell me!"

The Flash looked at the bright brown eyes of the other.

"You'll shoot me through the head," said he, "and then you'll cut the cords around my wrist, and put a revolver in my hand, and tumble me on the floor. And when the others hear the revolver shot and come running, you'll point out the fellow who intruded into your room in the middle of the night, while you were quietly sitting here and smoking a cigar, and reading your newspaper. It won't be murder. Only self-defense. Nothing could be easier than that, of course."

Winter sighed.

He put his hands together, joining fingertip to fingertip, accurately.

"I ought to do it," he said, "and yet I can't. I really cannot bring myself to do it!"

The Flash stirred a little, and smiled.

"You will, though," said he. "You'll manage to bring yourself to it. You know the necessity."

Winter slowly nodded.

"If I could put you off, frighten you into good behavior in any way, I'd do it in a moment. I don't want to clutter my way with a dead man, just now. But I see that you're of a superior cut. You intend to cut my throat for me, if I don't cut yours. Not that I blame you a whit. Not a whit!

I admire you all the more. But, as you point out, there is a necessity. Sammy, please carry our new friend over to the window, will you?"

The Flash rose to his feet.

"I'll walk," said he.

"Steady," said Winter.

He was holding a revolver which he had suddenly produced. He held it negligently, muzzle down, but his meaning was plain.

The Flash, however, walked toward the window, and turned about when he was near it. His plan was clear in his mind; he felt that he had the hundredth part of a chance.

CHAPTER XIII

"It's all right, you see," said the Flash. "Here I stand. The intruder into your room, ready to be drilled through the brain."

His host smiled almost tenderly on him.

"You're a delightful lad, David," said he. "But as you went toward that window, just now, you almost got a slug through the back of your head."

"I suppose I did," said the Flash. "But I couldn't stand the thought of being carried—I've been touched already—by your monkey man, yonder!"

And he turned his head, with a sneer of disgust, toward Sammy as he spoke.

The latter, however, did not pause to consider that his master was about to destroy the insulter. A strange whine came out of his enormous throat. He lurched from his place and went across the room in a sprawling rush, with his vast hands extended before him. And as he charged he did what the Flash had hoped he would do, the thing for which he had spurred the monster to frenzy—he came straight into line between Winter and the Flash.

That was all the latter wanted. He was already full before the open window. Now he simply leaned backward and hurled himself through it. If he landed on his head, it would mean a broken neck; but he managed to twist about in the air and strike the ground on his side. It was a heavy blow, but he rolled with it, and sprang to his feet.

Behind him, he heard the incredulous roar of Sammy. Behind Sammy he heard the calm, sharp remarks of Winter.

And as the Flash took to his heels as fast as he could

run, he saw Winter shoot through the window like a circus performer through a loop and land running, behind him.

The red men of the prairies used to run their foot races with their arms held stiffly at their sides. It was considered ungraceful to allow the arms to swing. But even arms carried at the sides are as nothing compared with hands tied forcibly behind the back. The rhythm and the swing of the runner are destroyed completely.

But the Flash went like his own name—despite all handicaps. He had not the wind or the endurance for a long effort. His muscles were not seasoned by labor or by training. His strength was like the strength of a great cat. The deer may run away from it in a quarter of a mile, but in the first hundred yards the leopard travels two feet to the deer's one.

So the Flash shot from the house of Moore and went arrowlike into the aspen grove behind the corrals.

Who has tried to pick up a pair of thrown reins and get them over the head of a horse—having no hands for the performance?

The Flash did it with a single gesture. He caught the reins on the toe of his boot and swept them over the head of the mare with one swing of his leg.

Who has tried to mount without hands?

The Flash did it. One bound into the air, and he caught the good mare between his knees. He almost spun over and off on the farther side, having no arms to stop his side thrust, but he managed to lean forward enough, and the pommel of the saddle struck him and stopped him with a shock.

Through the brush he heard Winter coming.

Even to the steady nerves of the Flash, it seemed that the devil himself was rushing upon him, and that he heard him panting in the underbrush.

So, with a shudder that racked him from head to foot, he gave the mare the word, and she shot away.

He blessed God and the gypsy who had trained her. She answered the pressure of heel and knee with a perfect readiness. She swerved through the aspens neatly, without jumps and jars that might have unsettled him.

So he swept into the open, and knew that already he was beyond any but the most distant and chance revolver shots.

He was in the open, and the mare was working like smoothly flowing water beneath him, carrying him back to safety. In all his risky life, there had been no chance so close as that through which he had passed on this night. There had been no threat so keen and so great.

He felt, in a way, that he had been in the presence of a master and an assistant devil. He had felt the mind of the

58

master; he had felt the hand of the slave. He could not call either of them mere humans. The apelike Sammy, who had not uttered a single word, might be from the East Indies or an island in the South Seas. Even there he must be a freak of nature.

And Winter himself? He was of no age, no blood, no country. He was simply evil, first, and last. It was the ground he walked on and the air he breathed.

Now, as he rode off into safety, the Flash looked back and saw the glimmer of the lights of Moore's house, and smiled a little. For Winter was Moore's most honored friend! And now, as he watched, he saw the light go out, and he smiled again. The household had gone to sleep, never dreaming that murder had almost been committed under its roof.

The Flash returned to Pazo.

He went not down the main street but by back alleys until he came to one very familiar to him. Down this he rode, and presently the mare stopped at a back door. There the Flash tossed his leg over the horn of the saddle and slipped to the ground. With his foot he tapped against the door—one tap, and a pause, and two more taps close together, and then another as for a grace note.

He waited. No answer coming, he repeated the summons.

At last a shutter was pushed open soundlessly on its well-oiled hinges.

"Si?" said a woman's voice, whispering.

"Juanna, open the door to me," said the Flash.

The window closed. There was no sound of footsteps within. But presently the door before the Flash opened. The form of the woman was dimly outlined by the starlight against the deep dark within.

"Have you a knife with you, Juanna?" asked the boy.

"Yes, senor."

"Cut these cords around my wrists."

He turned, and the thing was done. With the fingers of her left hand, she felt the way cautiously, using sense of touch as a light to see by, lest she should harm the skin with the keen edge of the knife. The cords parted. His arms were free again.

"Your hands are ice," said Juanna.

"Rub them," said the Flash. "Get the blood back into them."

He gave her his hands and she kneaded them swiftly, massaging the cold, hard flesh until it softened and the blood ran through the active fingers again with a painful tingle.

"That's better," said the Flash. "Now get your husband up. Is he sober?"

"Yes, senor. He has been lying awake, thinking."

59

"He'll think himself into prison, one of these days," said Flash David.

"Yes, senor," said the woman, submissively.

"Go call him, then."

She disappeared. The sound of her step was merely a light whisper in the house, a hiss in the darkness.

The Flash turned about and eyed the stars. Boötes had swung, now, far toward the west, and there were new stars soaring in the east. It made a good clock, that procession of the stars, and he saw that he had talked with Winter longer than he had guessed.

Now came a heavier, padding footfall behind him, but he did not turn. The voice of Beckwith muttered at his ear.

"Hello, Flash. What's new?"

"I'll go in and sit down with you," said the Flash. "We have to have a little chat."

"Come along. I'd rather talk to you, Flash, than anybody in the state."

Beckwith led the way down the narrow, cool hall. The thick dobe walls of the building shut out the day's heat, and now the coolness of a cellar, and the dampness of one, breathed through the place. He opened a door, lighted a lamp, and would have sat down.

"Close the shutters," said the Flash.

"It'll keep out the cool air," said Beckwith, but he did as he was told.

When he had finished, he found the Flash seated by the table, making a cigarette which he lighted. As he puffed at it with long inhalations, he began to hum and to drum on the edge of the table. Beckwith fastened his eyes on the youngster with a sort of awe, and sat down opposite him.

He was so quiet, so respectfully attentive, that one might have thought that he was a child in the presence of a father or a tutor, and unsure of his lesson.

"I've lost my guns tonight," said the Flash.

Beckwith closed his eyes and opened them again. He began to stroke his drooping, pale mustache and he said not a word.

"They were taken away from me," said the Flash, "by a man that I'm after. Have you seen him? I mean a newcomer who's staying at the house of Moore."

"I've seen him," said Beckwith.

"What did you think of him?"

"Muy diablo," said Beckwith, with conviction. "How did he do it?"

"He has a servant along with him," said the boy. "A queer, big devil with the strength of three men in each of his hands.

60

My shoulders are aching, where he grabbed me, and so are my arms. He handled me like a baby. And he took the guns away from me and tied my hands behind my back. Juanna has just cut the cord and rubbed some feeling back into my fingers.

He spread his slender hands before him on the table, and worked the fingers, attentively. And Beckwith watched, as an amateur might watch the exercises of a great pianist.

"Do you know anything about that fellow—that man, Winter?" asked the Flash.

"No. Not a thing. Never heard of him before."

"You'll hear of him later on," said the Flash. "He's on my trail. I'm on his. And I want to keep in touch with him. Get a man up to the Moores' place. Have you got a good fellow to send?"

"I've got a half-breed," said the saloon keeper, "that could put on hip boots and a high hat and walk under the crack of a door, or dive through a keyhole. He can speak three languages and understand thirty. His father was a gunman; his mother was an Indian witch; and his uncle was the devil himself."

"Then," said the Flash, "perhaps he's bright enough to learn something about Winter. But I doubt it. Anyway, the Moores always need new hands. They work them, up there on the ranch. Get your half-breed together and tell him to go up there and keep his eyes open, day and night. For your own sake, too, Beckwith. Because if Winter finds me in your place, he may blow you and the house up along with me. He's thorough. That's what Winter is."

CHAPTER XIV

The Flash went to bed. Beckwith did not.

First he went into a low, rambling shed near his house and roused two men who were sleeping in it. One was as withered and tough as an old goat; him the saloon keeper posted outside the window of the room in which the Flash was soundly sleeping. The other was a supple, slender youth, yawning, but courteous. He wore an air of distinction, owing to his hawklike nose and his erect carriage, and he had a pair of sleepy, coal-black eyes.

To him, Beckwith said: "Manuelo, there is a man at the Moore ranch about whom we want to find out a few particulars. Savvy? You get yourself up there by the crack of dawn and take a job."

Manuelo groaned deeply.

"You'll get something out of it," said Beckwith. "You're working for the Flash. You understand? That's sure to mean money, and it's sure to mean a fight, I'd take it, before the finish. You know the Flash, don't you, you snake in the grass?"

Manuelo smiled. He drew in his breath with a sound like one drinking water noisily.

"I know him a little," said he. "I go gladly to the ranch. I become a puncher again, senor?"

"You become anything. A house mozo, if they need one. You can do anything. Try to get near the house and stay there. The man's name is Winter. Now get out of here and sharpen your wits. Winter is a man in ten thousand. You've got to be better than he is."

After these not altogether explicit instructions, Beckwith went back into the house, but still he did not intend sleep.

He took a chair which he placed exactly in front of the door of the room in which his guest was sleeping. He had a lantern on the floor of the hall, between his feet, and by the light of this he looked over his revolver, made sure that it was in good condition and ready for instant service. Then he put out the light and sat in the darkness, with the gun in his hand, and the barrel of it resting on his knees.

All the rest of that night he sat there with ceaseless vigilance, now and then turning to this side or to that, in case the whispers which he imagined he heard should develop into dangers creeping upon him down the corridor.

Then the gray of the morning filled up the doors at each end of the hall. At last the light entered, dimly. Juanna got up and, before starting the day's work, she came to her lord and master. She stood beside him, and whispered softly:

"What is it?"

"I dunno," said Beckwith. "Hell's popping. I dunno just how. But the Flash is in deep. He said that his hands was tied."

"Yes. I cut the cords."

"Might have been better if you'd cut his throat!" said Beckwith, with a sudden bitterness.

"The throat? His throat?" whispered the woman, horrified.

"Ay," said Beckwith. "He'll make us stumble one day so hard that we'll break our necks!"

"Would we have necks sound and whole today," she asked, "except for the Flash?"

"Ay," said Beckwith. "I know what I owe him. I ain't one

to forget, either. But I'm drawed so tight that the flick of a finger would break me in two."

"I, also," said Juanna. "I have not slept all the night. It was the Flash—and his hands were tied together. Who could have tied his hands?"

"The devil himself, I guess," said Beckwith with a sigh. "It beats me!"

"How did he manage to get away from the danger—after they made him helpless?"

"How did he manage?" muttered Beckwith. "D'you think that he'd talk about that? That ain't worth his time. That's nothing. The thing's behind him, and he'll never mention it again. Go make some coffee, and make it double strong. I'm gunna need it. But make some tea for the Flash, and make it weak. He likes it better that way."

Juanna moved away.

And so, a little later, after the Flash had risen and bathed himself in half a washtub of cold water, and dressed, and come out of his room, he found the fragrant tea waiting for him and sat down with Beckwith to sip it.

They said nothing. Beckwith was looking out the door at the increasing glaze of light on the whitewashed faces of the dobe buildings. And the Flash seemed interested only in the flavor of his tea.

"It's gunna be hot," said Beckwith, after a long pause, as he finished his third cup of coffee. "It's gunna be hot as the devil, today. Juanna had oughta close up the house."

"Juanna is a charm," said the boy. "There's no one like her. She has a voice like a dove and a touch like a magician. What a lucky thing for you, old son, that her cousin was thrown in the same hoosegow with you. You never would have seen her, except for that."

"A lucky thing for her cousin," said the saloon keeper, "that he threw in with me while we were in that jail. Or you'd never of taken the trouble to turn him loose when you called for me!"

The Flash shrugged his shoulders, and seemed to make the past slip smoothly from them.

"What was her cousin in for?" he asked.

"Oh, nothin' much," said Beckwith. "He slipped a knife into a Yaqui. It was just some little thing like that. Call it murder, if you want, because he done it from behind."

The Flash yawned.

"I slept like a dead man," he said. "You have a good house for sleep, old son."

The saloon keeper grunted. He did not tell his young friend that he and another man had watched all during the night over his welfare. From time to time, these two had done much for one another, in the paths which are straight and in the paths which are crooked. Their mutual obligations they mentioned rarely.

A barefooted boy suddenly appeared before them.

The doors of the house had been closed to shut out the increasing heat of the day, and the flash of the outer light as the boy entered, and then closed the door behind him, was almost blinding.

"A Senor Winter asks if he may come in to speak with Senor Baldwin?"

"Go tell him to come in," said the Flash.

The boy disappeared.

"I told you he was the devil," said the Flash, showing his white teeth as he smiled at his friend.

"Now," said Beckwith, leaning a little toward him, "I'm ready to take him off the board so as nobody will ever guess that he ever played checkers. I'll wipe him out. I'll take the risk. D'you want that?"

The Flash looked thoughtfully at him, and said nothing.

"All right," said Beckwith. "You go on and be proud and upright, you safeblower, you gunman. One of these days, these little tricks and proud ideas, they'll get you into a pack of trouble."

"I'll trouble you for a gun," said the Flash. "Now, vamoose. Good-by, Beckwith. You keep out of this until I tell you to take a hand."

Beckwith disappeared just as the street door opened again, and through the blinding flash of the outer light Thomas Winter walked into the hallway and down it toward the boy, who had risen to meet him.

Winter came straight on, until he was only a pace away. Then he halted. He held out his hand.

"A flag of truce," said he.

The Flash sighed.

"All right," said he.

"Hadn't we better shake on it?" said Winter.

"Shaking hands," said the Flash, "is a mighty bad habit, when the weather gets as hot as this. Down here we mostly just give the other fellow a high sign. That's all. Sit down, Winter."

"Thank you," said Winter.

He took a chair opposite to the boy, and after regarding him for a moment he actually smiled and then chuckled softly. "I should have done it," he said.

"What?" asked Flash David.

"I should have shot Sammy down in order to get him

64

out of the way and take a crack at you. The big fool—blundering in between us like that! I don't know why I didn't put a slug through him, and then another into you."

"You might have been too late to catch me," said the Flash. "And that would have been ugly—Sammy dead on the floor, shot through from behind. I thought of that, when I worked the little scheme out."

"It was a good scheme, a bright scheme, in fact," said Winter. "It's plain that you use your brain. They tell me that you never work with your hands. Instantly I understood the point. A man who works with his hands is apt to allow his brain to grow stale. But yours is fertile and worth while. I tell you again, I am proud and happy to have you among my acquaintances, David."

"Thank you," said the Flash. "Now, about this truce that you come under. I don't know what's in your head, Winter, but I'd like to point out that we've got a lot of space, out there, and as good places as you ever could find to fight it out."

Winter gaped at him; though perhaps his astonishment was not as great as he pretended.

"Do you think, Flash," said he, "that if we're to fight it out I'll meet you on equal terms? No, sir. If it's to be a battle, then I use everything I can against you—trickery, deceit, hired hands, anything that I know of to brush you out of the way. Fight it out on equal terms? Why, my boy, you must think that you're talking to some proud duelist of another century! No, no, David. You're mistaken about me. You take me too lightly. You really do."

The Flash nodded. And his grim eye bored into the brown, bright eye of Thomas Winter.

"I believe you," he said. "I think that this is the truth."

"Of course it is," said Winter. "I told you before I would never lie to you about an unimportant thing. And now for the business that brought me here. First, as to these."

He took out a pair of long Colts, the very ones which the Flash had left behind him.

"I wanted you to have them again," said Winter, with a charming smile.

"Are they loaded?"

"Yes, yes. Exactly as you left them."

The Flash looked the other straight in the face, leveled one of the weapons suddenly, and fanned the hammer back with his thumb. It fell again with a dull click. The cartridge had not exploded.

CHAPTER XV

When the revolver was pointed at his head, Thomas Winter twitched a hand suddenly inside his coat. A gleam came in his eye. But the hand immediately came from beneath the flap of the coat again, and the light went out of the brown eye.

As the hammer fell with a harmless click, he actually smiled at the boy.

"One never can be sure, you see," said he. "I expected that you might be tempted, and therefore I made temptation a harmless thing. You'll understand that, of course?"

The Flash smiled.

"I wasn't tempted, Winter," said he. "You'll understand that, too. I knew that you wouldn't leave the gun intact. That would have been a reasonably cheap way out, for you. Suppose, for instance, that we walked out to settle this little argument together? No, no, Winter, I think that we understand each other better than you think!"

Winter laughed softly. "I've admired you from the very first, David," said he. "And now I admire you more than ever. Of course I had that in mind, too. If you crowded me against a wall, then I wanted to take every advantage that I possibly could."

"I see that," said the Flash, without anger in his voice.

He merely considered the other with a bland curiosity, as though he never had seen such a man before, and this was in fact his feelings.

"Suppose," said Winter, "that we get on to the business that brought me here?"

"By all means," said the Flash.

"Very well, then. You realize that I know you're a dangerous lad to have against one?"

"Thank you," said the Flash.

Still he waited, watching the older man without enmity, as a safe bird might watch the stooping of a hawk in the sky above him.

"Now, then," said Winter, "since I realize the danger that may come at my head from you, I've called on you to see if you can't be persuaded to make a truce with me, and out of the truce we may build up a regular treaty of lasting peace."

"You ask for a truce?" said the boy.

"That's exactly what I ask for."

"And why should I give you a truce, Winter?" said the Flash.

"Shall I tell you? But of course you see for yourself," said the other. "You feel that you have a deathless duty—which is to hate me. Am I wrong?"

"Not to hate you," said the Flash. "I don't hate you, Winter. But I'm going to do my best to kill you."

Winter nodded.

"You put it in the best way," said he, "and of course I appreciate the difference between the two viewpoints. However, let me suggest that though you have seen me in a pair of rather vital situations, still you don't entirely know me?"

"That's true," said the Flash. "It would take years to get even an inkling about you."

"It would. And more than years," said Winter. "Because I don't really understand myself. But I know this much—that I would have a chance to appear to you in other lights, if we could patch up a short truce between us. The advantage of the truce would be that you might have an opportunity to learn that, if I am a disagreeable enemy, I can also be a valuable friend."

"Just a moment," said the boy. "You've shown that you're ready to double-cross anyone at any time. Now you ask me to take your word that you want a truce. What would happen to me the first moment that my back was turned?"

Winter nodded gravely.

"I understand why you feel this way," said he. "But try to understand this. To my enemies I can be a steady foe. To my friends, I can be faith itself. I'm asking you to believe that. If you'll reflect for a moment, you'll see that this must necessarily be true."

"I don't see that point," said the Flash.

"Then, look at the thing in this way. When a man leads a life of crime, he must have friends, must he not?"

"I suppose so," said the Flash. "Yes, I've found that to be true. I suppose that a crook needs friends even more than an honest man."

"More?" said Winter. "But of course he does. The honest man has no real need of friends. Friends are a luxury to a fellow who's safely bulwarked behind the law. But to your hunted criminal, a friend is a helping hand, safety, wisdom in a time of need, everything that the heart desires. I'll tell you, my lad, that once I was riding through the snow, against a blizzard, near Winnipeg, and behind me there were two fellows of the Northwest Mounted. And all of those policemen, up there, are hawks, with wings that never grow tired. But *my* wings were tired, believe me. And I came through the storm to the house of a friend. I told him what had happened and what was behind me, and he put on my coat, got on my horse, and acted the part of a lure to get the police on *his* trail. Now, that gives you an example of what friendship has meant to me."

"And what did it mean to your friend?" asked the boy.

"It meant that they caught him, and put him in prison for a year, on some charge or other. But if they had caught me, they would have hanged me, Flash David. Which makes quite a good deal of difference, one way and another."

"No doubt," said the Flash. "But I'm a little curious. What did you do to pay back your friend that went to jail to save your neck?"

"I paid him," said the other, "with blood out of my body, and with cash out of my pocketbook. But more than that, I paid him with the only real coin that he was willing to accept —a deep, undying affection, faith, and trust."

"That lasted to this day?" murmured the Flash, sneering.

"It lasted for only three years," said Winter calmly. "Then the temptation grew too great for him. He knew that he could make a great deal of money by turning me in, and he turned me in. I managed to ecape by the breadth of an eyelash. And my friend—" here he looked the Flash straight in the eye— "repented so much what he had just attempted to do, that he committed suicide."

The Flash smiled, and Winter went on, with a voice like an iron bell: "At least he was shot with a bullet from his own revolver."

"I thought so," said the Flash.

"But don't miss my point," said Winter. "As long as a man lives outside of the law, the very breath in his nostrils is friendship. I try to tell you that I understand this. I ask you to believe that my faith to a friend can be as inviolable as a Christian's love for his God. Do you believe me when I say it?"

"Yes," said the Flash, slowly. "Perhaps you're only hyp- notizing me with words. But I *do* believe what you're telling me."

"Thank you," said Winter. "Now for the next point. I'm asking you for a truce, Flash, so that I can show you the sort of friend I would be to you. I put such a value on you, Flash, that I would go to any lengths to secure your friendship. Let me try to put myself before you in the best light. After- ward, you can say yes or no."

The Flash shook his head.

"Don't be hasty," urged Winter. "Think it over a little, I beg of you, before you make up your mind permanently. If you are fixed and final in your resolution to be against me, then I assure you that there are black days ahead of you."

The Flash nodded.

"You're acting like a madman," said Winter. "If only I could let you see the needless danger—if only I could let you see, on the other hand, how I could help you, teach you, instruct you in the easiest way of living—"

The Flash held up his hand. And the words stopped.

"It's pretty much of a compliment," said Flash David, "to have you call on me and talk like this. I think you mean it. I think you would actually like to have me as a friend. If I were a shade different from what I am, I'd accept what you offer. It would be a great game to work on your side in anything. And I know that I'm bound to step outside the law, sooner or later. I couldn't find a better partner than you'd be. But the trouble is that you killed my father, Winter. And that fact burns in me wtih a light that will never go out. You've murdered a man who happened to be *my* friend. And if you were the devil himself, or an angel out of the sky, I'd never stop trying to get feathers or bat wings to fly after you. That's pretty final, Winter. I won't change my mind on the point."

Winter sighed, and his sigh was almost a groan.

"I dare say that it's ended, then?" said he.

"It's ended," said the Flash.

For a moment the older man kept his eyes on the floor, apparently reaching deep and more deeply into his mind in search of other temptations and other arguments.

"Suppose I tell you this," said he. "I have under me a complete and complicated system. I can stretch one hand to New York and another to San Francisco. I can touch a fellow in New Orleans and another in Chicago. I have this power to do you good, David. I have the same power to do you harm. I give you my word of honor, that if you throw in against me, you will not be living and breathing ten days from this. I know that the job will be a ticklish one, so I give you ten days of life. But that's absolutely the end. I beg you to think once more!"

"Winter," said the boy, "I've never even been tempted by what you say. I would rather shoot myself through the head than associate in any way with the man who murdered my father."

"Ah, ah, ah," murmured Winter. "There we are—the old, childish prejudice of the ages—as though blood relationship were the relationship which counted! As though it were not a mere fiction of the imagination! There is no more real tie between father and son than there is between the oak tree and the pine, though both of them come out of the same soil. But

I won't argue any longer. I've never before begged any man for his friendship. I see that I was wrong to offer myself to you. Good-by, Flash David."

"Good-by, sir," said the Flash.

Winter paused at the door, holding it a fraction of an inch ajar. He looked back almost tenderly upon Flash David.

"Poor lad," said he. "God pity you, as I pity you. I could have made you a tower of flames. Now I can only see you burn for one instant, and consume yourself in your own brilliance. I'm sorry, David. I swear that I'm sorry to the bottom of my heart."

But David, leaning a hand upon the edge of the table, smiled fixedly, and said not a word.

Winter stepped out into the street, and the door closed softly behind him.

CHAPTER XVI

Great events, when they go by us, may pass as silently as the night itself, but they are apt to leave the mind a melancholy blank, as the eye and the ear are left after a great overland rushes through a little way station and the watchers see the dust cloud, the fluttering flag, the swaying observation platform diminish rapidly in the distance.

So the Flash felt lonely, deserted, cast out from the main currents of life, when the door closed and shut Thomas Winter away from him. With that man for a partner, he could at once have entered a wild swirl of excitement. With Thomas Winter at his side, they might have ripped open treasures and walked a tightrope around the world, never falling, never failing.

He was sure of it. And when Winter left him it was as though a picture of ten thousand joyous faces grew dim before his eyes and ten thousand gay voices faded on his ear.

So he clenched his teeth, suddenly, and turned his attention to the guns. It did not take him long to remedy the defect. It was a simple thing to put them right.

He was still working over the weapons when Beckwith came in, holding by the scruff of the neck a little wizened, yellow-faced fellow who alternately cowered and snarled.

"Do you know this fellow?" asked Beckwith. "Ain't this one of these here gypsy friends of yours?"

"He's the fellow that I won Rags from," said the Flash. "What's he up to?"

"He was just payin' a call on Rags," said Beckwith. "He

was out there talkin' to her, in a whisper, as you might say. And so's she could hear him better, he unties her head rope, and he starts her toward the back door of the stable, so's she will be able to see him by a better light. And just then that kid that works for me, that Juan Pedro—you know him?—"

"The kid with the scar?" said the Flash. "Yes, I know him."

"Juan Pedro sees him, because Juan is up in the mow of the bar—stealin' pigeons, most likely—and he jumps, lets himself go and drops off the edge of the hay and lands on this gypsy with both knees and knocks the wind out of him and bowls him over. So he picks him up and hands him to me. D'you want him, or is he just one of your discards?"

"Let me look at him," said the Flash.

He stepped close to the other. The little man had a sick look in his face, and his head was down. Only through the brush of his brows did he turn his eyes up toward the Flash.

"Why did you try it, brother?" asked the Flash.

"Brother?" echoed Beckwith. "Brother—to dirt like that?"

The Flash lifted his young hand imperiously. Beckwith was silent.

"Why did you do it?" repeated Flash David.

"I dunno," said the other, softly.

"Even if you had her," said David Baldwin, "even if you had her under your saddle, and an open road before you, don't you know that I would have caught you—this year or next year—or sometime? Don't you know that I would have broken your neck?"

The gypsy nodded. He raised a hand as dark and as dirty as the claw of a buzzard.

"I know," said he.

"And still you came for her?"

The gypsy raised his head and looked for an instant toward the ceiling.

"Yes," said he, simply.

"Why?" persisted the Flash.

"Because I could not stay away!"

The Flash made a face of pain. He began to walk up and down the room.

"Steady!" said Beckwith to the gypsy. "If you make another move like that last one—I'll let light clean through you!"

The gypsy leaned against the wall. His clawlike hand was still fumbling at the soiled yellow rag that was knotted about his throat. And his eyes were as empty as unlighted windows.

The Flash paused suddenly before him.

71

"That mare," said he, "what's she mean to you?"

"She?" said the gypsy.

He sighed. His eyes half closed. His face flushed a little.

"I saw her when she was a foal beside her mother," said he. "I saw her. I dreamed of her. The next night I stole her. She has lived with me like a daughter ever since."

Beckwith laughed loudly.

"The crook admits that he stole her—the dirty hoss thief! The skunk!"

"Be still, will you?" commanded the boy.

"Yes," said the other. But he scowled and sneered at the gypsy.

"Listen to me," said the Flash very gently. "It happens that just now I have a great need for her. Perhaps not for long. A few days. Ten days, I should say, at the most. After that time has ended, I'll give the mare back to you. You won't even have to turn a card to get her!"

Beckwith listened to this conversation with a shake of his head, and with blinking eyes, as though he could not comprehend the words which his ears were hearing. The gypsy, however, listening with a face which gradually changed and with eyes that widened to round black moons, yellow stained. He put out a hand toward the boy. It was the gesture of a beggar who asks for charity and does not expect it. The Flash smiled reassuringly.

"I'll give her back to you," he said, "sound in wind and limb. Unless she's dropped dead under me!"

It seemed to Beckwith that the gypsy was about to fall his length upon the floor at the feet of David Baldwin, so deeply he bowed, and so slowly. When he stood erect again, he said: "They told me that you were to the others like a king to ordinary men. I was a fool and did not believe. But let me speak to you, master. You saw the light in her, shining through. You knew her, although she is not beautiful. Let me tell you still more. Her blood is the oldest line in the world. Her blood is more priceless than jewels. Keep her and use her, and God give you good out of her. But think of her as of a whole treasure house, filled with jewels."

The Flash laid a hand on the lean, bony shoulder of the little man.

"I love her already," said he.

And the gypsy, looking back at him, had softened eyes. It seemed to Beckwith that there were even tears in those eyes.

And, a moment later, he was gone. Beckwith had reached out a powerful arm to stop him; but a sign from the Flash made his hand fall. So the horse thief who had been taken in the act was turned loose unharmed. To Beckwith it was almost as a matter of sacrilege.

"I'd have peeled the hide off him like a rabbit," he declared. "Here you go and turn him loose and even promise to give the hoss back to the sneak. What's the matter with you, Flash? Tell me what's the matter, will you? Didn't the damn mare beat Hal Morgan's racer? Don't everybody know that?"

"I'll tell you what," said the Flash. "I've come to the point when I need friends, and that's the answer."

He sat down and picked up one of his revolvers again, and finished assembling the parts, which he had been cleaning and scrutinizing carefully.

Beckwith looked on with fascinated eyes.

"Seems to me," he said, "that I never seen that top notch before, Flash, and what is it for?"

"That?" said the boy. "Why, that was for a day when a gang of revolutionaries got hold of me, away south."

"Hai!" exclaimed Beckwith. "You been mixing up with revolutions, and such stuff?"

"Oh, it was a long ways off," said the boy.

"Mexico?"

"No. Beyond that. The less you know about it, the less you'll have to worry about, old son. Anyway, I got jammed between two gangs of them one day. And I had to take sides, and my side was so badly licked that you never saw a crowd more badly scared. We were pinched, with our backs to the wall, and the gang that had the upper hand began to butcher my friends. Just slaughtered 'em. And the cowardly beggars, they simply fell down on their knees and waited for the knives to go into them. I used up my ammunition and emptied the magazines of a couple of rifles that lay around handy on the ground. But it was no good. The other fellows had seen the red of the blood running. And they came in with a whoop and a rush, like wildcats. Well, that was time to get out. And still, it wasn't such an easy thing to get away. I mean, we were jammed right up against a wall of the rocks, do you see? And there was no trail to the top."

Beckwith moistened his lips.

"And what the devil did you do?" he asked. "Put on a pair of wings?"

"No, I hitched myself onto a kite," said the boy.

"Come along! You want me to believe that?"

"Well," said the Flash, "we had some goats with our party, big full-grown wild devils. I knew that goats can climb where even a fly gets pretty dizzy. They were already pretty nearly mad with fear because of the roar of the guns,

73

and the dust and the smoke. Their blatting was what put the idea into my head. So I roped 'em together, all three of 'em. And I turned 'em loose. And they ran the only way that was open to them to run—straight up the face of that bluff, with me as the tail of the kite, hanging onto the fag end of the ropes. I keen, they zigzagged a good deal, but they went fast enough to bark my knees and shins for me. Half of the time, I was hanging in the air, with my feet on nothing thicker than hope. But I got to the top, and by the time I got there the other devils had stopped shooting at me. I looked over the safe edge, and there they all were below me, gaping, and looking up where they had seen the miracle. I'll bet that by the time I get back there, they'll have a shrine on the spot, and a Saint of the Goats legend all worked out. I was a pretty good miracle, at that. So I just sat down there among the rocks and vowed that I'd never eat goat meat again, and cut a notch into the handle of the right gun."

Beckwith grinned. Then he sighed.

"Lemme see the gat, will you?" he asked, taking the weapon into his hands. "Sometimes I wish that I was with you, on some of your parties. But I've been with you enough, and I know the pace that kills without riding it. And here's the notch you cut after—hold on, Flash!"

"What's the matter?" asked the Flash. "You look half sick."

"I'm *all* sick," said Beckwith. "These ain't your guns at all! The notches is all imitations! Because here's the V notch that you cut, and the ends of it overlap, the ways yours didn't!"

CHAPTER XVII

The sheriff who represented the right and the left hand of the law in Pazo was a chunky, wide-shouldered, deep-chested man by the name of Bill Dines. Bill had never been a sailor, but he walked with a swing and a swagger that would have become the long, heeling deck of a clipper such as in those days raced around the world and wallowed at eighteen knots an hour through the southern seas, running her casting down. The reason for Bill's swaggering stride was that he had been put on the back of a horse when he was three years old, and he had remained in the saddle some twelve hours a day ever since. So the soft bones of his legs had bent, in that early trial, and his knees had not come within six inches of one another for a long number of years. The arch of his chest, the calm of his eye, and the swing of his walk had gained for him the nickname of "Crusty," and as Crusty Bill he was known for a thousand miles of the range.

Crusty was a man not only of action, but of ideas. His preferences were early established, powerful, and never changed. When he was a little boy, lads of his own age often attempted to bully him because of the shortness of his stature. His early life was one prolonged battle, and from these battles he usually emerged victor, because he had the build and temperament of a bulldog. But these experiences placed him solidly on the side of law and order. Fighting was to him a disgusting thing, unless it were undertaken on the side of right, and then it became a fragrance in his nostrils and a song in his heart.

Crusty Bill Dines loved to talk both at length and slowly. Three of his anecdotes could fill an entire evening. This was a quality valued on the range and detested in town. He was considered the most delightful companion of the trail, where he took the place of both books and newspapers; in town he was a dreadful bore. Some people said that they continued to vote for him for sheriff simply in order to escape from his arguments. They voted for him and told him they would vote for him, merely so that they could prevent him from giving his reasons why they should.

He was an eminently fair man, both to criminals and to his political opponents, but, the instant he was convinced that the other fellow was really bad, he went to all lengths to worry him. He rarely raised his voice. His swagger was entirely in his manner rather than in his words. And the softness of his ways had fatally deceived many a desperado.

Crusty Bill Dines, on this early morning, was standing on the porch of his home, ready to go out behind the house and saddle his horse, smoking his after-breakfast cigarette, and watching a twist of wind carry up the street a pale phantom of dust. The sheriff watched with contentment, for he had had a good month. He had run down two long-wanted men; he had rustled several others out of the big county; and he had shot the hind legs, so to speak, off Quicksilver Mac-Grey, the Tucson gunman.

So the world was a bright scene to Crusty Bill, and he inhaled his cigarette smoke to the very bottom of his lungs.

Then he heard the beat of hoofs down the street.

Before he could see the rider, he said to himself: "Trouble. Drunk or sober, it's trouble!"

Then the horseman came into view, spinning around the corner of the church fence, his horse skidding in the liquid dust of the road. It was a little horse, a mare pony and it was running all straightened out with speed. The man on his back had a green cloth twisted around his head in lieu of a hat; something twinkled at the lobes of his ears, green sparks of light.

"A damn gypsy!" said the sheriff, and spat over the edge of his veranda.

The gypsy pulled up the running pony in front of Dines' house. He leaped to the ground, light and agile as a monkey, in spite of his age, and then came running up the path.

His talk was chiefly with hands and gesticulating arms. His eyes flashed and rolled, until the sheriff almost thought that there was nothing but whites to the eyes of his caller.

The truth was the sort of truth that usually came to a sheriff: a man was dead—murdered. It was one of the traveling band of gypsies.

The sheriff said nothing. He merely went back to the little corral behind his place, and he yawned as he saddled his horse for the day. It may be explained that the sheriff, though shrewd in some ways, had prejudices against all peoples of colored skin. They might be high-bred Mexicans of chiefly Spanish descent. They might be upper-caste Hindus, or Indians, Negroes, Chinese—it made no difference. There was only one complexion which the sheriff envisaged when, to himself, he defined the term "human being."

"A damn gyp is bumped off, and now I gotta ride on his trail!" he said to himself.

He swung himself into the saddle with that frictionless sway which one sees nowhere east of the Mississippi, nowhere in the rest of the world, except on the steppes of wild Russia in Asia. Then he rode out with his informant to the gypsy camp. In the distance, he heard the wailing of a woman. He shrugged his shoulders and bit his lip.

In these affairs of men, he almost always forgot that there was usually a woman attached to the tragedy. Always the sad, dim eyes of a woman in the distance, watching him.

He tried to shrug his horror away, but it would not depart; and so they arrived at the camp.

When they came into the willows, he found the whole gypsy band standing in a loose circle, silent, attentive, around a clump of brush out of which the wailing poured like a wild, dreary song. They showed no sorrow. They were merely interested. One might have thought that they were criticizing and enjoying the woman's lament, like connoisseurs of music.

Their heads turned toward Crusty Bill when he came.

There was no anger, no thirst for vengeance in their glances. They simply looked blankly at him, without even

76

curiosity. His guide led him straight into the clump of shrubbery. In the midst of it there was a little clearing. On the ground of the clearing a woman knelt, rocking herself back and forth with an almost automatic motion, her head thrown far on her shoulders, her raised face corrugated with grief, her eyes closed, her hands clasped at her breast.

She had torn her hair into a wild disorder. She had ripped at her clothes and at her flesh with her long fingernails. And as she rocked back and forth, her keening voice gave a rhythmical utterance to her grief.

The sheriff guessed that it was really an almost automatic, a traditional, gesture that she was making, but the sob that choked and bubbled in her throat kept the chills working in his spinal marrow.

On the ground at her knees lay a little, skinny form of a man on his side, his heels kicked up under him, his hands gripped on his long, greasy black hair. He was in the attitude of one about to scream with agony. But the sheriff saw with a glance that the feet which had kicked away the grass from the ground would kick no more, and the hands, of their own volition, would never untangle their fingers from the black hair. And the voice would never again leave the throat of the man.

For he was dead.

The sheriff's guide was explaining that nothing had been touched. All was as they had found it, shortly after the shot had been fired. He, in person, had forbidden anyone to touch the body, lest the ways of the law and the upholders thereof should be thwarted, mysteriously. For his own part, he came from a far land, and he had seen many countries, north and south. But he knew that in the United States there was justice, even for the humble, and the life of one man was worth the life of another.

The sheriff looked with rather hazy eyes at his informant. He was thinking, just then, of what that declaration meant; he was thinking also of his oath of office.

And what was he to do about the death of a greasy gypsy, murdered by some hateful companion?

He would almost as soon have investigated the death of a rattlesnake.

He was led to the side, and his guide pointed under a bush. There the sheriff saw a revolver lying on the ground.

"A plant," said the sheriff calmly. "Nobody would kill his man and leave his gun lyin' behind him."

"Look," said the old gypsy.

He pointed to a willow twig, broken, and with some of the bark skinned away from a side of it. Then he indicated the

77

trigger guard of the fallen revolver. It was stained and soiled with the unmistakable willow bark.

"There!" said the gypsy.

The sheriff grunted.

He felt rather shamed at having these clues pointed out to him by one who was not of the legal profession, or of the man-hunter class. He himself should have seen such a sign as this.

So he dropped on his knees and stared at the revolver while, with half his attention, he listened to the words of his informant. It had all happened in the early morning. The sun was up. It was already blinding bright, and it was beginning to send its heat through the dense, silver mists that rose among the dank willows. And the dead man had issued from his tent, at this hour—

But what was he? The sheriff broke in on the tale. What sort of a man was he?

A man, came the answer, who could read the very mind of a horse at half a mile. A man who knew the very language of horses. The greatest jockey, horse thief, and scoundrel in the tribe—the very greatest genius.

The information came in not exactly those terms. But is was so that the hard-minded sheriff translated it into his own thought.

It was this dead man, in short, who had owned the mare which beat Hal Morgan's beautiful gray gelding. Surely the sheriff had heard of that race? Yes, this was the man who had owned the mare, and a white man had taken her away on the turn of a card. That had been a game worth seeing!

So much had the dead man loved the mare that, after her loss, the loser had lain in his tent for four-and-twenty hours and groaned, and beat his breast, and wept like a sick child.

The sheriff hardly heard the words, for he was gazing with enchanted eyes at the revolver that lay under the bush. At last he picked it up, gingerly, with both hands.

"I'd rather," he said, "have found ten thousand snakes in my way on a dark night, than to of found this here gun. Because it's the beginning of a whole hell of trouble for men and the county, and the whole range. That's the gun of Flash David Baldwin."

CHAPTER XVIII

The sheriff stood up, still holding the weapon in both hands. He saw with a vague eye, that the woman had stopped keening beside the corpse. She was gone. From behind the brush he heard a soft, continued murmur of many voices. They were the outlanders, the despised people, who now waited for justice to take its course.

The old gypsy beside him was nodding, without emotion, now that he had told his tale.

He was saying that the thing was very clear. Baldwin was the youth who had taken the mare from its owner—probably through some crooked trick with the cards. He had the slender, active fingers of a professional gambler, that young man! Had not the whole tribe noticed this—and envied?

And, when the rightful owner, the lover of the mare, had begun to make trouble and to ask questions about that trick of the cards, the young American had decided to put an end to all talk, all question. He had done a bold thing. He had come down into the willows in the brightness of the full daylight, and he had murdered his man behind the screen of the willows.

He would have come off without leaving a trace behind him, but God had intervened and, through the willow twig, He had snatched the weapon from the hand of the slayer, and left it lying there on the ground!

The sheriff listened. He was not impressed. He was simply stunned, as one who had felt the stroke of a great calamity.

So much did he show it, that the old gypsy, bending a little, looked up into his intent, solemn face:

"Is it a friend of yours?" he asked.

The sheriff sighed.

"Look," he said, more to himself than to the other, "nobody's the friend of the sheriff. Because every man's walkin' along a mighty rough road, and one stumble may put his knee on the neck of somebody. And if the neck breaks, the sheriff's after him. So nobody's my friend. I got acquaintances. I got no friends, God help me! I got friends on election day. That's all I got."

"He's not a friend?" said the gypsy, keeping close to the particular and avoiding the general. "Well, then, why do you care?"

"Why do I care?" said the sheriff.

He looked calmly on the other, the calm of a man who is filled with more than words may express.

Then he said: "You know what sort of a man this Flash David is?"

"A quick young man. He's quick with his hands and his eyes. He's quick with his tongue, also," said the gypsy.

The sheriff smiled at the understatement.

He held out the Colt revolver which he still was supporting with both hands.

"You see this?"

"Yes."

"That's his left gun."

"Hai!" said the man of the dark skin and the rolling eyes. "Do guns have faces, that you recognize them so easily?"

"The guns of Flash David have faces," said the sheriff, rather bitterly. "Because he's carved features on 'em, if you wanta know. Some of them features I know. And every man in the county knows 'em. The left-hand gun —his right one is the real dynamite—but even this left-hand gun, it's done its little trick. You see this nick here in the handle, high up?"

"Yes," said the gypsy.

"What do you think it's for?"

"It roughens the grip. It keeps the hand from slipping," said the other.

The sheriff actually laughed aloud, and his laughter was as harsh as the croaking of a crow.

"There come a time," said he, "when the kid was only thirteen, I think. And all he had in the world was a pair of gats that he got the year before and had lived with ever since. He got those gats by swiping one of his pa's horses and trading it in for the guns. Damn good guns, right new and straight shooting. He knew guns already well enough to tell 'em. So he picked the best, and he turned in the hoss, and he got his hiding when he come home. He got his hiding and laughed as the welts was bein' raised, because he knew that he'd had his own way. And the next year, when he was thirteen, he goes down the street and he hears a yelling and a wailing and a smashin' and a crashin' in Dan Wiley's saloon, that used to stand down at the south end of town, the nearest to the river. When he heard that, he listened for a minute, and seen a couple of gents bolt out through the swingin' doors. And then what did he do? Did he run home to tell his ma that things was goin' wrong downtown? No, sir, he just up and stepped through them doors, and the first thing that met him was a stink of burned gun-powder, and the second thing that met him was a forty-four caliber slug out of Hi Jackson's gun that tore through his right shoulder, and knocked him flat as a pancake on the floor.

"Because the two Jackson boys were havin' a little party, down there at the saloon, and they was runnin' the place, and breakin' the mirrors, and drinkin' free drinks. They was a pair of high-grade mulattoes from over the Munroe way, in Louisiana. And they'd come far enough west to feel pretty free and easy. And they up with their guns and bust things up a good deal in the saloon.

"And the last thing that they busted was this kid. Which I'll tell you why. As he was fallin', he dropped that right-hand gun, and he gets his left-hand gun out from under his coat, where it was makin' a sizable bulge on the kid's anatomy. And just about as he hits the floor on his wounded shoulder, he turns loose with that left-hand gun that he had pulled out from under his right armpit, and he shoots Hi Jackson between the eyes. It wasn't no chance shot. It was mighty accurate. It just popped Hi Jackson right between the eyes, as if he had measured out the place, first, and made sure that it would be exactly right. With a pair of dividers, he couldn't of hit the place more center fire.

"Well, there's Hi Jackson down, and down forever. And Sam Jackson, he lets out a whoop and a couple of bullets, and one of 'em plows all the way down the kid's back. And Jeff Snyder, that was lyin' under a table in the corner of the place, he says that the kid just smiles and steadies his hand, and he takes a good, careful aim, while Sam Jackson is shooting him up, and he shoots Sam Jackson right where he'd shot Hi. He didn't seem to think that bullets would kill, unless they went through the middle of the brain. And he hit Sam Jackson at the base of the brain, and the bullet, it mushroomed, and it took out most half the top of Sam's head on the way to gettin' free from him.

"And that's how that we got to know the kid for the first time. And for three months he laid around and took things easy, and got his right arm to workin' again. And then we heard that he'd put a notch into that left-hand gun of his. Not two notches, for two men. But one notch, and he said that he'd made the notch to remind him of some trouble that he'd got into, one day! Mind you, it ain't a big notch, nor a deep notch."

"No," said the gypsy.

He lighted a cigarette. His skinny, yellow-brown hand was trembling a little. His eyes seemed to sink deeper in his head. And he studied the face of the sheriff with careful, attentive eyes, as though he was reading a rich will which might affect him nearly.

"No," said the sheriff, sighing again, and carrying on in his many-worded way: "Fact is that's kind of a skinny scratch on the handle. And here's another just below it that's deeper only a mite. Mind you, it wasn't an American. The kid says that he's never killed a man in Pazo. Because he don't count foreigners. But there was a high-bred lookin' fellow come through—a Spaniard or Italian, or Frog, or somethin'—"

The nostrils of the gypsy flared suddenly. He looked down to the ground.

"And," continued the sheriff, "this here foreigner was kind of in a hurry and he wanted to make good time, and he had a reason, because there was half a dozen gents that had trailed him all the way from San Antone, and when they caught him they meant business about some little checks that he had kited, up there in San Antone. And so the guy, he hops a dead-beat hoss into a field, and he leaves the hoss, and flops his saddle onto the back of a fresh pony that he finds, and he ties fifty dollars into the mane of his own hoss to pay the boot for the one he swiped, and away he goes, kind of regular and honest, the way I look at it. But it just kind of happened that the hoss that he borrowed was a hoss belonging to the kid—to Flash David, and Flash didn't figger that there was enough money in the world to pay for his own pet pony. And he got onto the back of one of his dad's ponies, and he followed that gent for three days across the desert, and he found him, and he come back with the pony that had been swiped, and when the gents from San Antone found their check raiser, it was kind of hard to read his face, be- cause the buzzards had seen him first. And when he was buried, this here kid, this Flash David, he gets fifty dollars' worth of flowers, and he sends it to the funeral.

"This is only my way of tellin' you what kind of a boy he is and always has been!"

The gypsy, listening, nodded gravely and slowly.

The sheriff went on, as though he had not made his point.

"Then Flash, he begins to find that the home pastures, they're kind of cramped. He wants to get into some bigger fields, and his way of figgerin' is that they's a lot of elbow room south of the Rio Grande, and so he drifts out one day and he comes home six months later with a limp in his right arm, again, and a limp in both legs so bad that they had to lift him out of the saddle. And they put him to bed for a while, and he lays there and reads his damn books—education is the sickness that gets the brains of the young men, I tell you!—and all that we ever know about his trip to the south that time is the scars of four bullets, and two knife cuts in him, and on his revolver handle, there's a good, deep, sizable notch filled in, which it's this here notch that I'm pointin' to now. And God only knows what he done to Mexico that trip. He's been back there since. And we've heard some kind of whispers and rumors about the things that he's done down there. But we don't know nothin' very much for sure. We only see notches, now and then——"

His voice trailed away. His eyes grew absent.

"Do you not see it, Mr. Sheriff?" asked the gypsy, humbly.

"Do I not see what?" asked the sheriff, testily.

"My people, you see, are also foreigners!"

The sheriff spat upon the ground before he answered.

"Oh, I seen that the first look I give," said he. "I seen that, and I seen the worst bundle of trouble ahead of me that ever was handed to a law officer in this neck of the woods. God help my unlucky soul, and God help the poor kid, too. Because one of us has gotta go!"

CHAPTER XIX

Crusty Bill went about the arrest of the Flash in no haste. He had not the slightest intention of rushing to a glorious martyrdom in the execution of his office.

"The minute that I'm dead," Crusty Bill used to say, "maybe a doggone sight worse gent will hang his heels on the edge of the sheriff's desk!"

For that was where Crusty's heel reposed when he was in his official room.

So he went back to the town from the gypsy camp, and on the way he passed young Tom Pertwee, as sassy and gay a youth as rode the range near Pazo. His hat was always at an angle opposite to his cigarette, and his spurs were decorated with little bells that jingled whenever he rode or strode. He had a tidy little record piled up in the matter of gun fights, and it was said that he was ambitious to increase his account.

The sheriff welcomed the sight of him as of a visitation from heaven. He pulled rein and shouted, and young Tom Pertwee jerked his galloping horse back on its haunches.

"I've got a little party on," said the sheriff. "How would you like to take a hand, Tom?"

Pertwee grinned from ear to ear. He grinned so very broadly that his freckled nose wrinkled a little.

"You bet!" he said. "Are you after the gang that raided the Langford place?"

"No," said the sheriff, "I'm only after one man."

The boy wheeled his horse and rated it along that of the sheriff's.

"You say when to start!" said he.

"It's the Flash," said the sheriff.

He watched the face of the other fall suddenly.

"The Flash?" gaped Tom Pertwee. "What's he gone and done?"

"He's gone and got careless and killed himself a gypsy down in the willows," said the sheriff. "Come along, Tom. We'll just run him in for the job."

He watched, askance, the sudden falling of Tom Pertwee's face.

"I'll tell you what," said Tom. "I'll be right into Pazo as soon as I've seen the old man. He sent in for me, real particular, and I've gotta see him. When I get back, I'll sure give you a hand if you ain't finished the business by that time."

He turned his horse abruptly, waved, and galloped off up the road. His head was hanging a little, but he did not change his mind and return. Nor did the sheriff expect him to.

Crusty Bill merely grunted to himself, and then he started down the road at the dogtrot of his mustang. He was not greatly depressed. He remembered that Steve O'Malley was newly in from the Mogollon Mountains, and Steve was a man who never had backed up in his life. Men said of Steve that he would fight a charging railroad locomotive with a pitchfork.

So, on the outer edge of Pazo, he stopped at Steve's shack, and young Mrs. Steve was outside of the house, doing the washing under the shade of a cottonwood tree—poor shade though it was—while her lengthy husband stretched himself in the cool and smoked cigarettes, and spoke not at all.

He had been away six months, and he had brought back sixty dollars. But his wife adored him.

The sheriff reined in his horse at the picket fence and called across to the two of them.

"Hey, Steve, whatcha doin'?"

"Aw, nothin' much," said Steve, without lifting his head. "How's things, sheriff?"

"I got a job for you," said the sheriff.

"I'd eat a wild cat for ten dollars," said Steve, yawning.

"I'll give you fifty bucks for one day's work," said the sheriff.

Steve rose to his feet as though a rope from an invisible derrick had lifted him.

"Say that again!" said he.

"Fifty bucks for a *half* hour's work," said the sheriff. "The Flash has gone and killed himself a gypsy, down yonder. And I want company to keep things from getting dull when I go and call on Flash David. Will you come along? I got the fifty bucks here in my pocket."

"No!" screamed the young wife. "No, no, Steve. Don't you do it. Don't you dare to—oh, that murdering, terrible devil of a boy—don't you go near to him, Steven O'Malley! He'll kill you sure. He'll—"

Steve himself, when he heard the name the first time, had jerked back his head as though a fist had struck him. But now he seemed to recover his courage.

"Aw, quit it," he said to his wife, "quit yer yappin', will you? I'll be back in half an hour with fifty dollars and—"

The girl screamed at the top of her voice. She flung her arms around the strong shoulders of her husband.

"Steve! Steve! Steve!" she wailed.

Steve shook his head sadly at the sheriff.

"You see how it is, sheriff, don't you?" he said. "I'm crazy to go, but the wife won't have it. I'm doggone sorry."

"So'm I," said Crusty Bill. "It's about the first time that I ever heard of your wife keepin' you at home."

He could not avoid the final dig, but he jogged his horse on into Pazo with very little content in his gloomy heart.

The bitter point was that if he could persuade nobody to help him, he would have to attempt that arrest single-handed. And though he was somewhat vain of his shooting prowess, and rightly so, he was not fool enough to class himself with the Flash. He went into his office. Two men, he noticed idly as he went in, were clowning in the vacant lot, laughing loudly, and playing silly tricks on each other.

Well, let the world remain young. But *he* was growing older. He sat down to think over the list of fighting men in Pazo. There were many of them. Pazo's reputation was as high as that of any other Southwestern town, considering the prowess of its males. But he could not hit on the name of a man who would be apt to ride with him against the Flash. Not for fifty dollars an hour—not for fifty dollars a minute!

He began to feel that his death warrant had been signed the moment he looked under the willow bush and identified the revolver of young Flash Baldwin.

The ugly clangor of revolver shots made him look up and through the window. The pair of strangers were still at their foolish tricks. One of them was now heaving rocks into the air, and both of them fired at the spinning targets.

"Drunk, and nacherally foolish, anyway," said the sheriff. "I'd better give 'em a run out of town!"

Then, suddenly, he saw one of the rocks disappear at the height of its rise. It was snuffed out like a light, and the sheriff rubbed his eyes and gaped. He knew that a bullet hit that stone and knocked it to smithereens.

Suddenly he jerked the window up and bawled up: "Stop that fool noise, will you?"

One of the strangers turned his head. It was not a pleasant face that he showed to the sheriff. It was scarred and twisted, as though horses had trampled it underfoot.

"Who wants us to?" he asked, insolently.

"The sheriff wants you to," shouted Crusty Bill, furiously. "But hold on—you fellows lookin' for work?"

"Yeah, I dunno but what I'd take a job," said the man who had first turned his head. "What about you, Hank?"

"I might saddle up, Jim," said Hank.

They turned toward the sheriff.

"Come in here," he said.

They strode to his door.

"You know Flash David Baldwin?" he asked them.

It seemed to him, when he thought back to the thing afterward, that they exchanged odd looks with one another, but at the time he hardly noticed the alteration of their expressions.

"I'm new here," said Hank. "So's Jim, my side-kick. I never heard of Flash Baldwin. Who's he?"

"He's a flash," explained the sheriff. "And he's under danger of arrest, and I've gotta have help in servin' of the warrant, because he's sure to fight. I'll take you boys along. I'll pay you—ten bucks. It'll only cost half an hour."

"Ten bucks for a man to get himself shot at?" said Jim.

"Aw, shut up, Jim," answered Hank. "You can have my ten, too. I'll do the job for fun. What's the matter with Pazo, old son? Ain't you got no ambitious young men around here?"

The sheriff looked mildly down at him. "Not ambitious like that," said he. "You know what you're doin', do you? Suppose that there has to be sad letters wrote to relatives—"

Said Hank, grinning, "Our relatives was through with us before we was through with them. There won't be no sad letters wrote. Where's this son of crime, eh? Lead us to him."

"Hold on," said the sheriff. "Are you two brothers?"

86

"Yeah, you might call us that," said Hank, grinning again. "We're closer, some way, than brothers."

"What brung you here to the town?" asked Crusty Bill. "Hosses."

The sheriff laughed. He felt that he knew his men as completely as though he had heard their stories told in detail from impartial lips. They were rough, wild sons of fortune, with the stain of many a sin on their souls, and no care for God, man, or devil in their minds.

But it seemed a rare miracle of chance that had placed them in that vacant lot adjoining his office at the very moment when he had need of them. Or could it be chance, altogether? He did not believe in such coincidence, that honest Crusty Bill; but he reserved judgment and determined that he would wait and watch and listen, and hope to pierce through the mystery, if mystery there was.

In the meantime, his hand was filled with two excellent workers, and he set his face forward, with determination, toward the work which lay before him.

He asked to see their guns. And each of them brought forth a pair of blue-shining Colts.

The sheriff looked over those weapons with a practiced eye. "You'll do," he said.

"These here," said Hank, "is self-shootin' guns, and the only reason that they stay with us is because we treat 'em real affectionate. But if we got a job on hand, you tell us when to start, and we're gunna go."

CHAPTER XX

Trouble, in the opinion of Beckwith, was sure to follow for young Flash David, the instant that he learned that the guns were imitations of the originals.

His advice was that David should mount his horse and shy for quieter regions, until they learned that all was well in Pazo for him.

The boy listened with interest. At last he said: "I think that you're right. I ought to slide out. And there are some places in Old Mexico where I would like to spend a little time. But the trouble is that I have a job to do here in Pazo that can't be done in any other place. I've got to stay. You're wise. You're right. But I've got to stay!"

So he remained in Beckwith's place.

To kill the time he dozed a little in the patio shade behind the house, until the flies found him and wakened him.

Then he got a guitar from Beckwith's wife and began to strum it, sitting always there in the cool of the patio and looking up toward the roof lines, above which the birds were floating and dipping. He sang to the thin blue of the sun-flooded sky. He sang to the birds. He sang to his own careless soul. And the music came lightly and easily from the guitar, and his voice sailed lightly over the accompaniment.

Mrs. Beckwith stood behind a shuttered window and listened to that music, and drank of the Spanish words, and wept softly to herself. Presently, she heard the soft clattering of hoofs on the dusty path that ran behind the house, and into her view raced a girl riding on a little mule that seemed half wild, for it bucked and shied at every shadow in the path.

When the rider came to the patio of Beckwith's house, she leaped down from the saddle and ran in, dragging the unwilling mule by the bridle reins behind her.

She was an oddly dressed girl. Her skirt was a blue rag. Her blouse was a red one. There was a hole in one stocking. Battered slippers were on her feet. She wore a twist of cloth around her black hair instead of a handkerchief. She wore a parti-colored Mexican sash for a belt, and in the belt she carried a formidable-looking knife with the air of one who knew how to use it.

Her skin was the color of old ivory, pink tinted in the cheeks. Her eyes were utterly night-dark.

There was much to displease Mrs. Beckwith in the appearance of the damsel. Even at a distance, for instance, she could guess that the clothes were not overclean. But that was not all. She seemed a bold minx. She carried her head as high as any boy. She did not simper. She did not look on the ground. She stepped like a proud young horse that is ready to race or jump.

Moreover, two bits of green light shone at her ears, and some rare instinct told the Mexican woman that these were real emeralds.

Real emeralds!

Furthermore, whether in sun or in shadow, her beauty shone by its own light. Rags could not cover it.

Mrs. Beckwith smiled, and her smile showed that her teeth were gripped hard together. Then, half closing her eyes, she cast all of her faculties into the sense of hearing, and saw little, and heard much.

When Flash David saw her, he finished the line he was singing and let her drag her horse halfway across the patio

before he spoke. Then he did not rise—the young impertinent!
—he merely sat up a little and waved to her.

"Hello, Sonia," said he. "Sit down and catch your breath.
Have a drink of something. You look hot."

She paused before him, breathing hard, staring at him
fixedly.

"Stand up, then, if you want to. You look better, standing.
You look as though you were about to slide out into a dance,
Sonia. Have a smoke?"

He extended brown wheat-straw papers and a half-finished
sack of Bull Durham.

"Sweet, cool and wholesome," said the Flash, as he made
his proffer. "Try a Bull Durham."

"I don't smoke," said the girl. "You know I don't smoke.
Whatcha wanta talk like that to me for, Flash David?"

"I always wondered," said he, making a cigarette for himself, "where you learned to speak English so well."

"I don't speak it very good," said she. "But I learned it in
a reform school."

"What sent you there, honey?" said Flash David.

"I was slow on my getaway," said the girl, with a shrug
of her shoulders, "and the fellow, he caught me by the
thumb as I was jerking my hand out of his pocket. There
was nothin' in the pocket, neither, mind you. I thought I
seen him drop a watch into it. Well, I was pretty young then.
I was a fool. I'm still a fool; I'm wastin' time on you!"

"You're all heated up, Sonia," said the Flash. "You look
grand. You look as though you'd spent a month in mountain
air. That's the way you look."

"Always bright and easy, ain't you?" said the girl. "Well,
I'm gunna put a smudge on your brightness, maybe. I got
something to tell you, handsome!"

"Go on and tell," said the Flash. "You ever hear that song
they sing down in Vera Cruz about the fish that—"

"Bah!" said the girl.

He struck a few soft bars on the guitar, but he did not
commence the song. He was listening to what she might have
to say.

"Bah! Vera Cruz—fishing songs—*you* will have a hanging
song, Flash David!"

"Hai!" said the Flash. "Who's going to hang me?"

The girl's face grew ugly.

She twisted her mouth into a grotesque horror and jerked
her head over to the side.

"They'll break your neck for you. They let you dance on
air. That's what's gunna happen to you, Flash David!"

"Are the gypsies going to lynch me?" he asked, mildly curious.

"Gypsies? You laugh at us!" cried the girl. "Our people are older than yours. They're just as wise. We've been kicked around a lot, but we're as good as any of you! And if only—"

"I know," said the Flash. "They're all good, but you're the best. You're what I chose, and to hell with the rest of the tribe. I choose you, Sonia, because you're such a lamb —such a little woolly lamb, with tan claws on each hand. But I'm glad to know that the gypsies are going to hang me!"

"You fool!" cried the girl. "I about hate you! I just about hate you, when you sit there and grin and act superior! You're not superior. You're nothin' important."

"I know that," said the Flash, still only mildly curious. "What's the matter, Sonia? Sit down here and tell me."

"Why did you do it?" cried the girl. "You had his horse. Why did you have to harm him any more than that? You'd broken his heart, taking the mare away. Why did you have to go back and kill him? Were you afraid because he may have threatened you, or because he tried to steal the mare? He was a coward and a weakling and he never would have been able to harm you, really. You oughta know that. But you had to go and murder him—and they're gunna hang you —and I hope that they do! I'll dance under the rope!"

"The gypsies are going to hang me, are they?" said he. "And who put the murder on my shoulders?"

"Do you deny it?" asked the girl, suddenly and coldly quiet. "Why, they picked up your gun among the bushes. Do you deny it?"

He looked down at the sunburned floor of the patio. Not even weeds could endure the summer heat.

"No," said he, "I don't deny anything. I'm a murderer, am I?"

Suddenly the girl moaned and struck her hands together above her head and clasped them there in an agony.

"Why did you do it, Flash?" she cried to him.

"Listen to me," said he.

"Ay," said she. "Go and lie to me. I'll listen, because I wanta believe in you."

"I didn't kill him," said he. "Another man dropped that gat of mine on the spot. The same one that faked the marks on the new set of guns he framed up for me."

He drew one from under his coat and showed her the notched handles. Then he made the weapon disappear once more.

She, her hands still locked together, pressing hard across her head, looked down into his face in an anguish. Suddenly she dropped to her knees and laid her hands on his shoulders.

"You wouldn't go and do a thing like that, Flash? You're wild, but you ain't mean!"

"Look at me, Sonia," said he.

"I'm lookin'," said the girl. "Where else in God's name would I wanna look, but to see if you're honest, Flash?"

"No," said the boy. "I'm not honest. I'm a pretty good liar, Sonia. But I don't lie about this. I'll tell you something. Not so long ago, I promised that I'd give the mare back to him, when I'd finished the use I have for her now. That's true, also. Would I lie like that, for the fun of the lying?"

All at once, she began to smile at him.

And Mrs. Beckwith, pressing closer to the shuttered window, ground her teeth together.

"I believe you, every word," said Sonia. "And that's why I came, because I knew that you'd make me believe. And I want you to tell me, Flash, that you'll start now, on that same mare and ride, and ride, because the law's after you, and this time it'll surely get you. They been after you before. But your time's up. Your bad luck's beginning."

"Do you know that?" he asked her gently.

"I've cast the horoscope," said the girl. "I know—oh, I know things that make me sick, thinkin' of 'em. But I know that there's a lot of misery ahead for you—and misery for me, too!"

He stood up, and he raised her with him.

"Do you think that the law is going to take this up against me?" said he. "Or is the tribe going to handle it?"

"The law!" said she. "The sheriff's been out there. He's seen the gun. He seen it more'n an hour ago—"

"More than an hour?" said the boy.

He was plainly startled.

"What's he doing, then?" murmured the Flash. "Getting an army together to come after me? Sonia, you're a jewel. But I wish that you'd come a little sooner!"

"I wanted to. They knew that I would. They tied my feet together. They put a man watching me to keep me there. And I chafed through the cord that tied my ankles. I rubbed it through against the rough edge of the rim of the iron tire on the wagon I was sitting under. And so I got away. And—"

Her voice died away to a gasp. Into the open gate of the patio had stepped Crusty Bill, and his two new helpers behind him.

CHAPTER XXI

The Sheriff and both his men pulled out their guns with a single gesture which certainly denoted a single mind.

"Stick 'em up, Flash!" called the sheriff.

And even the ambidextrous Flash was no whit better than a dead man in that moment, and well he knew it, unless he should raise his hands above his head. But then the grace of two seconds was given to him, for the gypsy girl sprang in front of him with her arms stretched out the better to screen him, gasping in her fear and her excitement: "Run, Flash!"

He did not wait.

His first leap brought him behind a pillar. The sheriff still thought the girl too near to risk opening fire. But Hank and Jim were less tender minded. Each of them put in a slug. Jim's flew an inch wide. Hank's chipped off a handful or so of the dried adobe that made up the pillar. But all three of the men, at the same moment, ran forward to get behind that same pillar.

They came in view of what lay behind it in time both to see and to hear the back door of the house slam shut. They even caught the last twinkle of the flashing spurs of the fugitive as he darted through into the dimness of the interior, and the sheriff, groaning, split the center panel of that door with two shots fired in rapid succession. Those bullets went through just breast high—an admirable tribute to the marksmanship of Crusty Bill, for he was firing as he ran at full speed.

He himself was fairly sure that he must have struck the target. He had a vivid mental picture of the Flash struck by the shots, and staggering against the wall of the corridor inside, bleeding, dying on his feet.

He saw Hank, with a brutal side stroke, cuff Sonia out of the way. Then Crusty Bill himself reached the door and cast it wide.

The interior was so dark that, compared with the dazzle of the sunlight outside, it was almost deep night. The sheriff rushed in, and his two eager henchmen came rushing behind him, keen for the fight. Neither of them held back half a step, and a thrill of pleasant confidence passed through the heart of Bill Dines as he heard them stamping and breathing behind him.

Then the door which had swung shut behind them opened

again. The sheriff glanced over his shoulder in time to see a slender form leap out—to see the gleam of the spurs, the glow of the bright colors in which the lad was dressed.

And he groaned again!

The thing was too maddeningly simple. It was the oldest trick in the world. The Flash had simply flattened himself against the wall behind the door and remained there as the others thrust it open and poured through. Then how easy it was for him to double through behind them!

The sheriff, shouting, cursing as he checked himself, found that he did not have to tell his lieutenants what had happened. They were already spinning about, growling like two blood-thirsty dogs. Hank got in a snap shot through the center of the door as it slammed shut, and then all three fell into a tangle, hindered by one another in the narrowness of the hall.

The sheriff and Jim got to the door together and gave it their shoulders.

The door sagged, but held firm; they heard the clank of the outside bolt which held it!

Then they shouted, all three of them, and gave their united weight in a charge against that flimsy obstacle. But it was made of well-seasoned wood and, though it groaned and creaked, it held against them.

The sheriff put the four remaining bullets from his gun through the place where the bolt was fastened. Then, striking the door heavily with his shoulder, he made the wood give way, and they blundered out into the brightness of the patio.

Alas, for the course of smooth-flowing law! At that very moment across the entrance to the patio dashed a rider on a racing horse. The brilliance of the rider's clothes attested his name. It was the Flash!

And so they ran, jarring a groan out of their throats with every footfall, until they pitched into the lane outside. The Flash was out of sight already, behind a shed!

They did not even follow at once. They merely stopped and stared at one another, each with a dumb, amazed look, each with a future consideration in his eye, as though they guessed what unbottled troubles were now ready to sweep over the landscape and employ their time.

"Sheriff," said Hank, snarling deep in his throat, "we've missed him now. But I'm gunna stay with you till we corner the rat. He tricked us. A cheap fox can fool the best dog now and then, but I'm gunna get my teeth in him one of these days. Mind you that!"

"I'm with you," said Jim, "till my hind teeth fall out of

my jaw! They're crackin' now. I wanta get even with him for this!"

The sheriff said nothing at all. His heart was too filled with thanksgiving to have such followers and helpers. Of old, he knew fighting men, and the rush of these two had been like the charge of hungry mastiffs of the manhunting breed.

He went for his horse. But they were mounted before he had foot in saddle, and they both led him down the lane. He could not help wondering a little at the eagerness which they displayed. It was as though they were, of old, enemies of this lad. Perhaps they might be, for all the ignorance which they had displayed. The Flash had left at least as many enemies as friendships behind him; both had to be numbered by the score. No one could tell where they would turn up.

When they got well out from the last scattering of buildings behind the little town of Pazo, they saw their fugitive before them, sending his horse down toward the willows of the river bottom. He went at such a rate that it was apparent they could not overtake the flying mare in a single burst, so with an unspoken assent they rated their horses along at an easy lope, and Hank said: "If he gets pretty deep into those willows, maybe the gypsies will bag our fox for us. There's enough of 'em to pull him down, I reckon."

"He won't stay in the willows," said the sheriff. "He can be a hill wolf or a desert coyote, or a jungle cat, all right. But he likes the hills and the desert a lot better. Specially with that set of four legs under him that he's got now. Look at her flyin' the fences!"

"Where'll he be likely to head for then?" said Jim.

"I've gotta think," said the sheriff. "We'll never ride him down. We gotta outguess him, and that's all that they is to it. Where would he likely go? What friend would he likely hole up with?"

He pulled his horse down to a jog.

"We'll get into the woods ourselves," he said, "and then we'll off saddle and have a think."

That was what they did. In the green gloom of the willows, they stopped their horses and got down for a comflab. They smoked cigarettes, and listened to the sheriff thinking out loud.

It might be that the Flash had gone deep into the willows to hide. It might be that he had headed south for Old Mexico. It might be that he had chosen the Devil Mountains, or the ranges beyond. Or perhaps he intended to soak out of observation into the wide heart of the desert itself.

Which would he select?

"There's the gypsies agin the willows," said the sheriff, in summing up. "There's agin Mexico that he's only lately been down there raisin' Cain. And a good many hands are set agin him. He's been up in the hills only lately, too. And I guess for variety that he's likely to try the desert. If he goes out the desert way, what road will he take? Why, the opposite one to what he started on. He'll double straight back, the way that a good fox does. And if he doubles straight back, he'll likely hit the trail for San Jacinto del Rey. And if he hits that trail, about forty mile out—he'd hit the shack of old Jay Boomer."

Suddenly the sheriff broke off with a laugh. "I been havin' a little guessin' party, boys. Maybe my guesses run right along with the thinkin' of the Flash. I got one chance in about ten, I'd say, that I'm right. D'you fellows want to play my hand with me?"

"We'll play your hand," said Jim, "until we get something that sounds better to us. Am I right, Hank?"

"You're absolutely right," said Hank. "The sheriff, he knows this coyote. He can tell the henroosts that he's likely to rob. We go with him, and we stick with him!"

They waited there, quietly, in the cool of the woods. That was the sheriff's idea. They stayed there until the afternoon had well begun. Then they mounted their refreshed horses and headed in a straight air line for the shack of Jay Boomer, far off in the alkaline mists of the desert.

They rode on until the daylight failed. They rode with the sweat streaming from their bodies, drying on their flannel shirts, making cakes and streaks of salt. And similar salt streaks formed on the necks and the shoulders of the horses. Water ran down their hips and dried and turned white, and new rivulets washed channels through the old deposits, and the spirit left them, and they no longer tossed their heads and champed at their bits but went sullenly along with their ears canting out and their heads fallen, like plow horses which find no meaning in their labor except an endless pain—one foot in the rough furrow, one foot on the firmer ground.

The men were like their horses. They did not speak for hours. A faint wind was against them. It was not sufficient to cool their bodies, but it was enough to raise up the dust of the desert and its alkaline salts. To shut out these, they raised their bandannas so that the fold of the thinnest silk was over their mouths and nostrils. They rode like masked men. The dust turned the bandannas gray and dimmed the original bright colors.

But still these silent riders persisted. They had ridden like this a thousand times before. They knew their own endurance.

Weaker-minded men, and men with weaker bodies would have fainted. But they scorned surrender. They knew of old that there is a sweeter quiet after hard labor. Their encrusted throats would all the more gratefully receive the first drink.

And then, through the desert mist of dust before them, a single tiny ray of light appeared, twinkled, went out, and appeared again.

The sheriff lowered the silken fold from his nostrils and his lips. He rubbed the cuffed sleeve across his sweating forehead. He cleared his throat with a harshly rasping sound.

"That's Jay Boomer's shack," he said. "And maybe Jay is lookin' at the Flash by that same light."

CHAPTER XXII

They left their horses at a little distance. Then they spent a full half hour examining the place. The sheriff was the only one familiar with the outlines of the mare; but the other two, though they had had but fleeting glimpses of her, swore that they could recognize that low-running machine in the darkest midnight by the sense of touch alone.

So they hunted about the place for a sign of the great mare, if she were hobbled out on the good grass which grew in small patches here and there, where Jay Boomer's wandering handful of cattle had not eaten it down as close as sheep bite, well nigh. However, they had no sign of the mare. And she was not in the shed close to the house, and was not standing in the little corral either. There were other horses, of Jay's own string. But the mare was not among them.

Then the three forgathered where they had abandoned their own mounts.

"He ain't there," said Hank, gloomily. "We better eat some more dust and head back for Pazo."

"My hoss won't make it," said Jim, though not with an air of complaint.

Of the precious pair, he was a little the harder, the more supple sword-steel.

"Well," said the sheriff, "I reckon that you're right. But what's an old sourdough and measly squatter like Jay Boomer, what's he doin' with a light burnin' up good oil this late at night?"

The other two agreed that there might be something to this, unless Boomer had recently been to town and returned with a stock of magazines, papers, and such reading matter.

Instead of saving the treasure, he was apt to squander it all in a month's reading.

But they would stalk the house again. No, it was better to ride straight up to the door, two of them. And let a third man lie out behind and watch the rear door of the place.

Many of the wiliest of crooks had been caught by that simple device.

"The brightest foxes, they ain't lookin' for the simplest turns," said Hank, and the sheriff agreed with him.

He was appreciating his two helpers more and more during every moment that he spent with them. So he gave to Jim the important task of lying out behind the house, while he and scar-faced Hank went up to the front door. When they were a hundred yards away, they saw the light go out. But they knocked at the door cheerfully enough when they arrived.

There was no delay. A husky, nasal voice that had a metallic clank in it, like something long unused, called from within: "Who's out there?"

"Somebody that needs a set down and a cup of coffee," said the sheriff.

Then they could hear faint mumblings which were distinctly audible through the flimsy sides of the shack.

The front door opened, and the dull light of a lantern gleamed out at them.

"Hullo, Crusty," said Jay Boomer, holding his lantern higher. "What's fetched you out here? Have I been rustlin' a few mavericks lately? Get down and feed your hosses back there in the shed. I got a bite of barley there. Looks like your nags could use it about as good as mine can."

"Fetch the hosses out to the shed and throw down a feed for 'em," said the sheriff to Hank. "My old legs are about used up, and I gotta rest 'em. Will you take care of the hosses, Hank?"

"Sure," said Hank, and took the horses obediently away towards the shed.

He yawned as he went, he was so sure that nothing would come out of this cache which the sheriff had led them to. He yawned, and then he cursed softly. But being a man inured to the miseries of labor which is scantily rewarded he went on again, leading the horses. He found the shed, went into it, and then sniffed at the sweet smell of the hay which had been put up that spring, and at the scent of the barley, hot and moist in the feed box. And he felt better, and more at ease with the world, and he loosened his belt as he walked back toward the shack, in anticipation of food.

Inside, the sheriff was taking his ease. He had peeled off

his hat and actually kicked off his boots, and sitting back in a chair he spread his tired legs and leaned back his head against the wall, and was now firing up on his old black pipe. Every time he drew a puff he closed his eyes. Every time he breathed the smoke out, he opened them a crack.

Old Jay Boomer was smoking also.

"There's a lot of coyotes, though," the sheriff was saying, when Hank returned to the shack.

"Yeah, and who wants 'em?" said Jay Boomer.

"Why not?"

"They're mangy," said Jay Boomer. "That's what they are."

He shook his head. He was as thin as a radish, and as red. He had a fluff of hair over about half of his head, unevenly distributed. Stiff with alkali dust, it stood up, and shone in the lantern light. He was a little man. His back was curving into a hook, despite the meager weight of the head which bowed it. His eyes were covered with wrinkled lids. It seemed a distinct effort of the will that raised them, whenever he looked up. But generally he was looking at the floor.

"Well, you get a bounty," said the sheriff.

"Yeah. Sometimes. I'm kind of tired of mange and bounties," said Joy Boomer.

"Yah, a man gets tired of things," agreed the sheriff. "You get visitors out here though."

"I get too many," said the sour old man. "There ain't no time hardly for reflectin' on things. Along comes somebody and you gotta talk."

He lived forty miles from the nearest town!

"I know the way you feel," said the sheriff. "Me, I got my hands full of people all the time, except when I get out on a trail."

"Man trails are no good," said Jay Boomer. "Men, you take the way they are, they'll get the man that hunts them, one day."

"Yeah," said the sheriff. "And that's true, too."

"You oughta quit it," said the squatter in the desert.

"Someday I'm gunna quit it," answered the sheriff.

"That day," said the other, "you'll get a letter all wrote in lead. Well, what you boys gunna eat?"

"I ain't gunna eat," said the sheriff. "I'm gunna turn in and sleep. You mind?"

Old Jay Boomer raised a glance towards the ladder that led to his small attic.

"I got no place for you, boys," said he, softly.

"Any old place will do for me," said the sheriff. "How about you, Hank?"

"Aw, I could sleep on planks," said Hank. "I kind of prefer

98

'em. I'll just take myself out of the way and fetch up in the attic."

He laid hold of the ladder.

"Don't you do it!" said Jay Boomer.

Hank looked at the sheriff, and the sheriff looked at Hank.

"Why not?" asked big Hank.

"Why, look at me," said Jay Boomer.

"I'm lookin'," said Hank.

"I'm kind of small and weazened, ain't I?"

"Well, you ain't a heavyweight."

"But I'll tell you what," said Jay Boomer. "That doggone ladder, it just bends and squeaks and groans, when I get about halfway up on it. It wouldn't come no ways near to holding your weight, friend!"

Hank stepped back.

"That the last weight that it's held?" he said.

"Yes," said Jay Boomer, with a faint sigh. "Nobody ever goes up there except me, mostly. I been figurin' to put up a new ladder, but somehow it don't never get done. You know the way that things go when you're a bachelor."

"I know," said the sheriff.

He had drawn off into a corner of the room, well away from the square black hole which had been sawed into the ceiling. Now he looked at Jay Boomer with a faint smile, and Jay Boomer hastily began to refill his pipe, scowling studiously down at it.

"Built that attic, up there, without any windows, Jay, didn't you?" said the sheriff.

"Ay, nary a one," said Jay Boomer.

"Well," said the sheriff, "it ought to make a pretty good —cage, say?"

Hank stood also in a far corner, and he likewise was staring upward at the attic trap with a smile.

"I reckon that cage would hold a bird," said he. "What kind of a bird might be in it now, Boomer?"

"I dunno what you mean," said Boomer.

"Kind of a light bird, I reckon," said the sheriff. "Because the ladder's shaky, old Jay says."

He chuckled. Jay Boomer was sweating with distress. And the sheriff said in a changed tone: "You're all right, Jay. You'd stick by him, even when he got himself outside the law. You're the kind of a friend for a man to have. But we gotta have that boy, and we're gunna have him——"

A thin, distant whistle came off the desert like the call of a bird, except that no bird of the desert ever had such a note. When he heard it, Jay Boomer actually groaned with relief.

"All right, boys," said he. "Go on up and take a look at the cage. There ain't any bird in it, though!"

The sheriff started. Hank, with a grim look at Boomer, suddenly wrenched open the door and shouted at the top of his lungs: "Jim! Jim!"

There was no answer.

He and the sheriff seized the lantern and rushed out behind the house. Near the corner of the horse shed they found Jim lying on the ground, face downward. A streak of crimson was painted in a glistening stripe across the front of his head.

They turned him over. Hank, cursing bitterly, heaved him to a sitting posture, but his head fell loosely back across his shoulders.

"Dead!" said the gasping whisper of Jay Boomer, behind them.

But the great head of Jim now heaved itself up, and a groan bubbled on his lips.

Hank, on his knees, held the other by the shoulders and shook him frantically.

"Jim, Jim!" he urged. "What happened?"

The head of Jim still rolled from side to side, but in a flat, droning voice he answered, word by word: "It kind of rose up out of the ground. Like a shadow. It kind of rose up, and then it slammed me—"

He slumped forward again, into the arms of Hank.

CHAPTER XXIII

Surprises are less dramatic than long-expected calamities. Tragedy gathers around the sick man, who has fought for years against his disease. People hold their breath when at last he goes to bed. They shudder when his death is heard. But when your strong, robust fellow drops dead without warning in the street we shrug our shoulders, turn up our eyes, and say without conviction that one never knows what may happen. Public attention must be worked up in order to be held. There have to be two good preliminary acts before the tragedy.

So it was in the case of young Flash Baldwin.

He had held the center of the stage for a long time and prepared the public mind for just what had happened. They had watched him with a breathless intensity, as though he were buried powder, and a forest fire nearby. Now the word went out that he had killed a gypsy, made a fool of the sheriff and two good fighting men, and a second time in one day had escaped through their fingers.

The sheriff came back to Pazo looking somewhat dour. Hank had vowed never to leave this blood trail. And big Jim appeared with his head tied in a strong bandage. He said nothing. His looks were enough to show where his heart was.

No one was surprised that the Flash had escaped from the sheriff. Probably they would have been vastly disappointed in their hearts if Crusty Bill had captured the outlaw at the first stroke. That was not how the play was, so to speak, advertised. In the first place, the boy had pointed towards eventual outlawry for a long, long time. But his exploits had been contained within the mysterious realm of "self-defense," or else they had been performed south of the Rio. But now that he had broken through and struck the law in the face there would be no peace for him. It seemed absurd that the death of a mere gypsy should have been the cause of his outlawry. But, whatever the cause, it was clear that a man could be hanged for the killing of a gypsy as well as for the killing of a president of the United States.

And, now that the boy was cut adrift and was roaming at large, everyone looked forward to a long, long chase. People settled back and shook their heads with outward gravity and with inward smiling. If the Flash did not give them good newspaper reading for six months at least, they missed their guess.

Good old Crusty Bill—he would stick like a bulldog to the trail, and he would do his best—but, of course, one cannot expect a bulldog to catch a thunderbolt without being badly burned; and already Crusty and his party had been singed, so to speak.

So the downfall of the Flash called for neither great sympathy nor great surprise, but only a deep, deep interest. People nodded to one another. And there were only three people in the county who so much as guessed that the Flash was not guilty of the slaying of the gypsy. Everyone else took it for granted.

Even Jacqueline Moore took it for granted.

She was walking up and down along the veranda of her father's house this evening, with Thomas Winter, and their theme was the Flash. He walked a fraction of a step behind her, and this expressed the deferential and serious attitude which he had adopted toward her. It flattered the girl, because she knew from her father that Winter was a man of importance. To be sure, even her father did not seem to know very much about Winter's past, but he knew that celebrated names came readily and familiarly to the lips of Winter, and the man was familiar with the world from Cairo to Pekin, and from the Fiji Islands to London. If such a fellow had taken Jacqueline lightly and carelessly, she would not have been surprised; and therefore she was enormously flattered by the way in which he treated her as an equal. He never talked down. He never appeared faintly amused by her youth and its absurdities of thought. One would have thought, to watch him, that they had enjoyed equal years, equal experiences.

He seemed very interested in the Flash.

"Nothing is proved, in the first place," said he. "We really don't know that he killed the poor gypsy."

"Oh, stuff!" said Jacqueline, roughly. "His gun was found on the spot."

"Coincidence," said Winter. "A very odd coincidence. But still, one can't call that an actual proof."

"Humph," said the girl. "Well, it's enough to hang him! That little coincidence is enough to convince any twelve jurors in this part of the world. All I hope is that he puts up a good fight."

"Before he's caught, you mean?" said Winter.

"Yes."

"Perhaps he won't be caught."

"Oh," said the girl. "They're all caught, sooner or later. He'll be caught, too."

"Poor fellow!" said Winter.

"Why do you sympathize with him?" asked the girl.

Winter paused, and clasping his hands behind his back, he looked upward, in quiet thought.

"I'll tell you," he said. "When I first saw him, I took him to be a shallow young desperado—or hardly a desperado even. But when you told me that there was something in him more than met the eye, I looked again, and I thought I saw what you meant. There was an air about him that detached him from the other cattlemen. He seemed to stand by himself, aloof from the rest. There was something keen and fierce about him. Perhaps he was a robber, but he was also a hero, like one of the old Greeks that Homer loved to sing about."

"You put the Flash on a high plane," said the girl.

"But not on such a plane as you put him," said Winter. "Because he's your friend, seriously. Am I wrong?"

"Oh, no, you're right," said she. "He's my friend."

"And when one's intimate—" began Winter.

"Well, I can't exactly call him an intimate," she corrected

102

him. "You see, once we were as thick as thieves. We were raised together. But after I went to school we drifted apart a good deal. Now I never can find out what he's thinking about. He's grown ugly. He takes a pleasure in sneering at me."

"No, no," said Winter. "Sneering at *you?* Surely not that!"

"But he does!" she said.

"High young spirits——" said Winter.

"Just plain ugliness," said she. "The trouble with the Flash is that he's bad himself, and he thinks that everybody else is just as bad as he is."

"Of course you know him much better than I do," said Winter. "But there's an honesty about a lad who goes out alone, and throws himself on his father's grave——"

"Sentimentality," said Jacqueline. "Moon-staring romance, and all that sort of thing. Byronism. That's what it is! Nothing but that!"

"Jacqueline," said Winter, "you amaze me."

"How?" said she.

"By the keen, bitter way in which you look through people," he explained. "It's no good trying to hide weaknesses and follies from you. You see through them. You could look into the sun, easily enough. You'd see the spots on it, too. I've never known anyone like you, my dear girl!"

She was flattered and a bit abashed. She looked straight at him to discover mockery, if it were in his face, but his brown eyes were as clear as could be. It startled her to look into them, they were so unclouded, so boyishly bright.

"Uncle Tom," said she.

"Yes?" he answered, in that rather hasty, deferential way of his.

"Tell me how old you are?"

"Old enough," he said, "to have done more with my life than I've managed to do. Old enough to have found some surer and better form of happiness. Old enough, in fact, to be something more than an aimless wanderer on the earth, Jacqueline. And that's why my heart goes out so to poor Flash David. I can sympathize with him. I know the careless, wild impulses that must be working in him."

"*You* know!" burst out the girl. "As if you ever did a dishonest thing in your life! As if honesty doesn't simply shine out of you! Do you know what you are, Uncle Tom?"

"Well, tell me, Jacqueline," said he. "The preamble sounds promising. Don't let me down flat."

"You're just a big, gentle, simple-hearted boy, no matter what your years, or how far you've traveled over the earth, or what people you've known!"

Thomas Winter looked down to the board floor of the veranda. A distant roar and chiming of laughter swept towards them from the bunkhouse.

Then Winter looked up at her again.

"I would never give myself such a clean bill of health," he told her. "I really think, on the other hand, that if you'll consider Flash David——"

"I almost hate the name!" she broke out. "Flash David! I almost hate it. I'm tired of hearing of it. He's nothing to me, after all!"

"Ah, but he's a friend," said Winter. "And I think you were saying, yourself, that friendship is a sacred thing. You said it with your whole heart. I know that you meant it."

"I *do* believe it," said she. "Poor David. Of course my heart aches for him. Only—to murder a gypsy—a poor half-witted jockey of a gypsy whom he's cheated out of a horse before—I mean, that's too detestably low——"

"Don't call him all those bitter names, Jacqueline," said Winter. "But I see how it is. You really were very fond of the poor lad."

"Do you know?" she broke out at him, savagely, her hands clenched.

"Well?" said he.

"I can tell you," she said. "You're a grave for secrets, I know. And I'll tell you what. I loved him—I really did—I loved that horse stealer—that murderer from ambush——"

"Loved him? *Loved* him?" exclaimed Winter, appearing stunned. Then he added: "But I understand. He has one of the handsomest faces I've ever seen. Almost femininely fine features——"

"That's it," she answered, bitterly. "You say that I can see through people. I can't. There I was with my head completely turned by a handsome young rascal—a fellow worth nothing, not even to handle a lariat! Oh, I despise myself when I think of it!"

"But don't try to drive him out of your mind by looking at his faults. Keep the full, fair picture of him before you. And, after all, it was a grand thing that he did—giving the sheriff and his men the slip, like that."

"He is a fox, of course," said the girl. "And if only there weren't something about him that pulls at my heart—I don't know why—why, there's one of the men who rode with the sheriff!"

He came through the evening dusk a dim figure, but the white of the bandage around his head was clearly visible. It was Jim, the gunman.

CHAPTER XXIV

Jim walked up to the veranda and took off his sombrero, thereby showing a wider expanse of white bandage.

"Hello, Miss Moore," said he. "I come up here from the sheriff. I been ridin' with him. Which he sent me a message for you, ma'am, or for your father, rather. He says that the Flash is aimin' in this direction, and it seems like the Flash is likely to drift around about here. He just wants to send you a warnin'."

The girl smiled.

"He doesn't need to warn us against the Flash," said she. "David Baldwin is an old friend of this family."

Jim chuckled. It sounded like a snarl.

"You're talkin' about him the way he is before," said he. "He's a new lad now, ma'am. I can tell you that. He don't fork a horse the same way. He don't pull the same kind of a gun. He's turned sour, Miss Moore."

He rubbed his head, and added with another rumbling laugh: "I ain't talkin' about the slam that he handed to me. That's part of the game between him and us."

The girl nodded at him: "Everybody feels a debt to you and your partner, Hank. But you're wrong about the Flash, I think. He'll never be sour to anyone in this house."

Jim looked at Winter.

"I'll go and find father," said Jacqueline Moore. "He'll want to talk to you, I know. This is Mr. Winter, our guest. He'll be glad to know something about your adventures following this trail, I know."

She disappeared. Jim sat down on the high wooden arm of the steps that led to the veranda floor; Winter came down and stood before him.

"Well, Mr. Winter," said Jim. "What can I tell you about my adventures, and all such? You new to this neck of the woods?"

He began to manufacture a cigarette.

Winter regarded him without a smile.

"You've made a pretty picture out of yourself," he said. "And you've done a good job—you and Hank and the fool of a sheriff. I didn't know, Jim, that you've lost half your nerve and most of your brains, or I never would have brought you out here for this job."

Jim lighted his cigarette. The flame of the match revealed

a face contorted and dark under the white smoothness of the bandage.

He snapped the match far away. It made a dying arc of light that disappeared in mid-air.

"What kind of a job?" he asked. "What's to be had out of it? What's the good of it?"

"You're sick of it, are you?" said Winter.

"I'm sick of it," said Jim. "I'm sick of talking the lingo. I'm sick of swaggering around in chaps and all the rest of the paraphernalia. I'm sick of the whole mess and I want to get through with it. We're wasting time! I met that shyster from Denver, that Taps Isaacson—you remember? He came around and whispered a plant in my ears. It's a hundred-thousand-dollar pickup. We could make it as easy as taking candy from a baby. We could pull jobs like that, out here where we're not known. But you're blowing in our time for nothing at all. For nothing at all, except what *you* get out of it."

"Tell me, Jim," said Winter. "What do *I* get out of it?"

"Aw, I saw her," said Jim. "And I know you. You subtract the pretty girls out of your life, and you'd be worth a hundred million, and the rest of us would have a fat slice, too. But you can't go past a good-looking girl. They bring you up standing. Only, I point out to you that you hang around here and waste our time, while you grin at a girl and make fool talk to her, and send the rest of us out to head off the kid that she really has a liking for. Besides, one of these days they'll wake up and see the whole plant, the gun, and the dead gypsy, and the whole thing. It's pretty thin. It's pretty thin. I'll tell you another thing. Hank is kind of sick of it, too. This idea of going around and bumping off skinny gypsies that never did more harm than rob a henroost— well, we don't like it."

Winter nodded at him again.

"This is why I like you and trust you, Jim," said he. "Because you get into words everything that's on your great big manly, open heart. Because you're such a straight-forward man with your grumbling."

"Go on," said Jim. "I expect to hear a lot worse than this."

"Because you've been rapped over the head and made a fool of by a half-baked lad in the West," said Winter, "now you come to me with your tail between your legs whining."

"All right," said Jim. "You can say that, and a lot more. All I want is a straight crack at that wildcat. But he's as shifty as a ghost. He has his claws into you before you know that he's about."

"And Hank has enough, too?" asked Winter.

"We both have enough," said Jim. "I've talked it over with him. There's no use throwing your purse away to get back a dollar that you've lost. This kid, the Flash—let the regular law handle him. For all the good that you can get out of him, you'd better try to live on cactus thorns, I'd say. He's made up of nothing but rawhide and steel springs, and that's a fact. You'll never harvest anything but trouble out of him, chief."

"Are you through with your advice?" asked Winter.

"Yeah. I'm through."

"Then listen to me: you'll stay after the Flash until you've nailed him."

Jim grunted. Then he shrugged his shoulders.

"If I have to, I have to. And that's the end of that," he said gloomily.

"It's not on account of the Flash that I sent for you," said Winter. "It's something a great deal more important and a great deal worse."

"There's nothing worse," said Jim stiffly. "You don't know him. But I've chased him, I've eaten his dust. And I've seen the speed of him, when he's close up. He's nothing but sleight of hand, if you want to know the truth. When he got at me that night, I grabbed for my gun with one hand and made a pass at him with the other. It was like trying to put out a star. I just over-reached myself punching the air, and while I was off balance he slammed me. He could as well have sifted some lead into my system. It might have been fast work for another fellow, but for him it was dead easy. He could afford to yawn, think it over, and make up his mind between moves. That's how fast he is. Now tell me what's worse than that?"

"There's a plague," said Winter, "that makes the Flash seem like no trouble at all. You forget."

"Ay. You mean Old North?" said Jim. "But he's no nearer than Pekin, I guess."

"Our detective friend North," said Winter, "will be here inside of two days!"

This word raised the other slowly to his feet, with a sigh that was half a groan.

"Old North? Here?" he muttered.

"That starts your hair lifting, I dare say?" suggested Winter.

"And what about your own?" asked Jim.

"He's hounded us long enough," replied Winter. "But now he oversteps himself. A Chinese junk, or a South Sea Island, or a nest of beachcombers, or city streets and crowds—he can work in places like that. But he doesn't know the West. He's overstepped himself, Jim, and we're going to polish him off. We're going to erase him. We're going to wipe him out, Jim. Do you hear?"

Jim grinned widely.

"I'd rather do that," he said, "than have a brownstone front on Fifth Avenue, with two butlers, and a turnout for the Park, and all the rest, including a box at the opera. I'd trade all that to see Old North turned into a stiff, and a cold one. Damn him!" he concluded with a soft vehemence.

"Yes, damn him!" agreed Winter. "I tell you, Jim, that my luck is in. I feel it in my blood and my bones. I feel it in my heart. We're going to polish off Old North, because I've laid the lines for the job. He thinks that he's taking us by surprise. Instead, we're going to surprise *him!*"

"When do we start?" asked Jim.

"You start tonight. Collect Hank. Tell the sheriff anything you please. I'll make my excuses here for a couple of days' absence and join you about noon. I'm riding from here towards the Ralston Buttes. I'll expect you there."

"I'll be there, and Hank with me," said Jim. "And God help Old North if we have a fair chance at him. How many has he got with him, and do I know any of 'em?"

"Let me tell you something," said Winter. "You won't believe me, but it's true. He's alone!"

"Hold on!" exclaimed Jim. "That can't be straight. Not alone! Not Old North! The old boy must have weakening of the brain before he'd tackle us all by himself!"

"I've told you the truth," said Winter. "Tell Hank what I've said. We're going to crowd him into the last corner this time, my lad! Now, get out of here. No, you've got to wait for Miss Moore."

"I'll wait for nothing," said Jim. "This is news that will make Hank stare! I'm gone. So long, chief!"

He strode hastily away, got his horse out of the heart of the twilight, and rode away as Jacqueline Moore and her father came out from the house.

"He's gone," said Winter. "He said that he couldn't wait. He simply wanted to leave the warning."

"A very odd thing," murmured Moore. "Why the devil should Flash David turn against my house? What has he against us?"

"When milk turns sour, it's sharp to every man's tongue, you know," said Winter. "However, I'm sure that the sheriff is wrong. The boy can't be as bad as that!"

"Of course, he can't," said Moore. "Winter, you always show refreshing common sense. God bless the man who puts down scandal."

"Did you talk to that fellow?" said Jacqueline.

"Quite a little," said Winter.

"What did you think of him?"

"Rather a grim figure of a man, I thought," said Winter. "I'm not surprised that he's a man hunter!"

"He's a true Westerner, though," said the girl. "Take him away from chaps and ropes and spurs, and he wouldn't know what to do witht himself. He's as Western as salt is salt!"

"I suppose you're right," said Winter. "You have a way of looking through people, Jacqueline!"

CHAPTER XXV

The day had been blinding bright in the morning, and the sun a power so great that every spot on the earth seemed a focal point upon which its force was gathered as through the lens of a burning glass.

Through this heat rode Old North.

Even a stranger would have picked out the word "old" for him at a glance. To be sure, at a distance, he seemed almost like a youth, a mere boy, so short sat he in the saddle, and so lean and finely drawn was his face. But when one came nearer one saw that his lack of height was owing to the bend in his spinal column which thrust his chin forward and gave him the appearance of one about to break into a run. There were few lines in his face, but a closer inspection showed that what appeared a smile was merely the double, deep furrowing of wrinkles on either side of his mouth. And though the rest of his face was not plowed by time the complexion had an unnatural, fiery red, and the brows had been burned white by sun and time. At a distance, he seemed a youth. At close hand, he appeared aged by centuries. He was like a crimson mummy. He was like a body from which the epidermis had been flayed, and the underskin had hardened from exposure and was ready to crack at the first touch.

The mount of this old man was not a horse, not even a mustang. Instead, he had chosen a mule. It was a fine animal of its kind. It was a little inclined to knock-knees, as so many of its species are, but its head was small, the ears comparatively delicate, its neck very lean, is loins and quarters powerful. It went with a short, precise step, sometimes fetlock deep in the sands. But it kept patiently at its work, and an expert could have told at a glance that this animal was accustomed to desert life and to desert ways.

The rider allowed the reins to fall loosely upon the neck. Only now and then he corrected its course a little, but the mule knew how to accept a distant landmark as a goal, and to keep on steadily toward it.

The equipment of Old North was a battered felt hat with a high crown and a wide brim that flopped a little above his eyes, a dusty flannel shirt, old blue jeans by way of riding breeches, wrinkled, obviously secondhand boots, and no spurs shining on their heels. Hooked over the pommel of the saddle there dangled a quirt with only one of the several lashes remaining. There was a time-and-weather-cracked slicker bound behind the saddle, and one of the saddlebags bulged slightly with a meager set of provisions.

One would have said that this was a mere beggar, a nameless, poverty-stricken man—or else a great miser. As a matter of fact, the second case was the true one. Old North could have spent tens of thousands of dollars upon his quest. He had a sufficient official backing to credit the expense, and he would not be esteemed more highly for the lack of large expense accounts. Rather, the reverse would be true. But his very soul loathed extravagance. He loved to make five cents do for him what a dollar did for others. It was something of the same spirit, perhaps, which had made him detest crime all of his days; and since his youth he had been a man hunter.

There was only one item upon which he had spent money without reluctance.

Running through a long holster that extended down the side of the saddle under his right knee was the finest rifle that money could buy. One could see that it was cared for as a treasure. The protruding wood of the butt, at easy handgrip from the rider, had the appearance of having been well oiled recently. And the metalwork shone, when a touch of the rider's gloves brushed the surface dust away.

As a matter of fact, the life and the future of Old North might depend upon the goodness of that rifle, almost as much as upon the skill he possessed in the use of it. So he had not hesitated to spend money for his weapon.

He had another gun. It was not visible, being hidden inside his clothes, but this weapon was so old that it hardly deserved the name of a gun in other hands than his. It was a short-nosed bulldog revolver of an antique pattern. It shot high and to the right. Its range was very short. But he knew all of its defects, and constant use of it during a period of some thirty-five years had made it like part of his flesh, a thing that responded to his will almost without the aid of his hand. It had the virtue of shooting a large-caliber bullet hard enough to knock down a man at twenty yards. And its short barrel made it handy for a quick draw. In the agile, clawlike hands of Old North, the only part of his body which had not begun to stiffen with time and years, that short revolver had accomplished wonders.

So equipped, Old North rode stolidly through the blasting heat of the morning over a desert which was in part a torrid red sand and in part a pale, dazzling gray, with lines and streaks of greasewood running like smoke in the hollows that collected the few drops of the spring rains.

In the afternoon the atmosphere grew misty, but not with water vapor. It was only the fine-flying desert dust which filled the sky, drifting in from the wake of some far-distant storm, perhaps. This clouding of the air did not seem to decrease the heat of the sun. Rather, it brought home the heat as with a blanket, and a fine, imperceptible fall of the desert dust worked down inside the bandanna which was bound about his throat—a faded, secondhand bandanna, also—and irritated his dry old skin.

He cared nothing for this. Physical discomfort up to the suffocation point he had endured too often before to be troubled by it now. He went on with a steady head to his direction, and cared nothing for his body. So he had done all his life.

His attitude was that of a seeker. And the direction of his gaze was toward the horizon, the mysterious and misty line which divides earth from heaven, infinitely fine, infinitely soft, infinitely deep, the mock of all landscape painters. One might have said that he was searching for a distant mountain head, a desired landmark to make him sure of his course. In truth, he was seeing only before his eyes the unforgotten image of Winter, his old enemy, whose trail he had followed so many years.

He had done other things, also, in the meantime. He had done enough to build up a tidy little fortune for himself, not invested in dangerous securities, but locked up in secure four per cents, as invincible as the rock of Gibraltar. But ever and anon, he returned to the great quest, the endless effort, like Palomides forever returning to the trail of the Questing Beast.

Now he felt in his heart that he had come near to the end. He was growing older and older. He could not deny that his crooked back grew every year yet more crooked. Sometimes when he sat down to a supper, he found his right hand trembling. And a man whose right hand trembled, either day or night, had no place upon the trail of Thomas Winter.

This would be about the last time that he would be able to make a determined effort to gain a hold upon the great

111

criminal. And he felt a sense of fate—that either he or Winter must go down in this final trial—as if God himself must pay some heed to the efforts which had been invested before, and decide either for or against him, not allow him to slip into a green old age with the one desire of his heart unfulfilled!

In the middle of the afternoon, he came to a sharp-shouldered mesa and stopped in the shadow of the eastern side of it. There was no breath of air here. The instant he paused, the sweat began to course down his face, mingling with the alkali dust to scald his skin. The mule broke into a profuse sweat also.

However, legs cannot go on forever.

He got some greasewood, made a wretched fire, and over it prepared some coffee, which he drank with hard, dry biscuits, real ships' biscuits, generally considered indigestible except on the high seas in the mouths of true tars.

He had two canteens of water. He used just enough to make his coffee. The rest he poured down the throat of his mule. And the mule held the mouth of the canteen nicely, accurately between teeth and lips, not crushing the fragile metal, and then raising its head and drinking without the spilling of a drop. It was plain that this mule had traveled the desert many times before and knew that water is better than food—better than wine.

When the coffee and the hardtack had been eaten, Old North lay flat on his back.

He did not want to lie down. He did not feel like sleeping. Small insects, whirring through the air, lighted hungrily on his face. For a time he brushed them off. Then he realized that he was growing jumpy and that all his nerves were taut. So he closed his eyes, bent the full power of his will upon sleep, and all in a moment he was profoundly slumbering.

The well-hobbled mule strayed only to a little distance, reaching for the casual spears of dead grass that grew here and there. And not until the sun was down did the sleeper waken.

Then he resaddled and unhobbled his mule. He would have been heartily glad of a drink of water. During the latter part of his sleep, his mouth had been open, and for that reason his throat was dry as a bone and gritty with sand. But there was no more water, and much of his march still lay before him.

So he calmly mounted and jounced himself in the saddle. The mule flattened its ears and humped its back.

At this, Old North smiled.

"Good!" said he.

For a mule that is ready to buck is a mule that is ready to work. He resumed his journey. The day faded. A dull red came up like a dismal smoke in the west and spread drearily to the zenith. The light dimmed still more. The darkness came.

He no longer guided the mule, but let it follow its own sense of direction.

Then, gradually, the stars appeared, and after the stars the pale, broad face of the moon moved up the eastern sky and gave a ghostly light to the desert.

The mist was still everywhere. Through it now and then appeared the faintly glistening outline of a Spanish bayonet, like a stalking body with arms upraised. And now the square head of a mesa loomed quite suddenly before him.

He had not wasted any time or effort. The mule had kept to its course wisely and well, and now as the moon brightened he could see the loom of more distant landscapes. For his ship there was now almost a harbor in sight.

On through the night he went. The way began to climb. The sand gave way to naked rocks underfoot, still hot from the day. The rocks cooled. The night grew old.

And so he came to a narrow defile that opened through the heart of a dreadful region of broken rocks. He checked the mule. Should he go through it, or should he take the safer and longer way around?

CHAPTER XXVI

Old North looked up. He could see the dim disk of the moon, fast making its westing, and beside it a small star, lost, refound, and lost again.

Again he looked down at the small defile, narrow, closed with rocks as with teeth, and he shook his head. So he started the mule on the wide detour which was necessary if he was to avoid this traplike place. The tired mule stumbled over a rock half hidden in a patch of sand, and this changed the mind of Old North. Some concessions must be made to weariness, on a long march. So he turned the mule back, and straight down the defile, first loosening the rifle in its holster, and touching the handles of his old revolver to reassure himself of its readiness.

Then, all eyes, all keen attention, his head thrusting forward and his eyes noting every shadow to the right and to the left, he went down the little pass. The rocks grated and clicked under the hoofs of the mule. Once it brought down its iron-armed hoof on a stone surface so hard that the clang sounded in the keenly attuned ears of the rider like the stroke of a bell.

All his nerves jumped at once. His heart began to race, but he argued that this was a foolish apprehension, and that if he had been upon the trail of any person other than Thomas Winter he would have had no fear, no jumping of the nerves whatever.

So he went on. He had come to the very middle of the pass when he straightened in the saddle. He glared before him among the rocks. There was nothing to be seen, but an electric sense of danger filled his brain and his body.

Then a quiet voice said: "Don't turn your head, old fellow!"

He had his right hand frozen upon the handles of his revolver. He considered casting himself from the saddle among the rocks nearby, but he controlled the impulse rigorously.

His bones were old and brittle. He could not play cat as he had in his younger days. And that was the voice of Thomas Winter, which had spoken behind him!

Another voice, almost equally familiar, now said: "Shove up your hands, North. Hank, take a look at him, will you?"

"Take a look yourself," said Hank. "I'm not going to touch the old spider."

"Draw a tight bead on him. Get a little closer," said Winter. "I'll fan him myself."

The two gunmen stepped nearer, their guns ready, and Winter walked up to his quarry. He reached instantly for the revolver, as one who well knew where it was concealed. Then he drew the rifle from its holster.

"Is that all?" he asked.

"That's all," said Old North.

"No knife—no little trinkets of that sort, North?"

"No, none at all."

"Then you might slide off your mule and sit down and have a smoke with us."

"Not a bad idea," said Old North. "Give me a hand down, will you? I'm pretty stiff. It's been a long ride."

"But you're going to have a long rest, now," said Winter, carefully handing the old man down from the saddle. "Sit down here. And take this, North. You'll like it. It's a real Havana. As good as they come."

Jim and Hank, standing near by, kept their rifles at the ready, leaning over the crook of their arms. And they glared down at Old North with a strange, patient joy. A collector who at last has found the picture which his heart desires,

114

at a price endlessly beneath his expectations, would stare in this manner at the prize. So stared the two gunmen, drinking in the face of their victim, and removing their glances from him only to flash at each other looks of intimate appreciation and understanding.

Old North paid no attention to them at first. He was refusing the proffered Havana.

"Let me see that thing," said he, taking the cigar. "Now, I can tell by the feel of it, and the handmade shaping of it, and the smell, too, that it's a high-priced cigar. That cigar, now, would cost as much as twenty cents, wouldn't it?"

"Twenty-five," said Winter.

"Take it back!" exclaimed Old North. "Thinking of smokin' money like that—hard-cash money! Why, I couldn't do it. You look at this—"

He drew from a pocket a thin black stick, which he broke in two. It snapped like a bit of rattan.

"I know that kind of a cigar," said Thomas Winter. "I even smoked part of one, once."

"You didn't like it, maybe?" asked Old North.

"I lost most of the skin off my tongue," said Winter. "Otherwise it might have been a good smoke, except that it choked me after two or three puffs."

"You're joking, I see," said Old North. "You always would have your fun, Tommy. But the fact is, why does a man smoke? Because he wants to get some nicotine into his system. That's the real reason. Now, there's more nicotine in half of this here cigar than there is in the whole of that fat one you're biting the end off. That's a fact. And I get these here cigars for ten cents. Three for ten cents. About twelve per cent of what you pay, smoke for smoke. I tell you, Tommy, it's the ruin of you, the way that you smoke up money. You take my advice. Save the pennies. The dollars will watch themselves."

Winter sat down on another stone opposite the old fellow. He nodded at him, saying: "You're wonderful, North. There's nobody like you. But it's not carelessness with money that's been the ruin of me. Want me to tell you what *has* been the ruin of me?"

"Oh, I see what you mean," said Old North.

He accepted the light which his enemy was holding, and puffed vigorously. The end of his broken cigar became a glowing, crimson coal, but only thin wisps of smoke issued from the lips of Old North.

"I see what you mean," he said. "You mean me. You mean that I've kept you rolling, kept you from gathering moss, eh?"

"That's what I mean," said Winter. "That cigar pulls rather hard, doesn't it?"

"Well, it takes kind of a bit of patience," said the old man. "But I don't mind. You gotta have patience in this here world of ours. The harder the shell, the sweeter the kernel."

"That's true," said Winter. "You've been a hard nut to crack, but I'm certainly enjoying you now, North."

"I reckon you are," said North, placidly.

He pulled so hard on the narrow cigar that his face swelled and his neck turned red.

Then he went on: "I've enjoyed you, Tommy. I've enjoyed you a whole lot."

"I imagine that I'm getting enough pleasure now to make up for it," said Winter.

"Ah, Tommy," said the old man, "you're young, and that's what makes you talk like that. You think what I've thought for a good many years, that it's the end that counts. It's not, however. It's the work that gives one the pleasure. Here I sit, a dead man. But what's death? Only a twinge. And in the meantime I've had—how long has it been, Tommy?—about twenty years of pleasure hunting you like a fox."

"Ay," said Winter. "You've been running me and some of my friends for about twenty years."

"And what a run," said Old North, closing his eye and inhaling to the bottom of his lungs with satisfaction. "What a grand run—what bursts across the open, what beating of cover, what getting to earth, what tricks, what doublings, what thin scents and what hot ones! Oh, it's been a grand run. Ask the old sportsman as he lies dying of a fall if he regrets his life because it has had to come to an end. Then ask me if I regret the long chase after you! No, no, Tommy, I don't regret it. I'm glad of it. You'll need to live another twenty years to have the fun that I've had out of you."

"No regrets, eh?" said Winter.

"Well, hardly any," said the old man. "Of course, it would have been extra sweet to land you in jail, to sit in at your trial, and hear the judge condemn you. But I wouldn't have wanted to be at the hanging of you, Tommy. No, because that would have meant the end of too much. I would have felt that my own life was close to its finish! Nothing interesting left to do. However, I don't regret much. I've spoiled some of the best years of your life. I've wrecked twenty of your schemes, I've saved the world millions of money, and though you've made your thousands, and even your hundreds of thousands, here and there, still, I've kept the fox lean, be-

116

cause I've run the fat off him after every meal. Am I wrong, Tommy?"

Winter, his jaws locked hard together, could not answer at once. Then he said: "It's pretty true, old fellow. You've run me hard. You're absolutely right in everything you say—except in one respect."

"Then tell me what the one respect may be?" suggested Old North.

"Only the matter of your dying," said Winter. "It won't be one twinge."

"No?" said Old North, "Something barbarous, my boy?"

Winter nodded.

His two gunmen drew closer, like hungry dogs expecting to be fed.

"Something barbarous," said Winter. "That's what I'm turning in my mind."

"There have been Indians out here who could give you some good ideas," said Old North. "Tying to a stake—or a rock, if a stake is not handy, and then shooting out bits of the victim. That's a good dodge."

"Yes, that's a good dodge," agreed Winter. "But I have something better than that. I'm not going to tie you up."

"No?"

"No, in fact, I'm going to turn you loose."

"I don't understand that," said Old North.

"You will, when the time comes. Have you finished that cigar?"

"As much as I care about just now."

"Then we'll ride on a little distance."

Old North carefully put out the fuming coal on the end of his cigar, looked at it attentively to see that not a spark remained, and then put the butt into a pocket.

After that, he cheerfully put his foot into the stirrup and dragged himself rather painfully up to the saddle. He sat there, panting somewhat, while the other three rode out around him in a close escort, on fine-limbed horses.

Then they passed out of the throat of the pass, and into the moon mist that lay over the plain beyond.

CHAPTER XXVII

On that same evening when Old North rode on his jogging mule into the dull desert twilight, the Flash came out of the sandy leagues mounted on the good mare, Rags, and made for a light in the midst of the plain. As he came on, he heard a cow bawling in the distance, and a coyote was yelping farther off.

These signs of life made the Flash think of food. He was very tired and he was very hungry. He was learning rapidly that the Land beyond the Law is a hungry domain, so he freshened the pace of the mare and at a long, rolling lope he came up within dusky sight of a small shack.

There was not a shed, not a barn near it. There was only a corral fenced with barbed wire strung on crooked sticks of mesquite. It was a mystery that such a place should have been taken for a human habitation. The explanation was simply that in this district, for unknown reasons, more grass grew than in the surrounding landscape. Perhaps there was an upward shelving stratum of rock that came close to the surface and brought with it a slight subsoil irrigation. At any rate, the grass was there, not in close-growing lawns, but in ragged patches here and there. A corn-fed cow would have starved to death here inside of a fortnight. Even desert cattle could not fatten on the land, but they kept skin and bones together, and put out long shanks, and ranged fifty miles for their rations, and at last came to a marketable size.

Even so, it was a precarious business. And the Cary family knew many seasons of famine. They could not have told why they persisted in living in this place instead of driving their herd farther north toward better-watered land, better grass, easier living, larger and surer profits. Something had come to them out of the desert like a spell, and it held them still. It held old Pa Cary, and his slovenly wife, and his three gaunt sons, who were as black as Mexicans and as lazy as the heart of "Tomorrow."

When the Flash rode up, he dismounted and threw the reins. Then he walked in and leaned in the doorway, making his cigarette, and giving the family a careless word. They all got up to receive him. One of the sons went out to unsaddle the mare and give her a feed out of the single half sack of barley which they possessed at the time.

Said Mrs. Cary: "Not that you ain't welcome, Flash. But it always seems kind of a shame to me, feedin' hosses on what's plenty good for people to eat. But go right ahead, Charley. Here's come a time when the poor Flash has gotta depend on a fast hoss and a strong hoss, and whatever we've got is his, God knows!"

Said her husband: "Ow, shut up, Lou, will you? Shut up and give your face a rest. Set yourself down here in my place, Flash. No, you set yourself down here. I don't want no more. I'm all finished. Set yourself right down here. Ma, put on some more potatoes to fry, will you? Is that steak cold? You better wait till we heat it up a mite, Flash."

The Flash took the proffered chair, with some unwillingness. But since the other insisted he sat down. He declared that the steak was exactly as he liked it—lukewarm, and he shoveled onto his plate two slices as thin as the sole of a shoe, and almost as tough, with strips of yellow fat decorating the edges.

But quality in food made no difference to him. Nourishment was all that he wanted, and this he could receive even at the Cary house.

He was made as much at home as they could. It was not the first time that he had used their house as a stopping point when he crossed this section of the desert. And, whenever he stopped, it meant a small but important present of cash to the head of the family.

After he had finished solids and descended to a third cup of black coffee and Bull Durham cigarettes, they opened fire with many questions and many comments.

"All this for a damn gypsy!" said the head of the family. "I dunno what people are thinkin' of, Flash. I dunno what's come to the West. There was a time when a man was a man, and he was allowed to take his pleasure, like a gentleman had oughta be allowed to do. If there was a few Injuns or such in his way, nobody asked no questions about what happened to 'em. They'd as good ask why he smashed the beer bottle out of which he'd drunk the beer. What difference, so long as he paid for the beer? But things is different. There's too much law. There's too many old hens around. Always scratchin' and cacklin' and tryin' to raise trouble. I never seen nothin' like it. It pretty near makes me sick. All this for a damn gypsy. I'm sorry for you, Flash. I'm sorry that you wasn't a boy twenty years back!"

"They've stuck a price on my head, now," said the Flash.

"Come along!" said Mrs. Cary.

"They've put five thousand on me," said the boy. "And the fact is that I didn't kill the gypsy. But that doesn't matter. The gun that was swiped from me was found on the spot. However, that don't matter. Five thousand is what they've put on me, dead or alive!"

"Five—thousand—dollars!" said Mrs. Cary, and her eyes glanced aside, as though she saw a ghost.

"That's plain murder!" said the father of the family. "That'll get you done in, one of these here days. Mind what I say. It'll get you done in one day! Somebody you think is a friend'll stick you between the ribs!"

"Five—thousand—dollars!" said Mrs. Cary.

"It's enough to set up a ranch with, about," said one of the boys under his breath. "You could just soak in that money, and—"

"Pete!" said the mother to him sharply. "You go and fetch in another cup of coffee for Flash, will you? What good are you for, anyway, settin' around, mumblin'."

"He has a turn for business," said the Flash carelessly. "He's thinking how far five thousand dollars would go around. Well, folks, I'm going to turn in."

They led him up the ladder to the attic, and there he was shown a bed which was merely a pallet of straw laid on the floor with a roll of blankets ready at the foot. Such as it was, it was the best bed in the place, and in the coolest place, for the wind blew through a small window at one end of the attic.

There the Flash turned in, and felt sleep come over him in a numbing wave.

But, at the very instant when unconsciousness was growing, a thought struck him like a spur. Suppose that danger came upon him while he slept, here? Suppose that the patient sheriff or Winter, or the two of them together, should round him up in this place? He would be no better than a dead man, of course.

He tried to force himself to sleep, but sleep would not come. And at last he simply surrendered to the jumping of his nerves. He did not go down the ladder. The creaking of it would waken the sleepers beneath him and force him to answer embarrassing questions. He simply pushed his pack out the narrow attic window, lowered it to the ground with a cord, and then followed in person, climbing down the sheer face of the wall like a cat.

Near a corner of the corral, he unrolled his blankets and lay down. And Rags came instantly to watch over him, sniffing now and then at him, as far as she dared to reach her head toward him through the pronged strands of the wire.

It seemed warmer outdoors than it had within. Heat still appeared to be breathing up from the ground. But the open, secure face of the starry sky was above him, and Rags was near by. She lay down with a grunt, and a moment later he had closed his eyes, and slept.

He wakened with a start.

It was not the dawn light which had startled him. It was the sound of voices, murmuring close at hand. And he lay wide-awake, with all his senses keen as a freshly sharpened knife.

The first voice that he heard he knew. He turned his head and saw two men dismounting from their horses close by the corral. They were hardly ten steps from him, and the voice was that of Pete Cary.

He was saying: "Come easy out of that saddle. He's a cat. He's got a cat's ears. Step easy out of that saddle, because the creak of stirrup leather would be enough to bring him up, all standing."

"I dunno that I care," said another familiar voice; for it was the sheriff who spoke. "I dunno that I care. Now, with us on this side of the house and the rest of the boys on the other side, I reckon that we can take care of him, no matter how stiff he comes up standing. What guns did he pack upstairs with him?"

"He's got no rifle," said Pete Cary.

"Then he's got no chance!"

"And what about them five thousand dollars?" asked Pete Cary, softly but eagerly.

"There's four of us, countin' you," said the sheriff. "You'll get your share. You'll get your split. That's all!"

"I oughta get more. I oughta get a half, anyways!" said Pete. "Look at what'll happen. Pa'll hate my spots as long as I live. So'll both my kid brothers hate and despise me, kind of. Only ma—she won't mind so much."

Said the sheriff, gently, with a sort of pity in his voice: "Tell me, old son—it was your ma that put you up to this, wasn't it?"

"Now, how did you guess that?" demanded Pete, his astonishment very easily read even in his gasping whisper.

"I seen the hungry look in her eye, once," said the sheriff. "Trust a dog, but never you trust a she cat that's got young. It's time for us to get in on the game. I'll tell you what. You'll get two shares. You'll get your quarter, and you'll get my quarter, because I don't sort of cotton to takin' money out of a thing like this."

"Now, what d'you mean by that?" asked Pete Cary. "Would you turn down pretty close on to fourteen hundred dollars? And what for, I'd like to know?"

"Why, son," said the sheriff, rather sadly, "I dunno that you'll ever quite understand. But this here business that I'm in, it kind of gives me the creeps, now and then. Let's close in on the house. We've talked enough—enough for me, anyway!"

They moved on toward the house. They did not turn to look back, for they might have seen a figure like a ghost rising from the ground.

They did not turn back, and it was not until some minutes later, as they crept closer beneath the imagined peril which the house contained, that they heard the beating of hoofs, and then, looking off toward the horizon, they saw a horseman, riding slowly, on an animal which galloped with a long, easy stride, swaying across the horizon stars.

The sheriff stood up with a grind of his teeth.

He said nothing, but young Pete Cary, who also had seen the passing phantom, knew perfectly well that the departing rider was none other than the man he had attempted to betray, and that his betrayal was known, and that he had damned himself as an honest man forever and ever as a mere traitor, without a traitor's reward.

CHAPTER XXVIII

The Flash went on slowly, for he was too deep in thought to pay much heed to the way before him. His main interest was in what had happened the night before, and he saw clearly that now he had reached a time when he must distrust every man. Old friendships were now of little value. He must judge every man and regard every woman with a new eye, for what they had been before they might no longer be now.

Five thousand dollars!

He could remember, now, how the words had come lovingly off the tongue of Mrs. Cary, and the brooding light which had been in her eyes, as she re-echoed and re-echoed them.

Money had ever been, to the Flash, merely something to fight for, play for, gamble for. It was stuff which glittered as it was thrown away, so to speak; but it was not worth working for, not worth keeping. For what could any man desire more than clothes enough to cover his back—gaudy ones when his fortune was ripe—and boots on his feet, food enough to fill his belly? As for the money which other men loved to put in the bank, which they treasured up and loved and fought and died for—it was foolish stuff! And yet now it was revealed to him that others who were even his friends could treasure the stuff more than they treasured human affection, human blood.

He was like a wolf, like a coyote. There was a price for his scalp!

He did not blame Mrs. Cary very bitterly. He could remember in the past small acts of kindness, almost of affection. He could not doubt that from time to time she actually had felt an honest kindness for him. It was simply that she loved five thousand dollars more than she could love honor and friendship.

It was a hard and bitter lesson for the Flash. It had been not too hard for him to think, in the other days, of the time when he might be living outside the law. But the actuality of that domain was a thing that bewildered him with its lonely hardness. He rode by himself. He lived by himself. Even Don Pedro Beckwith, as most people called him, probably could hardly be counted upon now as a true friend.

Five thousand dollars—that was the rock upon which all man's honor might be wrecked!

The sun brightened, grew intensely hot above him. And then he turned the head of Rags straight toward the house of Winter. That account he must clear off at once, and having accomplished this he would leave the country. He hardly knew in what direction he would head. It must be simply away. He wanted a new sky. The very sight of the Devil Mountains seared his eyes and made his brain ache as though the naked range itself were hostile to him.

There lay before him a peculiarly bitter tract. Even with Rags beneath his saddle, he shook his head and frowned as he looked forward to it, for it was a stretch of rocks and gray sand with little or no vegetation. Only here and there a stubborn cactus had treasured up inside its rind a few drops of water from the rainy season, and here and there a wretched mesquite showed a tuft of yellowish leaves, a small token of the many yards of rootage which stretched underground toward moisture.

But he put Rags at this bitter reach.

The sun, as it neared its zenith, became scalding strong. It was like a continual dripping of powerful acids over his head, his shoulders, his back. He had to shrug his shoulders to loosen the flannel shirt. He felt that his skin was blistering, even beneath the cloth, for here there was not a breath of wind. The distant foothills cupped the sun and fenced back the winds. A weight of heat like the pressure of a hand bore steadily down upon him. Even Rags was feeling it, tough daughter of the desert that she was, and shook her head with such impatience that her bridle chain jingled against the bit.

The Flash had been across that torrid strip more than once before this, and he knew its distance exactly, he knew the rate at which they were traveling, and could accurately gauge the length of the journey that lay before him. This was what kept him resolute. Otherwise, after a small dip into that furnace, he would have turned back and taken the much longer but cooler way around the rim of the fire.

Right up above his head, finally, the sun stood still, and his shadow disappeared under the moving horse. And it was at this moment that the Flash had his first sight of what he considered a mirage, at the moment.

The loom and glint of a moving creature came to him, far away. He stared at it.

It was neither antelope nor wolf. It moved so slowly that he had to watch it fixedly before he was sure of the motion. He shook his head, at what he considered a mere optical illusion, and continued on his way. He forbade himself to glance in that direction. But when he glanced again there it was, and much nearer. He had drawn even with the thing, and now he knew beyond a doubt that it was not a fiction of his mind.

So he turned the head of the mare toward this moving object and his increasing curiosity made him bring the mare to a canter. He swept rapidly nearer and, as he came on, his bewilderment increased.

For it seemed to be a man—or, at least, a creature that moved upon two legs only! It gleamed in the sunlight. It seemed naked. But the Flash told himself that this was madness. He became cautious. The thing could not be a naked man. No naked man could live many hours in the midst of this fiery furnace.

He rubbed his eyes. He forced Rags to a full gallop. And sweeping up on his goal at last he could be sure.

He was right. Incredible as the thing appeared, it was a man, a naked man!

Some old prospector had gone mad in the quest for gold, perhaps, and tearing off his clothes had walked out to find the most horrible of all deaths, more horrible than death in the flames, because the torment was so infinitely more prolonged, so delicately gradual in its accumulative effect.

A madman would take some handling perhaps. A tap over the head with the butt of a revolver might be necessary. But the Flash did not shrink from his duty; he could not have left even a cripple dog exposed to this frightfulness of misery.

He rode straight up to the sufferer, and now what he saw made him dizzy with the horror of it.

It was an old man, a very old man. His back was humped by the cruel weight of time. His face jutted forward, a crimson face, with deep lines beside the mouth that gave a horrible suggestion of smiling. There were white brows, time-faded, and a strange look about the features as of a predaceous creature. Naked and helpless as he was, there was something formidable about that poor old fellow, slogging across the desert. His face was resolutely turned toward the cool blue shadows of the distant hills. It must have been clear to him that he would drop down before he could reach them, but still he went on with shortening steps, plodding steadily along.

What a will was here! It made the heart of the boy leap. In one instant he dismissed from his mind all thoughts of madness. Such a man could not be mad. He was thousands of leagues from insanity.

At first the Flash thought that a thin white cloth, like a shirt, had been draped over the shoulders and the hump of the naked back, but as he came right up, he saw that the white was merely that of a continuous blister. Such an agony of pain must possess this aged fellow as would have made many a younger man scream with the suffering, but the wrinkles beside his mouth merely deepened.

The Flash leaped from his horse and threw the reins. But he had to step straight in front of the old man before the latter would halt. As he halted, he wavered weakly. He put out a hand as though to brush the interruption from his path. Then he seemed to recover himself and his presence of mind.

"I thought you were one of them," he said. "I'm wrong."

The voice was such a thing as the Flash never wished to hear again. The swollen tongue only dimly, thickly divided the syllables and sounded the consonants. And the words came slowly, with a croak, out of the throat of the sufferer.

The Flash was ripping the slicker from the back of his saddle.

The only thing he said was: "Somebody stripped you and turned you loose?"

A dull murmur of assent answered him. And the Flash said no more. He was merely blind with rage. He wanted to do murder—a thousand murders on every one of the scoundrels.

He carried with him a small can of salve. It was little Senora Beckwith's panacea. One could apply it to wounds, skin troubles, insect bites. One could make small pellets, for taken inwardly the effects of this marvelous medicine were beyond belief, according to the Mexican woman.

Some of this salve, hastily worked soft in the palm of his hand, the Flash rubbed over the scalded parts of the man's body. Upon the head of the old fellow he placed his own sombrero. He drew off his trousers and made him draw them on. No close-fitting garment could be allowed to touch those broiled shoulders and that back. Therefore, the slicker was draped over the hat, and hung as a shade over the upper body.

Then the Flash helped the other into the saddle.

Two things impressed him.

The first was that he received not a word of thanks or of joy from the old man. The other was that the veteran continually stared straight before him, toward the cool of the shadows among those distant hills, as though he were steadying himself with a fixity of distant purpose.

Then the Flash ran bareheaded at the bridle of the mare and went straight toward the goal.

When he looked back, he could see the tortured rider clinging to the pommel of the saddle with both hands. His smile had deepened to a grin of constant agony, but not a murmur came from his lips. Every half hour, the Flash paused and gave his companion a small swallow from his canteen. Too much of anything on the stomach, even water, would be dangerous to a man in this condition. And so they crossed the final stages of the desert. And, at last, they were climbing the hills.

The bared head of the Flash, well thatched as it was with hair, had begun to sing and ring before they finally were struck by the God's mercy of a breeze that meant more to them than cool water to the drought stricken. Straight before them, the Flash saw a small grove of pines. He reached the edge of its shadow before he heard a faint sound behind him, and looking back he was barely in time to leap and receive in his arms the limp and unconscious body of the rider.

CHAPTER XXIX

In the swooning middle of the afternoon, at last the Flash brought his half-conscious human cargo into the highlands where the steady, cool wind promised pleasant nights, and where the pines drenched the air with their fragrance.

He had turned straight off from the beaten track where he might more quickly have found aid for the sufferer. It was not mere kindness and attention, it was expert help which he knew the sick man needed, or else the sunstroke would end his life.

For his pulse was feeble and irregular. His body was clammy to the touch. And his wits had quite left him. What he spoke conveyed no meaning. Most of the time his eyes were closed. When they opened, they rolled straight up and displayed a ghastly ball of white, like the eyes of a statue.

Most remarkable of all, even when he was entirely unconscious, held a limp bundle upon the back of the mare by the strong arms of the Flash, he still uttered not a groan, not even a whisper of complaint.

But, at the last, they came in sight of a small shack which

was huddled against the side of a hill, with a green drenching of trees around it. To this shack, the Flash carried his companion.

On the threshold sat a half-breed Indian, his legs crossed, a long-stemmed pipe in his mouth. He was a man gray with time, with a battered face and a dull eye.

He arose, a lofty form, wide shouldered, grave of aspect, and in his powerful arms he received the limp burden of the sick man, tenderly, strongly, and bore him into the house. The Flash followed.

There was only one room. And this was arranged like an Indian tepee. Five beds were made, their heads against the walls, the feet projecting toward the center. Between the beds were screens with willow frames and woven grass mats for centers. At the foot of the beds stood posts from the pegs of which various accouterments hung, such as bridles, ropes, clothes. The shack seemed at first glance to be an infinite confusion. In fact, it was meticulously ordered. It was the arrangement which allowed the inclusion of enough gear in that one room to have filled three normal rooms in a white man's house.

Upon one of these beds—his own—the proprietor of the house laid the senseless form of the old man. At the same time, from the back of the room rose a short, squat, waddling form—a full-blooded Indian squaw with a face which looked as though she had slept on a plank all her life, so flat were the features. She put aside the sewing which had employed her and came instantly to the side of the sick man. The Flash turned him on his face, and raised the slicker. The shoulders and the hump of the back were no longer white. They were an ugly crimson, and where the slicker had touched, here and there, the outer skin had been chafed away and blood was flowing.

It seemed that the squaw was more interested in the ointment of Beckwith's wife than in the condition of the patient. Where it had run down onto the uninjured skin, she rubbed some off on the tip of her finger, scowled at it, sniffed at it, and finally actually tasted it, smacking her lips in order the better to sample the ingredients. The Flash shuddered a little at this naïve performance.

But the squaw began to nod.

"Very good!" she said. "Very good. Some wise man. Some very wise man!"

She held out her hand to the Flash. He put the little can containing the salve into her palm.

She nodded again. Then she continued her examination of the sick man while her husband went to the door and blew on a horn which sent a deep-mouthed, reverberating call down the canyon.

The Flash wondered at this, but said nothing. Something told him that even five thousand dollars would not tempt this half-breed to betray him.

In the meanwhile, the woman was listening with minute attention to the heart of the sufferer, her ear pressed close against his body, while with a raised forefinger she counted the tremulous vibrations. Stretched prone, intent on her work, her body sprawling, for whole minutes she continued.

Then she sat up, not bothering to brush the dust from her clothes, for the floor of the shack was simply hard-beaten earth. She shook her head, and her husband, returning, saw the gesture.

He took her roughly by the shoulder and shook her.

"He will live," said the half-breed, as his wife looked angrily up to him.

She shook her head.

"I say it," said the half-breed. "I, John Cray, say it. He will live. You will make him live. If there is life inside your nostrils, you will breathe it into him, and make him live."

Mrs. John Cray looked no longer at her husband. Instead, she stared fixedly at the Flash. Eventually she shrugged her massive shoulders.

It was as though she admitted that miracles may be.

"He is old," she said, and simply that.

In the meantime, there was a sudden rattling of hoofs on rocks, a beating of hoofs on earth, approaching the cabin, and the Flash found his nerves tingling. He jumped to the shadow beside the door, and the half-breed said to him, quietly: "My three sons!"

They came with a rush. They leaped from the backs of their half-wild horses. They were half wild themselves, or more than half. They might have ranged from sixteen to twenty years of age, but all were of a single cast. Nothing of their flat-faced mother appeared in them. They were as dangerous as beasts of prey. Their long hair swept down over their shoulders, held from their faces by bands tied around their heads. As they leaped down from their horses, they stood looking fixedly at their father, who had appeared in the doorway.

John Cray made a silent gesture. His wife instantly came beside him, and then he made a little speech, a unique thing.

He said: "All young men are fools. John Cray was a young man. He was a fool, too. Then he grew older. He had a wife. He had three sons. He was still a fool. He went to Pazo. He drank whisky. It made his belly hot. The smoke from his belly went up to his brain. He saw everything through smoke and flames. He wanted to fight. So John Cray, he fought. He fought everything. He fought with his feet and his hands. He fought with his knees and his teeth, and his elbows, and his nails. He fought like a dog. He fought like a bear. He hurt many men, and he smashed many things. He made a great noise, and all the people came running to see. They got clubs. They got guns. They began to beat John Cray. They began to shoot at him. He was about to die.

"He fought out of the saloon. He got to the street. But there were very many men. They were angry. They were trying to kill John Cray. He began to stagger."

He put up his hand and touched a long scar on his forehead.

"Blood was running down into his eyes. Blood made him blind. He only saw shadows and hit at them. Blows fell on him out of the darkness. He knew that he was about to fall and die.

"Then people shouted. They ran back. Horses had come, galloping. A horse stopped before John Cray. He jumped on it. He was too blind to see, but anther hand led the horse by the reins, galloping. Bullets followed but they sang the wrong song. John Cray heard all the noise finish behind him. He wiped the blood from his eyes and sat up in the saddle. Then he saw beside him someone he never had seen before. Somone had taken pity on him because he was fighting so hard and so many men were against him. It was not an old man or a very big man. He was younger than you!"

He pointed to his youngest son. The three of them were standing like statues, devouring with their ears, with their great dark eyes every word that fell from the mouth of their father. The wife listened, her nostrils quivering like the nostrils of a dog when it smells blood.

But that was all.

John Cray pointed toward the Flash, to finish off this singular speech, and turning on his wife he said: "That is why his friend has to live!"

The woman said nothing at all, but she gave the Flash one look and then hurried back to the side of the sick man.

John Cray stepped from the door and waved his hand to his sons.

"My friend is hungry," he said. "His belly is empty. He longs for venison, and the hills are not empty."

The three boys stared at the Flash for a single instant, as though there were something in his face which had to be memorized and there was only a single vital moment for the task. Then they sprang on their horses and were off with a rush. The trees closed behind them; the noise of the crackling

129

twigs died out, and only the whisper of the wind remained in the ear of the Flash.

The half-breed touched his arm.

"It is time to sit in the shade and smoke," said he. "Wisdom comes to a man when he sits with a friend and the smoke goes upward in still air."

So they sat in the shade, Indian fashion, not side by side, but facing one another.

The peculiarity of Indian conversation is this: that it is largely composed of pauses, intermingled with speeches. Ingenious narratives are spun out of the simplest events. As with Hindu jewelers, priceless truths are strung beside tawdry lies, and no one cares so long as the effect is good.

But, on this occasion, there was chiefly silence. At length John Cray said: "They give five thousand dollars for your head?"

"Yes," said the boy, startled. "Has that news come up here?"

"Ah," said the half-breed. "You know: good news is lame, and walks on the ground. But bad news is a wild hawk and goes across the world in one stroke of the wings."

"Yes," said the Flash. "They've offered five thousand dollars for my head, living or dead. A good deal of money, Cray."

The half-breed made a gesture to the quiet canyon and the shadows which were crawling to the east. In the stillness that followed, they could hear the musical trickling of water through the hollow.

"Here," said John Cray, "there is no money. Money cannot build this, and so money cannot buy it."

The Flash did not answer, for he felt that he had heard something too profound for comment. It stood by itself, like divine revelation. But from this, too, he was shut out. He could remain here only for a breathing space, for the searching hand of the law would find him out.

So neither of them spoke, and in the stillness they could hear the voice of the squaw begin inside the shack. She was singing a soft hymn, a monotonous and droning thing which the spirits must hear, so that the life of the sick man could be spared. And the boy, as he listened, felt with a strange security that her song would be heard.

CHAPTER XXX

Thomas Winter felt largely at ease with himself and with the world. And, in particular, he was pleased with his two subordinates, Jim and Henry, now termed Hank. They had returned with him to the vicinity of the Moore ranch, from which they would ride on to make a rendezvous with the sheriff and resume their man hunt. They had stopped at the big barn behind the house and there the two men stripped the saddle and bridle for their master's horse.

"What's the next step on the program?" asked Jim.

"Can we talk here?" asked Winter.

"Nothing could be near us, unless there's somebody in the harness room," said Jim. "Take a look, Hank."

So Hank stepped to the door of the harness room and gave it a fatally careless glance. For the room was filled with racks from which hung down stirrup leathers, and trailing tugs, and chains, making a dense screen behind which lurked a quiet figure. It was not strange that Hank did not see the form. Besides, it was the dim and quiet time of the mid-afternoon, when the heat is greatest and a drowsy numbness holds the brain.

He turned back with a yawn.

"Nobody there," said he.

"Well," said Winter, "there's nothing on hand, for the present, except the trail of young Baldwin. Get him, and you've got a prize for me, a prize for you, too; because since you started after him he's as hot to get you as you ever could have been to get him."

"You talk," said Jim, "as though it's an easy job, just because there's only one man."

"Man, man," said Hank impatiently to his partner, "what's the use of worrying about anything, now that we've got Old North out of our way?"

"I'd rather of seen him down and done for," declared Jim, the pessimist. "That's the way I feel about it."

"If you saw a man shoved in through an oven door, and the door closed after him," said Winter calmly, "would you still have your doubts?"

"No man's dead until he's dead," persisted Jim. "A lot of strange things happen. Somebody might come along and find him——"

"A buzzard. That's the first thing that'll find him," declared Hank. "It kind of choked me a little and gave me a chill, I admit, when we turned the old geezer loose with no clothes on, and that sun to scald him to death. It takes a man like Winter, here, to think up that sort of torture. But he's a dead one, Jim. He's off our trail for good. He's hounded us for the last time, and he'll never again have a chance to dangle a hangman's noose close to our necks!"

Jim shook his head.

"You've been low in spirits," said Winter, "ever since you were tapped over the head by Flash David Baldwin, but you'll cheer up later on. Trust to me and my luck, Jim, and let your doubts go. We'll have the kid done for in no time. Since I put up most of the five thousand that is being offered for him, dead or alive, his friends have dropped away from him. The people he used to trust are ready to trap him, now. And it won't be long before he's ours. Only stay on the trail, and keep the old fool of a sheriff at his work. He needs encouragement as much as he needs brains."

"He needs encouragement, all right," said Jim, "because down in his heart he seems to know that the Flash is all right. He seems to guess that the kid never would have bumped off the Mexican like that. I tell you, chief, if the people around here ever have more than half a guess about the truth—if they ever get any inkling that *we* killed the gypsy, they'll turn out, man and boy, and never stop until they've run us down."

"They're never going to have an idea," said the older man. "Let me run this affair to suit myself, and we'll all come out on top. Now, you fellows hit the trail. You can get a change of horses in Pazo. You'll need some spending money, by the way. Split this thousand any way you wish. So long. Now get out, and get fast!"

They left the barn, saddled, and rode off, humming.

Their chief watched them go, contentment in his heart. He had one hand upon the latch of the barn door and was about to slide it shut, when he saw a shadow standing at the door of the harness room.

His heart leaped, stood still. It was Moore himself!

"Why, hello, Larry," said Winter easily.

He wondered how loud had been the voices of Hank and Jim, how loudly had he himself spoken?

His doubts were instantly put at rest.

"You dirty scoundrel!" said Lawrence Moore.

Winter dropped his hands into his coat pockets. There was a gun in one of them. But he smiled amiably at his host.

"Bad names, Larry?" said he.

"I'm dizzy," said Moore. "I'm staggered by what I've heard. Winter, is it true that you're responsible for the murder of the gypsy—and that you did it to throw the blame on the shoulders of poor young Flash Baldwin?"

"You're not a youngster, Moore," said the other. "You don't stand there and actually ask me to admit something, do you?"

Moore nodded.

"I understand you," said he.

He drew out a revolver and held it with the muzzle covering Winter.

"Put up your hands, Winter," said he. "I'm going to have the sheriff look into this precious business of you and your men."

"Stuff," said Winter, unperturbed. "You're a good fellow, Larry. A little shy in your sense of humor, but a good fellow at heart. I love your simplicity. If the sheriff began to question me, what is the first thing that he would find out?"

"That you're a murderer!" said Moore.

"He'd find out about you, first," said Winter. "I'd tell him a mighty interesting story about the way the Arkansas Express was stuck up, those years ago."

Moore shrank.

"Nothing would come of it," said he. "I've paid back that money, every penny. Every penny has gone back to the company, with interest!"

"What difference does that make? In the eyes of the law, it doesn't make any difference," declared Winter. "You got your start on stolen money!"

"I've paid it back," reiterated Moore. "I was a young fool. I tell you, my heart has bled for what happened that day. But it happened long ago. The thing's forgotten. It's outlawed by time!"

"Murder's never outlawed," said the other, dryly.

"I didn't kill the messenger," said Moore, breaking into a sweat of anxiety. "Bud Topping killed him. Jay Shearer and Will Bartlett saw the killing. They know that Topping did the killing."

"Where are the three of them?" asked Winter. "Where's Shearer? Where's Bartlett? Where's Topping himself? Dead, Larry. Dead as the devil."

"They can't be. Not all three!" said Lawrence Moore.

"They are, though. Shearer died in prison. Bartlett was shot in Topeka by Little Sam Way. Topping died of tuberculosis in the Magollons. They're all dead. And when it's proved to a court that you were a member of that holdup gang, they're going to give you life or a rope necklace, Moore!"

Moore was silent, digesting the information, and the longer he brooded over it, the more simply correct it appeared to him. His conviction appeared in his face.

He merely said: "That killing was no fault of mine. I can prove that I've supported the messenger's widow all these years, besides."

"That's the proof of a guilty conscience," said Winter. "I'm glad you told me that, Larry. That makes the chain of evidence complete and perfect. Why, my lad, you're a dead man, the moment I choose to speak!"

The face of Moore grew purple.

"Winter," he said, "tell me what you want out of this."

"The best thing you have," said Winter. "You can guess what that is. I want the pretty girl, old fellow. I want young Jacqueline, and I intend to have her."

"I'd rather die," said Moore. "I'd rather swing on a rope. And you know it!"

"You're wrong," replied the other. "The fact is that when you think the matter over you'll change your mind. It's not a bad out for you. I've reached the period when I've decided to settle down, Larry. One more stake—and then I retire. I've brushed the main danger out of my path. The law will never trouble me again. I intend to retire, settle down with a wife, raise a family. And who can tell? I may make the best husband in a million, old fellow. Don't be downhearted. Look on the bright side. You've proved that a young crook may turn straight in time. Why shouldn't I do the same thing?"

"Because there's murder in you," said Moore, sternly. "And because—by God, I see a shorter way out—the only way with a fiend like you, Winter!"

And suddenly the revolver jerked up in his hand and he fired. Winter was flung staggering back against the wall of the barn by the shock of a bullet that glanced along the side of his head. He did not snatch his own weapon from his coat pocket, but fired with the gun still concealed, and saw Moore drop his revolver, clutch at his thigh, and topple slowly to the side.

He sprang to the fallen man.

"Moore," he said, "I give you a last chance. Think fast. Are you my man, or are you a dead man?"

Moore, his face white and twisted, looked up into the black muzzle of the revolver.

"I'm yours—and damn you!" said he.

"One word from an honorable man is enough for me," said Winter. "And now to let myself out of this, and into a little glory—"

134

He took another gun from his pocket, fired it twice in rapid succession, and then, throwing it into the air, nailed it with a bullet from his pocket Colt. The impact sent the gun whirling away. It clanged against one of the low rafters, and dropped with a crash to the wooden floor.

"Help!" shouted Winter. "Help! Murder! Murder! Help!"

He dropped himself to the floor, and when the first rush of people came to them they found Moore still clutching his rapidly bleeding wound, while Winter, his face covered with blood, was seen just staggering to his feet.

"Out the rear door, there!" shouted Winter. "He went out the rear door of the barn. A masked man. Murder, by God! He tried to kill Moore and me! There's his gun. I shot it out of his hand!"

There was a rush for the rear of the barn, where the door was found bolted on the outside. But someone paused to pick up the fallen Colt, which Winter had shot out of the air.

It was the ranch foreman who lifted it, and who shouted: "It's the Flash again! This is the right-hand gun!"

CHAPTER XXXI

It was the word of this dastardly outrage which brought the fame of the Flash to its lowest ebb. For what friend could cling to him, when he was suspected of attempting two such murders in the same instant, the destruction of two men, neither of whom had harmed him, so far as the world knew? To the boy was attributed a blind and brutal immorality. It was said that he killed for the sake of killing—that he was a monster, a true Frankenstein.

The excitement became immense, and it was shortly after this that a number of businessmen in Austin got together and, far as they were from the scene of the most recent crime, offered an additional five thousand dollars' reward for the apprehension of the criminal. Other contributions came in. More than twelve thousand dollars were offered for the death or the capture of the Flash. Or, since his capture alive was now a thing to jest about, more than twelve thousand dollars for the slaughter of the Flash! And this during a time when a single dollar trebled or quadrupled, in most respects, the buying power of the dollar of today!

Great as the excitement grew in more distant parts of the land, making the Flash into a byword and a byname for a fiendish malignancy, nothing could describe the emotion which filled all hearts upon the Moore ranch.

For though Lawrence Moore could be a sufficiently stern man upon occasion, yet he was celebrated for his charities, and for a true gentleness of understanding which had endeared him to all hearts.

He was not one of those people who give in order to win newspaper space. His name never appeared in published subscription lists. But to countless people he appeared like an angel of a special grace. He had aided Mexicans, Negroes, Indians, the nameless half-breeds of the border. He had aided good men and bad men. It seemed that Lawrence Moore did not give because he wanted to help good men, but simply that his anxious heart wished to relieve all suffering wherever it was endured.

And this man, this father of the range, was the one who had been chiefly attacked!

As for the other, it appeared that dauntless Thomas Winter had rushed to the assistance of his host in the most glorious and unselfish manner and that, had it not been for him, the murderer would surely have succeeded in his assault.

It was Thomas Winter who had leaped forward and who had drawn the fire of the inhuman lad on himself. He had fallen at the first fire, a bullet lancing along the side of his head. But the dauntless fellow had then opened fire upon the villain—opened fire while he lay stretched upon the floor of the ground, and with his first shot, by luck and by skill combined, his bullet had knocked the revolver from the hand of the miscreant!

Oh, lucky shot!

And there was the gun, now exhibited in the office of the sheriff, where all curious eyes could behold it—the right-hand gun of the Flash, well known to the entire range.

The riders who worked for Larry Moore, maddened with rage, desperate, and regardless of themselves, dashed across the hills and far out into the desert, searching for the hoof-prints of the famous mare, Rags. Her trail was well known by this time, for the sheriff had advertised the distance she stepped at a walk, a trot, a gallop.

Mysteriously enough, no trace of her was found, except in one place near the ranch house, and this appeared to be an old trail. But that was not exactly strange, for the malevolent cunning of the lad would have taught him, of course, to find the ways where the track of a horse would not appear among the rocks.

But no one on the range was so deeply affected as was the daughter of the rancher who had been shot down, the bullet passing through his upper leg. He lay on a bed of pain, and his daughter watched over him closely, her face grimly set.

She wanted to see Winter at once, but he avoided her, as it seemed, for two days. And when at last she managed to lay eyes upon him he was abashed and seemed to wish to hurry away.

"Why do you do it, Uncle Tom?" said the girl. "Why do you do it? You keep away from me, and you don't seem to want me to see you, Uncle Tom. It isn't fair. I've got too much in my heart. I've got to say something. I've got to tell you how I admire you. I've got to tell you what a glorious thing you've done for us! And for everybody. It'll teach every young man on the range what chivalry means. Why, it's the grandest thing I ever heard of—the way you stepped in against the inhuman devil—the fiend—!"

She stopped, panting.

"Well, Jacqueline," said he, "I had something to inspire me, you know."

"What was that, Uncle Tom?" she said.

She held him by both hands. Her eyes filled with tears of gratitude as she looked up to his face. "It was your affection for dad, of course," said she. "God bless you, Uncle Tom! God bless men who can be such friends to one another!"

"I didn't exactly do it for your father, either, Jack," said Winter. "But how is Larry today?"

"His wound is getting on beautifully, the doctor says. It's a perfect recovery. But there's something on his mind. He lies there with a black face, and a scowl on his forehead. Sometimes his hands are locked tight for long minutes together. Oh, it's a sad thing. Because friendship meant such a lot to him. Of course he has yours. But to think that a boy like the Flash could do such a thing—a boy who had run through this house playing with me, and sat at our table—and I remember a day when he'd cut his hand, and dad bound it up, and talked to him—and—"

Her voice trembled away to nothing.

"You know, my dear," said Winter, "that the very best of men sometimes give way to ugly impulses. Of course you know that. And the poor lad, the Flash, since he's been hunted and hounded from place to place—"

She jumped back from Winter. She stamped upon the floor.

"You're not going to defend him, are you?" she demanded. "By heaven, you are! You're going to take his part—the ungracious, bitter, cowardly, poisonous—oh, of all the people in the world, I never dreamed that one could be such a dastardly creature as Flash Baldwin! I detest the very sound of his name."

"Ah, poor Flash!" said Winter. "And still he's—"

He checked himself, and started away.

"What were you saying?" asked the girl. "Still he's— what?"

"I won't say it, Jacqueline," said Winter.

"Why won't you? I want you to. There's nothing you could say that I wouldn't be glad to hear!"

"Ay, Jack," said Winter, sadly. "There's one thing you would not be glad to hear me say."

This, and the hint it covered, struck her suddenly, and made her start away, with her eyes widening into a frightened look, but she forced herself to come straight back to him.

"You can say anything to me, Uncle Tom," said she.

"Why," asked Winter, smiling more sadly than ever. "Because I'm such a harmless old fellow?"

"Why, you're not old, really."

"I'm thirty-six," said he.

"Thirty-six? You're only a boy, really, then," said she.

She laughed a little, but her laughter was unsure. She remained there before him, and yet surely her eyes were begging him not to say the thing which she dreaded might be coming.

He said: "Well, Jack, I won't whine about it. Many a fellow has looked at the queen and sighed. So I dare say I have a right to look and sigh also."

She put up a hand to a place in her throat, which was aching. Such a pity for him came through her that she bit her lip to keep it from trembling.

"What do you want me to think, Uncle Tom?" said she. "Am I a fool if I understand you to mean me by that?"

"Tush, tush, Jacqueline," said he. "God made you what you are, and having made you so, men cannot help having a bit of an ache of the heart when they see you, and a rather bad homesickness when they've gone away from you. But don't take me seriously. I don't want to bother you. I don't want you to have me on your mind. My own trouble will pass away, I dare say, in good time."

He went on out of the room—at least, he had reached the door when her low voice stopped him.

There he turned, and looked back.

"Tut, tut, Jacqueline," he said, when he saw her face. "No pity, please, my dear."

"I'm not crying for pity, but from pain," said she. "And I want to tell you that only one man ever was nearer to my

138

heart. And he's gone out of my life and my mind. He's dead to me—he's dead to me—"

As she said this, she began to sob. At last, she covered her face with her hands.

"If I can be of the least use, I'll stay, Jacqueline," said Winter.

But she shook her head, and he went out, bowed and thoughtful.

He was away from the house and in the woods before he recovered himself, as it seemed, and then he walked straight forward, with a smile, and with a glint in his eye which few other people had seen there, but those who had seen it knew that it was the light of triumph.

As for poor Jacqueline, she hurried with a throbbing heart to the room of her father.

He was wide awake, but he looked at her with the unseeing eyes of thought or trouble.

"Dad," she said, "Thomas Winter is the finest man in the world, and the most perfect gentleman."

"He has his manners," said her father, slowly.

Then he looked at her with more attention.

"He's been telling you a good deal, I dare say," said he.

"About what? What do you mean?" she asked.

"He's been telling you that he's rather fond of you, Jacqueline," said her father. "Isn't that it?"

"How did you guess that?" asked the girl. "Has he spoken to you before? Has he asked you about it?"

"Humph," said her father.

He turned his head and looked up to the ceiling. She saw that his jaw was set hard.

"And if you were I, what would you say to him?" she asked.

"I'd tell him to be damned!" said her father, fiercely.

She laughed, softly.

"That's because you don't want me to go away," said she. "But seriously, what would you say to him, if you were I?"

But he made no answer. His face did not relax. And the long, silent moments went by between them.

CHAPTER XXXII

Mail came to the Flash, even in his retreat among the hills, though not through the regular channels of the post. On this day, he was sitting under the same tree under which he usually sat with the half-breed, John Cray. But now Old North was beside him. He had never spoken to his rescuer of the mission that brought him West. Instead, he seemed to prefer talk of the country around him, and he had endless questions to ask of the Indians and their ways. To flat-faced Mrs. Cray, he preserved an attitude of respect that was actually humble, and he seemed to treasure up her monosyllabic answers to his questions. He could spend hours examining the skins which John Cray and his three sons lifted from the deer and their all-wise knives. The manner in which Mrs. Cray dressed and tanned them was another mystery which absorbed him, and he would pore profoundly over the rubbing in of the fat and the brains, or the preliminary fleshing of the hides.

He seemed like a child, but the Flash began to feel that this was a very wise child who would put two and two together until he had added up his million before long. To the Flash he talked at great length about horses, about hunting, about guns, and about all of the interests in the boy's life. But he never referred by hint or outright word to the day when the Flash saved him from the most horrible of all deaths.

So he was sitting, on this day, quietly at the side of his young friend when a tattered Mexican, with a peon's round, featureless face, came up the canyon and stopped before them. He saluted the Flash with a broad grin and held out two letters.

"Senor Beckwith sends you these, senor," said he.

The Flash took them. One was in Beckwith's running, femininely small hand. The other was an address as sprawling as the handwriting of a child.

"Who sent you up here to find me, Juan?" He asked.

The peon grinned.

"No one sent me," said he. "But Juan followed his nose, and his nose brought him to a quiet place. You don't look for a deer in the middle of the day, but in the twilight. You don't look for a stag in the middle of the village, but off in the hills, senor."

With this oblique answer, characteristic as it was, the Flash contented himself, and sent Juan into the house to be fed. Then, with Old North's consent, he opened his letters.

He read that from Beckwith, first of all.

It ran:

Dear Flash,

The devil is to pay down here since you shot Moore. Winter didn't matter so much, I only wish that you'd put your bullet through his head instead of along side of it. But people take it badly, the way you took your slam at Moore. They can't see what you had against him. Neither can I, for that matter.

You'd better stay away from Pazo, for a time. There's a lot of bad blood up, and the price on you has gone up to close to fifteen thousand dollars. I never heard of so much offered on the head of any other man. I wouldn't trust my own grandmother, if I were you!

Down here, some of the boys might smile in your face, but they'd knife you in the back, if they had a chance.

Keep away till things quiet down. I don't understand what you've done, but I don't have to understand. I'm always for you.

When I say you have no friends, I go too far. I guess the little gypsy girl, Sonia, is true to you. She's just sent in a letter which she wants me to send on to you, and I'm sending off Juan with the two of the letters. I told Juan to follow his own wits. He's a better trailer than I could ever pretend to be!

The boy dropped the letter. He picked it up again, and scowled.

"Bad news?" asked Old North genially.

"It seems," said the Flash, "that I've shot up a brace of people since I've been out here with you, partner. Look at this!"

He gave the letter to Old North. Then he opened the one from Sonia. It said:

Dearest Flash,

I am in terrible trouble. Everybody is against me. Can you take me away, or send me away. I don't care where. My heart breaks here, alone. They hate me because I love you.

Sonia

141

He read this letter with the faint smile of a young man who had his share of personal vanity.

He looked up from the paper to see Old North staring at him out of narrowed eyes.

"Do you know Thomas Winter?" asked North.

"Winter? Why, you know him, and his first name!" said the Flash. "How does that come about? Of course I know Winter. I know enough of him to hate his heart. What do *you* know about him?"

"I know him so well," said Old North, "that he and his men turned me loose in the desert to die of the sun. And the reason they turned me loose there was that I knew 'em all so well."

The Flash gaped at him.

"Who are you?" he asked bluntly.

"Why," said Old North, "I'm a practical man with a hobby. My hobby is chasing criminals. And for twenty years I've been chasing the greatest of them all. I mean Tom Winter. I've broken up his games more times than one. And perhaps, thank God, I'll be able to break them up once more. What's Winter to you?"

"Why, he's the man who murdered my father," said the Flash calmly. "He's the man whose throat I'm bound to cut. That's all. But it seems as though we've got something to go on together, partner. By the way, you've not told me your name, yet?"

"My name is North," said the other. "Some people call me Old North."

"If I'd lived further east," said the boy, "I think I would have heard of you."

"You might," said Old North.

He waited for a moment, and then he said: "What's your next plan, my friend? Are you living up here outside of the law?"

"That's it," agreed the Flash. "I'm outside of the law. Someone worked a plant on me, and that someone was Winter. He wanted to get me out of the way, and he did it. He got hold of my guns. He murdered a gypsy with one of 'em. And now I suppose that he's used the other to shoot up Moore. Though how he got shot himself, I can't fathom. He's deep."

He's as deep as the ocean," agreed the detective. "But there are fish that live even at the bottom of the sea. What's your direction, my lad?"

"Back to Moore's house to find Winter," said the boy. "But first I've got a hurry call from a gypsy girl in trouble. I'll have to see her first. Here's her letter. There's only friendship between us, do you see? And she's been the saving of me, once."

Old North read the letter with great care. Then he looked off across the canyon with dreaming eyes.

"Who could have dictated this letter to her?" he asked.

"Dictated?" said the boy. "It's simple enough. All the words are simple enough for her to have written."

"She writes like a child," said the old man, "but she spells without a fault. There's no fault in that spelling, Flash."

"Well, she's a long distance from a fool," said the boy. "I don't know how much schooling she may have had. But what do you mean? If that was a dictated letter, then you think that she may be trying to get me back to a trap?"

"Fifteen thousand is a pile of money," said Old North. "It's enough to buy half a dozen souls at a time. Now look at the writing. It's hardly formed, but the letters are about of a size. They don't run very much uphill or down. Such an unformed hand, writing out of its own mind, would naturally be crowded here, and loose there. I'd say that this was written from a copy. Suppose that your friend Winter made such a copy for her?"

"It's Winter, perhaps," said the Flash. "But still I can't believe it. She wouldn't turn back on me. I've seen her offer her life between me and bullets, man!"

"Have you?" said Old North. "Ay, there are more twists and turns in a woman's mind than any man can follow very well! A lot more, I'd say!"

"I'll see Winter," said the boy. "I'll see him first, in spite of the devil!"

"Not a bit," said Old North. "See the girl first. That's your trick. A lad who loves to walk through the fire, as you do—that's the trick for him. Write to her that you're coming at midnight, and just arrive after sunset. That's the way for it. Then you can see for yourself, and hear for yourself, perhaps. And you might learn something worth knowing. I could go down with you, for instance."

"You?" said the boy, curiously. "When you can hardly walk, with comfort? To start on a long ride?"

"My skin is a little sore and peeling," said Old North. "But my heart's sound, and my lungs are sound. And God forgive me if I can't sit in the saddle as long as most men. Give me a slow pace and a steady one, and I'll go with you twenty-four hours, or my name is not Old North."

"But what would you do?" said the Flash. "It may be a tight place, and a place for a quick start and a fast run."

"Then," said Old North, "I'll have to go down, I suppose.

Or else, perhaps, I may be able to crawl into a hole, and let the hunt go by."

He smiled most genially at the Flash.

Said the Flash: "You've been in your close fits. I can guess that. But down there where I'm going—there's a lot of hard riding a good deal of the time, and a whole flock of guns—"

He paused. Old North was watching him with that singular and detached curiosity.

"Take me with you, my lad," said he. "Somewhere in your trouble is Tom Winter, probably at the bottom of it all. And nobody on the face of the earth, I think I can say, is able to crawl inside the mind of Tom Winter as I can crawl. And nobody can upset him at the last minute as I can upset him. For I've had twenty years of practice. You've taken me out of the fire of the sun. Perhaps I can take you out of a hell-fire, my son!"

The boy bit his lip, in the intensity of his doubt and of his hope.

"He's beaten me like a cur, so far," he admitted. "He's beaten me at every trick of the game. I've never so much as troubled him, except for a few seconds, here and there. And he's got in the law to help him hound me! Old North, come along with me, if you want to. You'll have the brains. And I'll be a pair of hands for you. Together we may beat him yet!"

CHAPTER XXXIII

Whoever had seen a lame old wolf come out of the hills onto the desert with a strong young companion would have thought of the picture again, seeing Old North and the Flash as they rode down from the highlands and struck out across the plains toward Pazo.

As they went, they did not talk a great deal, but enough was said to give North a perfect picture of the boy's life as it had been to that moment.

His comment was strange.

"You take most men," said he, "and they learn the cut of the lash so soon that they are still children when they have simply forgotten what it is to rebel against the ways of society. But now and again one runs into a fellow who makes a question of the old, accepted rules, and a fellow of that type is you, for instance. And if he is lucky, he

144

leads the happiest life of all. And if he is unlucky, he's like a blight and a damnation for everybody that's around him, and finally for himself."

This was not exactly a cheering verdict, but it was expressed from a viewpoint very different from that with which the Flash was familiar. For that matter, everything that he heard from his new friend was more or less unique. The man seemed to have his own individual starting point, from which he struck out with his own thinking. Schoolbooks and household morals did not seem to have penetrated into his consciousness at any time in his life. His conclusions were his own, based upon his own experience.

Then, from a low hill, they looked into the thick twilight of the flat valley, and saw Pazo glimmering like a patch of hot stars in a cloudy summer sky. They turned to the left, found the trees beside the river, and came winding up through them until they saw light ahead.

"It's a bonfire," said the Flash.

"There's no shake in the light. It's not a bonfire," said Old North.

When they came closer, they could see that he was right. For there were many points of radiance glimmering through the trees. They decided that something was ahead worth seeing, particularly when they heard the drone and whine of music. So they dismounted and worked gradually forward.

First they came to a number of ragged ponies, mules, and the undying burros of the West, staked out in small patches of grassland here and there, and for a guard each group had a small boy in charge.

They avoided the observance of the youngsters with care, and went on into the field of the illumination and into the sound of many voices.

"Gypsies—the gypsy tribe that I told you about," said the boy to Old North. "They're giving a shindig down here. That's all the party."

They came to the edge of a large clearing, and from a secure hedge of brush they could look out upon a strange scene of festivity. To the gypsies it was a harvest time. They had remained in the community long enough to know which people had money to spend and which people had not. They had remained long enough to stir up curiosity and not long enough to give great offense. Therefore they had established what was a cross between a fair and a dance, and they had advertised their merry-making through the countryside.

The countryside had responded.

Most of the people that the Flash knew in the region around Pazo were strolling about here and there, or filing in and out of two gaudy tents where fortunes were told, or making a circle around the pair of jugglers who spun knives and glasses into the air and caught them under their legs or behind their backs, and sent them flashing up and caught them again in their showering fall. Others were dancing, for a section of the ground had been beaten hard and smooth, and over it was a sheet of canvas, well waxed with candle grease. The orchestra consisted of an accordion, a violin, and a guitar, while a drum was worked in now and then by some other of the gypsies who had nothing to do.

Over in a corner, some planks had been raised on sawbucks, and here beer was served; for the gypsies knew that there is nothing like a little touch of alcohol to open purses and relax the spirit. For food, they kept a wide, low fire burning back among the trees, and here they roasted potatoes, and chickens, and small birds they had trapped, and rabbits, and they had a great pot of beans always simmering, giving out a spicy aroma, and another huger pot was black with soot outside and black with coffee inside, and pale ghosts arose in trailing robes of mist from the surface of that pot, and flickered away, and were followed by others.

The lights came from a number of lanterns which were hung more or less at random among the trees, and these lanterns had been draped with cheap, colored paper which the wind now and then set to fluttering and swaying, so that they looked like great, night-flying, self-illumined butterflies.

The beer was the master touch. If it had been whisky, the party would have burned in a furious flare for one hour; and then it would have exploded and wrecked the entire scene. But the milder beer prolonged matters and gave everyone a chance to open a purse not once but many times. Prices were never high, but there were many things requiring small fees; every dance cost something, and by the time the jugglers had been fed, and the palms of the fortune tellers had been crossed with silver, and coffee and food paid for, and beer bought, the funds of a cowpuncher were sensibly diminished.

But there were not cowpunchers only. Pazo really had turned out for the occasion. If nothing else, it was an oddity. And so the boy was not surprised to see substantial ranchers, and their wives and sons and daughters. He saw first of all, like a brighter star in all the happiness, Jacqueline Moore. And then, a shadow on his mind, Thomas Winter, who was her escort apparently.

The Flash looked at his companion, and he saw that the man was following Winter wherever he moved, with a quiet, delighted eye.

"Look at him!" said Old North. "There's the one man in

the world to whom I take my hat off. Look at that bright, honest, boyish eye! Look at that light, springing step! See the grace of him. See the modesty! How he steps back and watches the girl dance—who is the girl, Flash?"

"She? Oh, her name's Jacqueline Moore," said the Flash.

He tried to keep his voice casual in intonation, but he found that Old North had turned his head and was smiling at him. Enough light came through the shrubbery to illumine their faces.

"Ah," murmured Old North, "I see that you're not very fond of Winter. But I almost love him. He thinks that I'm gone forever, but even without me there are enough others in the world who know him. Every moment of his life, he's standing on the verge of a cliff. But you would never think that he dreamed of danger. He never seems to be balancing between life and death. And yet that's exactly what he's doing. But there he is, standing back and watching another fellow dance with the lady. Look at him nod, and keep the time, and smile, and encourage them. As if he had only a friendly interest in her—"

"Oh, damn him!" muttered the Flash, through his teeth.

"Tut, tut!" said Old North. "You mustn't judge him from the viewpoint of most other men. Do you blame a hawk because it murders other birds? No, no, Flash. But you see the falcon swish around the sky and rise to its pitch and then turn over and come down at its quarry. I've seen one turn over in the sky in that fashion and come down and knock the life out of a duck at a stroke—a wild duck, flying like a streak—just a gray pencil stroke in the sky— a wild duck, four or five times the weight of the little falcon. But the hawk's murder in the air, and we watch it, and wonder at it, and crane our necks to follow it, and call it the most beautiful bird in the world. Isn't that correct?"

"Humph!" said the Flash.

"Ay, but that's the way to look at Winter," said Old North. "Look, now, at the way he steps in and takes her for the next dance. See his quiet way. No flourishes. Nothing gay and new. No taking of the center of the floor, but quietly moving there on the outer edge, making himself small, as you might say. But suddenly—you see your Jacqueline growing interested? All at once she realizes that her partner is all silk— smooth, smooth, smooth, and always harmonious, just with the music. Oh, she's feeling, now, that she never danced before! That quiet fellow—well, let the other girls dance with the youngsters, *Jacqueline* knows a man when she finds one. And quite right she is, at that!"

He carried on these observations in a voice hardly louder

than a whisper, and it seemed that he was merely developing his own thoughts. And the Flash heard him with an abstracted eye, filled with misery.

Old North went on: "Now the dance is finished. He's taking her away. Oh, watch him closely. All young men ought to be raised in the presence of the great masters, and Winter is a great master. Now he brings her, as you see, far from the madding crowd. He'll tell her that he's old, probably, and likes to look on. I've heard him say that himself. It's his way of calling his attention to his essential youth. Here—I told you so—he's heading over here—this is about the farthest nook."

The Flash gathered himself as a cat gathers for a leap from all fours.

"Steady!" said Old North. "Steady, my lad. You've promised yourself to them at midnight. You don't want to appear too soon before that. And besides, see what a golden chance you have here?"

"Golden?" said the Flash. "Golden chance, did I hear you call it?"

"Certainly," said Old North. "For here you lie quietly in the shadow and listen to the talk, and see them all. Looked at from this angle, humans are mere dancing shadows, shadows of apes, prancing, and gibbering. See the grins of them. Look at the laughing. If men could see themselves laugh, they'd wear masks when they went to comedy. Gloomy men are fools. Gay men are idiots, more than half mad. There's no choice, except a Winter, in between the two, always perfectly in control of himself, because he never lets his real self show through. God bless one such man among a million. God bless him, I say, and multiply him."

The Flash listened to this outpouring with amazement. But he made no reply, for now, just as Old North had said, Winter brought the girl meandering through the crowd, and to the very log that stretched before the brush behind which the two of them were crouching.

And he saw that Jacqueline Moore was very happy, and that her hand rested confidentially upon the arm of her escort, and that her face was turned up toward him with affection, and with a rather awed respect.

CHAPTER XXXIV

Another thing perplexed the boy, and this was hardly less maddening than the sight before him. It was that Old North was looking askance toward him with a faint smile.

He could not understand. Old North, he knew, had spent twenty years in the pursuit of this criminal. Yet Old North seemed almost to love the villain. Old North seemed verily to rejoice in the social triumphs of the man!

This was another triumph. There was no doubt of that. When other young men, pursuing Jacqueline as every pretty girl is sure to be pursued, came close enough to see through the shadows her attitude toward Thomas Winter, they suddenly shied away like colts who see danger and had no more to do with her. The prettiest girl's popularity is half ended by her marriage. Jacqueline's popularity seemed in danger also.

"Jack is a fool," said the boy to himself.

But still his heart ached. He felt a bitter triumph. She who was so sure of herself, how would she feel when at last the truth burst in upon her understanding, and she knew Thomas Winter for what he was worth—murderer and robber as he was, and betrayer of men!

Then he found himself listening, intently.

"This doesn't amuse you, Tom," the girl was saying. "It's all too trivial and silly, and shallow to please you!"

She called him Tom, then. That title of "uncle" had been dropped!

"Of course it amuses me," said Thomas Winter. "It's an odd thing, Jack, that, well as you see through me, you should think that this cannot amuse me. Why?"

"Such rogues and rascals, these gypsies all are. And then the clodhopper cowpunchers—" said Jacqueline.

"They're all such good fellows, the punchers," said Winter. "And as for the gypsy rogues—well, they were raised to it, you know. What would you or I be if our fathers and mothers had been soothsayers, witches and thieves?"

"You're as open minded as the day," said Jacqueline Moore, and the Flash wondered that he never had seen any tokens of simple-mindedness in her before this.

"No, not so open minded," said Winter. "But after a fellow has been about through a good many nations, he finds that a Frenchman is after all not so much unlike an Italian, and the Italian is not very different from a German, and a German book translated into English is as apt to be a best seller in England and the United States as it is in its home country."

"I never would have thought of that," said Jacqueline, looking up to him, rather round eyed.

"Because you're a half-wit!" said the Flash fiercely to himself.

"Well, Jack," said Winter, "you almost professionally underrate yourself. And that's because you haven't seen so many other women, dare I say. But for my part—"

He stopped.

"What were you going to say?" asked Jacqueline innocently.

"Stuff!" said the Flash, to his dark heart.

"I was going to say—oh, well, I can't very well say it," said Thomas Winter. "Only," he added, "in all the years of my life—"

There was an emotional ring in his voice, like the ring of a bell. It died away before he brought his sentence to an end. And Jacqueline had looked down, flushing to the temples.

"I want to talk to you, Jacqueline," said Winter. "But my tongue is tied, somehow."

"You liar!" said the Flash, to himself.

Jacqueline threw up her head bravely.

"After what you've done for my father," said she, "is there anything in the world that you can't say to me, Tom?"

"Softening of the brain!" muttered the Flash through his teeth.

Winter raised his head also. An expression of suppressed pain was on his face, an expression of a grim resolution also.

"Suppose that I said, outright, that I love you, Jacqueline?"

She started, but not greatly.

And Winter, leaning forward, hurried on: "Not that I expect you to make any answer to me, Jack. Let it be as though I had not spoken. Only—do you see how it is?—there are some things that are rooted so deeply in a man's heart that unless he expresses them he's profoundly dishonest—to himself. Do you see?"

"You sneak thief," sighed the Flash.

And through the small gap in the brush he stared fixedly at the face of the girl.

She was looking, not at her companion, but straight ahead, toward the colorful swirl of the festivity.

"Don't answer me," said Winter. "I don't expect an answer. I know my age—the difference between us—and the pure soul that makes you a thing beyond my aspiration—beyond any man's aspiration. I know that. I don't want an answer,

Jack. I don't expect one. I've only spoken because I had to speak, as a man has to breathe, if he wishes to live. Forget what I've said, and forgive me!"

"Forgive you!" exclaimed Jacqueline Moore. "Forgive you, indeed! When the other men I've known, compared with you, are like grass compared with trees—forgive you, indeed! I don't know what else to say—only, this is the most wonderful moment in my life! I'm only a simple, silly girl, Tom Winter—quite apart from the thing you've made with your idealizing."

"Hush!" said Winter. "Hush, my dear! I know your great heart. There's enough pity and tenderness in it to move mountains. But I'm not a callow boy. I don't pretend that I'll die of a broken heart. Mind you, I'll swallow the pain, eventually. Some day, perhaps, I'll almost forget it. And I know that you are meant for your own kind—for youth, at least. There's something generous and strong and gay about youth for its own sake. And the young will turn to the young. Oh, I know what I am! I know that I never could stand for a moment compared with that handsome, brilliant lad—the Flash—"

"Stop!" said she. "I can't bear his name. I burn when I think of him—a murderer—my own dear dad—to have lifted a gun at him—and if you hadn't been there to intervene and take the fire on yourself, the next instant, don't I know that the first bullet would never have struck his leg? It would have gone through the heart. I know—because I know how the Flash can shoot!"

"You shouldn't be so hot against him," said Winter. "The poor lad's mind is addled, a little, with misfortune—"

"I'll addle you!" said the Flash, through his set teeth.

"I don't want to hear about him!" exclaimed the girl. "The detestable, unspeakable ruffian! Compared with you—but I wouldn't insult you, Tom, by comparing you with such a creature!"

"Here is someone to dance with you," said Winter.

"I'll not dance," said the girl. "I want to—"

"You'd better dance," said Winter. "You don't want to offend any of these good fellows, and—"

A cowpuncher came marching straight up to the girl, a big, bronzed, hawk-eyed youth. He came with a careless swing and a cheerful smile.

For a new note had come into the evening's procedure.

The gypsy men, up to this point, had been largely in the background, except for those who made the orchestra. Now they came to the forefront with a swirl and a rush. They were dressed in their gayest. They had on flashing silk shirts of

151

the gaudiest colors and jaunty hats, and earrings sparkled and swung above their shoulders, and every gypsy of the lot wore a small black mask that covered the upper part of the face, with the sparkle of the eyes shining through the eye holes.

Each of them picked out a gypsy girl, and suddenly they swung into an extravagant dance full of whirlings and boundings and a pattering of quicksteps in double and treble time that the eye could hardly follow.

Swinging out to the edge of the waxed canvas, they left the center free for the exhibition of a chosen pair. The girl was Sonia, magnificent in a red jacket and a thin, flowing yellow skirt with a blue turban on her head, set off with imitation jewels of a huge size. She had not appeared before this. But she appeared now to make a sensation.

The other gypsy woman danced well, but not like Sonia. And, in addition, she had a partner fit to set her off, for he was all in sky blue from head to foot, all in shimmering silk the color of the evening sky, and he wore a crimson mask and a yellow hat that sat at an angle on his head, with a long red plume floating and streaming down the side of it.

This gay fellow leaped farther and higher than any of the rest, and his feet were as active as the castanets which swung in the hands of the girl.

What a pair they made, as they went through the motions of a mad courtship, wooing, refusing, scorning, pleading, laughing, praying, rejoicing together, in the end.

The lips of the Flash curled. He had recognized the former wooer of the girl, now apparently taken back into her good graces. His lip curled, and then he smiled, in a stern disdain.

The exhibition ended.

The music kept on as the gypsies scattered, followed by uproarious applause. The girls were lost among the trees. The men went here and there, and presently they were dancing with the white girls who had come to the festival. If they had been unmasked, not a girl of the lot would have looked at one of the dark faces twice. But under the masks they were different. They were merely a part of the good time. It was foolish pride to refuse them!

At the same time, new dancers came onto the canvas and began a swinging two-step. Young Jacqueline went forward with her latest admirer, that same tall, hawk-eyed fellow who had just come up.

And the Flash, watching them go, felt some relief in his heart.

But he could no longer crouch there, at wait, and at watch.

He said so to Old North.

"I have to do something. I'm burning up!"

"Be a wise man," said Old North, "and stay away from them. Or else, be a wild man, and get right into the very heart of things. You may last ten seconds, before they begin to shoot. Go along, my lad, if you're that much on fire!"

The Flash rose to his knees.

"Take one of my guns," said he.

"I'll keep it like a treasure," said the other. "But I'd like to know if you have any idea what you're going to do?"

"I don't know," said the Flash. "I've no idea at all. I'm just going to follow my nose, the way Juan did. And I hope that it leads me into trouble. I never felt so much like trouble as I do just now!"

CHAPTER XXXV

He went through the brush with a step as soft as running water which slides down a smooth flume. Among the shadows he was a shadow. He moved, but so did the tree shadows shift as the wind bent the upper branches and set the colorful lanterns swinging.

He saw Sonia's old escort, the admirer whom he had displaced in another day, swinging jauntily through the dance with Minnie Grey, the daughter of old Sim Grey, the rancher. And, as the dance ended and the babble of loud talk and laughter broke forth, while some of the people went to the beer table, and others to the open-air kitchen, and others into the beflagged and bepainted tents of the fortune tellers, and while a pair of jugglers went through their tricks in the center of the dancing canvas, that slender sprite of a gypsy stepped back from the crowd into the deeper shadow at the verge of the trees.

The Flash stepped up behind him. He came so close that he could hear the fellow panting from his work in the dance. And no wonder—after whirling Minnie Grey about for a few minutes! It was as bad as a fast round of boxing.

The Flash took the narrow, sleek neck between his thumb and forefinger, and pinched. He laid the muzzle of a revolver into the small of the gypsy's back.

"Imagine that you're gagged," said the Flash, "because if you make a peep, the hawks will get you, pretty bird!"

The gypsy did not make a sound. He permitted himself to be drawn back deeper into the shadows.

The Flash turned him around and thrust his own face within inches of the other.

"Do you see me?" said the Flash.

The gypsy made no sound. His mouth parted vainly, and closed again. And all his body trembled violently.

The Flash reached behind the right hip of his captive, under the broad, brilliant scarf which was bound about his middle. He found the handle of a knife, warm from the body of the man, and drew it out.

"Now peel off your clothes," said he, "and peel fast."

The gypsy reached up to the button of his jacket, but his fumbling fingers could do nothing.

"Fast!" said the Flash, "and still faster, brother. The night's getting warmer, and you have too many clothes on. Get them off, or no doctor in the world will be able to save you. There's a mighty sudden sickness right at your elbow, brother. If it reaches you, you'll never even ask for help!"

The gypsy became as one inspired. The gaudy clothes dropped from him as though they were an outer shell which could be discarded by a shrug of the shoulders. The hat and the mask followed. A gaunt, pale specter stood before the Flash, shuddering. The boy could hear the light rattling as the teeth of the frightened man struck together.

"You've given your clothes to *me,*" said the Flash, "and when they find out that you've done it, they'll wring your neck, like the neck of a chicken, and drop you into the old Rio Grande to feed the fishes. Here's twenty dollars all in one round piece of gold. Take it with you, and make tracks. Better get south. The Rio makes good swimming, if your hands are not tied behind your back. Get out of here, and get fast."

He waved his hand, the big revolver flashing in it, and the gypsy disappeared in the direction indicated. He went with a rush and a bound, diving into the deeper shadows as though into water, his arms flinging out before him to embrace a surer safety at a distance from this terrible white man.

The Flash favored his departing companion with a faint grin. Then he stepped out of his own clothes and put on those of the gypsy.

They fitted well. Even the slippers encased his feet comfortably. And it occurred to the Flash, with a touch of melancholy, that he himself was not a very big man. Only around his hard, smoothly muscled shoulders the jacket pulled a little.

Then he put on the mask, and on his head the jaunty hat with the flowing, brilliant plume. It seemed to the Flash that he had placed a light on his head, when from the corner of his eye he saw the trail and curve of the feather in the air, always trembling, always alive with every breath of wind.

Now he was ready. But for what?

He hardly knew. He simply felt that he had a ticket of admission into a lion's den. Once his mask fell, every beast would be ready to rend him!

But in there with the swirl of the crowd he had to be.

He walked with an easy saunter from his sheltering shadows, and while he stood on the verge of the circle of the inner light he made himself a cigarette and surveyed the scene with the intimate eye of one about to take part. He was conscious of only one defect in his make-up. Under the pit of his left arm there was weight. More than that, there was a bulge that compelled him to carry his left arm swinging a little free from the body. He hoped that this would not be noticeable. For the rest, he carried the gypsy's knife just where the original owner had borne it. If they scratched him tonight, they would find a wildcat, with both tooth and claw prepared!

The jugglers had finished their exhibition with a few clowning tricks that brought out shouts of laughter. Then they began to circulate, passing their hats, deftly palming the coins as they fell, so that each donor would be made to feel that the rest of the crowd had been cruelly skinflint, and that the reputation of the American for generosity depended upon him.

In the meantime, the music began again, striking into a popular waltz. Waltzes were so written in those days that the feet *had* to step into the swinging rhythm, and the accordion and the complaining violin wailed and sobbed and hung on every beat.

Winter was walking through the number of those who hurried to get on the dancing canvas, and Jacqueline was on his arm.

The Flash was instantly behind the pair.

He did not know what he would do. He was drawn to them as to an irresistible attraction, and the very set of the shoulders of Winter made his fingers twitch and curl.

Winter drew from his breast pocket a handkerchief edged with a thin blue stripe. He brushed his forehead with it, replaced it in the pocket, and the next moment the Flash, edging near behind a passing puncher, had withdrawn the handkerchief dexterously between two fingers—dexterously and lightly —and let it fall upon the ground.

He stepped before Winter and stopped him with a bow. And then, pointing back, he said in broken Mexican: "Is it yours, senor?"

155

Winter glanced over his shoulder.

"Dropped my handkerchief, Jacqueline," said he. "I'll be with you again in an instant."

He turned back. The Flash stepped beside the girl and took her arm.

She looked calmly at him.

"Don't do that," she said in Spanish. "I'm waiting here."

"You're walking on," said the Flash calmly. "You're walking on with me."

She reeled, as a reed sways in the wind.

"Flash!" she gasped. "Flash! Flash David!"

"Come!" said he.

She went because he was taking almost her whole weight, and bearing her forward towards the dance floor.

"Not a step!" protested Jacqueline. "I give you a warning. You have ten seconds before I give the alarm. I'll call out! I'll give them to you!"

"You're better than you think, Jacqueline," said the Flash. "Here we are on the floor—there's the music humming—and here we are two—dancing—you see! Very easy! A little habit turns the trick—"

In the whirling of her mind she could neither protest further, for the moment, nor resist.

Her breath returned. But it still seemed to her that the gaudy lanterns were swinging in a circle, blending together at a dizzy speed. She could not help throwing her mind back to the only other man whose dancing had seemed to her perfection. But this was different. The other was smooth, easy, steady. In the step of the Flash there was a catlike grace, a tiptoe lightness, as though the next instant he were about to bound away.

She looked up at him, and she found that he was smiling, a small and mirthless smile. He stood very straight. The touch with which he held her was not the weight of a feather, and yet he guided her with an incomparable skill through the tangle of the careless punchers dancing.

"It's too late, Flash," said the girl, when she could breathe again. "It's a wild and terrible thing that you've done, to come down here and explain things to me in the midst of such frightful danger as you're standing in. Don't you understand? Fifty people here could recognize you in spite of the mask. They could recognize you because of the way you dance. No one else dances as you do—no one else has yours steps. You're walking through fire! And it's too late. I don't want to hear. Nothing you could say would be any good. After dad—"

Her voice stopped. Her anger rose, and the fire flashed in her.

"Murder, Flash! Horrible, damnable murder! That *that* could be in you—there's no use in words! I don't want to hear! I tell you that my heart breaks when I think of the old days, and what we were to one another. I tell you that I loved you as a brother. And something more! Yes, something more. I *did* love you. And there's an agony in me now, when I think of what you've fallen to! I can't believe it—but I've seen with my own eyes what you've done. Flash, this very minute, my whole heart goes out to you with a frightful pity. You could have been everything, anything. That you've come down here in the teeth of everything—that's enough proof of what you could have been. But for the sake of mercy, don't say a word to me—don't try to explain. Don't tell me that it was only a wild, horrible impulse. I'll be able to think more kindly of you, if you don't speak so much as one syllable of an explanation!"

She finished, and looking up to him she saw that he was still smiling and that his nostrils quivered a little, and the hand which was on his arm felt the stir of his muscles as they gathered, and slipped smoothly, one upon the other.

She had touched him, but she had not touched him in exactly the way she had expected.

"You've lost your wits, Jack," said he. "I haven't come here to explain to you. You're not worth an explanation!"

CHAPTER XXXVI

She looked suddenly away, as one does after receiving a blow, and she saw through the crowd that Winter was standing at the edge of the dancing floor, smoking a cigarette and looking over the crowd with the calm of a perfect good nature.

She felt a thrill of pleasure and of pride as she looked at him, so perfectly the gentleman, so at ease. Some other of the men on that canvas, some of those big, burly punchers, would have made a frightful scene if their lady had been taken away from them by a gypsy, whether with the lady's permission or not. But Winter was not perturbed. His trust in her was too entire for small shadows to fall and darken it, she knew!

And then her mind came back to the stroke she had just received. The Flash had come there not to explain to her—because she was not worthy of an explanation!

He was saying slowly, deliberately—and still his touch, holding her, was not a feather's weight—"You'd pick up the first

157

lie of the first stranger about me. And you'd believe it, against me. You've known me all my life, but you'd take a stranger's word about me! You'd take the word of Winter, yonder!"

"Not one whisper more against him!" she said. "He's tried to defend you. He's the one man to raise his voice in your behalf. Oh, Flash, if you knew what a man he is, you'd wither with shame!"

"He'll wither in hell-fire, for being the kind of a man he is," said the Flash. "But I don't care about you and your affairs. You've known me all my life—saving about a month or so of it! And yet you think that I'd murder a gypsy fool, and then step in on two unprepared men and take a crack at both of 'em."

She gasped.

"Do you deny it?" she exclaimed. "Do you mean to tell me, face to face, that your guns were not found—"

"I'm ashamed that I ever thought you were a friend," said the Flash. "There's no more logic in you than there is in a sparrow. There's no more faith in you than there is in a blue jay. You've dodged yourself out of my life—and I'm damned glad of it. I don't want you in it, and that's why I'm dancing here—so that I can tell you so."

"I'll dance the dance out with you," she said, controlling herself. "It's the last time that I speak to you, and you have another minute or so left to talk yourself out. Say what you please, Flash."

"I intend to," said he, calmly. "You're like the rest of the herd. You think that I'm the sort to drop a gun—one gun, let alone two. If I wanted to slaughter a gypsy, would I sneak into the woods and do it from behind? Do you know me? Have you ever known me? And can you think that about me? When before did I ever take men from behind? I've handled guns. I've faced men. Would I jump at a poor sneak from behind, like a wild beast?"

"Flash," she said, "I'll say this much. You must have been drinking. But your gun—"

"And after killing him," said the Flash, "I was so afraid of what I'd done, that I ran away, and my gun caught on a willow twig and was pulled out of my hand. And I went on and left it behind me! The rest of 'em believed that. But that *you* could believe it, though you know me. And you know that those guns were part of my heart's blood. *I* was so afraid of a pack of yelping gypsies that I wouldn't pause to reach down and scoop up my gun?"

Truth has a certain ring to it. And the girl thought she heard that ring in the voice of the Flash. He had been as one ten thousand leagues away from her, though she danced inside

158

his arm. But suddenly he came nearer in a single leap, and she was aware of him and felt the dead faith vaguely rekindled.

"Flash," she said, "if I could try to make myself understand —but my father, of all men in the world—"

"Who told you that I shot your father?" he asked her.

"Ah, Flash, Flash," she said. "Now you go too far. Are you seriously telling me that you didn't draw the gun—that it went off by accident perhaps—"

"No," he said, "I'm telling you that I was not there. I was sitting beside a sick man. And I could show the man to you here, tonight. I was not there."

She gasped.

"I have the word," she said, "of the most honorable man in the world! Flash, if you deny—"

She pushed herself back from him a little. It was not hard to do, for he made no attempt to hold her.

"Is that fellow more honorable than your own father?" he asked her.

She found her next words dying on her lips.

"Did you have the wit and the heart and the sense to ask your own father if I was the man who dropped him with a bullet?" asked the Flash.

And again, starting to speak, she stopped herself short. If it were not truth, it was incredibly brazen lying, a thing not to be believed in.

And all her old knowledge of the Flash rushed through her mind, and through her heart. He had been as bad a boy as the town possessed, but he never had been a sneak, he never had been a liar. He took his medicine standing up; he always had.

"You didn't ask him," went on the Flash. "You didn't care to. You took the word of that stranger—that honorable stranger of yours! But when you go in tonight, go to your father, sit on the edge of his bed, take him by the hands, look him in the eyes, and ask him in God's name to tell you the truth—tell you if I was the man who shot him down. Ask him, and I know that he'll speak the truth, unless I've been a fool about him, as I've been about you!"

"I want to stop," said the girl, faintly. "I want to stop. I can't dance, and listen. And I've got to know the truth—"

"When this dance is finished, I'll never have a word with you again," said the Flash. "You've said it before, and I say it now."

"The gun in the barn—on the barn floor—I saw where the bullet had struck it, close to the cylinder—"

"Look at my hand," said the Flash. "Is there a bruise on it? Is the skin broken? Could my own Colt be shot out of

159

my hand as easily as all that, without tearing my hand to bits —or else bruising every muscle of it? Look at my hand, and then tell me?"

She stared. The hand was immaculately free from scars, except for an old white one which ran from the palm up the inside of his arm, disappearing under the cuff of his jacket. But she knew how he had acquired that scar. Other men, also, know how he had acquired it, and still others had died while they were acquiring the knowledge.

"You want to know how the guns were stolen from me," said the Flash. "I won't tell you. Because you wouldn't believe, and it would have to do with the most honorable man in the world, the modest fellow over yonder who loves you so—you green-minded idiot!—the plain, outspoken gentleman who can swallow his pain, and almost forget you, some day. It has to do with him. You can believe him—and all his concern about me. But you don't know a whit about his past. You know mine. Ask him about his. If he feels like telling you the story, it'll be a long one. And if he doesn't feel like telling it to you, wait a while, and after you've married him you'll find a few of the chapters in the newspapers one day."

She started to break out into an indignant denial, but he stopped her, sternly:

"Don't answer me. Don't tell me that I'm slandering him. Whatever you may think, think it to yourself. That will be a very small difference to me. There's the end of the music, and it's the end between us, Jack. You've had my life in your hands, and I've had yours. We'll throw the memory of that away. We'll throw everything out of the old times into a junk heap, and turn our backs on it. You've done that already for me. And now I'll try to do it for you. Good-by, Jack."

The music ended in a long drone, and the Flash took her straight back to Winter and turned her over to him with a groan.

She looked after him as he went away. She would have run after him, and caught him by the arm, and made him stop to hear other things that she had to say. But she realized that such a demonstration on her part would call too much attention to the Flash. He had become prominent enough already in the eyes of Winter, who was saying: "Is that an old friend, Jacqueline?"

She wanted to laugh, to turn the question, but she knew that her laughter would be a feeble, shaking affair. Then she thought of saying that it was simply a foolish gypsy, but she knew upon second thought that Winter would realize that, though the other girls of the party might dance with a gypsy, she would hardly do so.

So she said, with a shrug of her shoulders: "It's only a foolish young puncher I know who's decided to disguise himself."

Winter nodded at her. He smiled down on her, also.

"These high-spirited lads—they give us all something to talk about and think about. There's an extraordinary boy, Jacqueline. Look at his step—like a young king among the others. It isn't inches that makes the man! What's his name?"

"That's Dave Shore," she replied.

The name had tumbled suddenly from her lips. She never had heard it before. And then she found that her heart was sinking. She had become involved in wretched lies and deceptions the moment the Flash appeared. Her heart swelled against him. He was not only full of evil himself, but he was the cause of evil in others. Suppose that Winter spoke that name—Dave Shore—to others? They would undeceive him. There was no rancher in that region by the name of Shore, and there was no young puncher either.

And then what would Winter say to her?

She was glad when Dick Mayberry came up and claimed her for a dance though, to be sure, Winter smiled at her departure with the youth.

And Winter himself?

His smile disappeared as he walked through the crowd that swarmed toward the dancing canvas. He passed on into the shade of the trees, and there he found Hank, his subordinate, waiting.

"How's everything?" asked Hank.

His chief did not answer. He merely beckoned, and when Hank came out to the verge of the trees Winter pointed to the form of the blue and crimson and yellow gypsy with the long plume floating beside his head.

"Watch that fellow," he said. "He's no gypsy. Find out what and who he is, if you can. Watch him like a hawk. I have a guess—but no—that's too wild. Watch him as if he were a million-dollar ruby!"

CHAPTER XXXVII

The Flash watched the next dance only long enough to allow his jangling nerves to become a little composed, and then he found his way back through the trees to Old North. He told himself as he walked that he hated Jacqueline Moore

161

with a profound hatred, and that she represented all that was fickle, vain, and light in womankind.

In the green screen of the shrubbery, he found Old North, lying on his elbows like a boy.

"What hunting luck?" asked North, without turning his head.

The Flash sank on one knee beside him.

"Suppose that it had not been I?" he said.

"If it was not you," said Old North, "then I was no better than a dead man anyway. So it was just as well to take things easily and speak to you."

"I've had luck enough," said the Flash. "I've had all the luck that I require. But now what about your own work? What about Winter? There he is before your eyes, and here I am to help you snag him. Why not step out and turn the trick?"

"If I could disguise myself," said Old North, "that would do well enough. We could walk out there and stand beside him, and ram a gun into his ribs, and take him along, perhaps. But you have to understand that he's not alone."

"He has a pair of thugs to help, those fellows, Hank and Jim. But I don't see either of them here."

"I suppose you don't," said Old North, "but they're hereabouts, you can be sure. He'd rather leave his arms and legs behind him than that team of rascals. But there are others, too. That little cowpuncher with the blue patch on his sleeve is one of Winter's men, and that pale-breed over yonder, leaning against the tree and grinning at the fun—he's another of Winter's men, and a damned dangerous one, too. And there are others. I've picked 'em out, here and there. Winter is like a king. He never moves unattended. And the moment that I shuffle out there into the open, they'll spot me as sure as fate by the crook in my spinal column. You can be sure of that!"

The boy sighed.

"There we have him pat!" said he. "We may never have as good a chance as this."

"I'm almost tempted," said Old North, "to level a gun at him out of the shadows, here, and send a bullet through that clever brain of his. Four times before, I've had him under my trigger finger, exactly like this, but I've never been able to fire. And still I'm not able to shoot."

"Why not?" asked the boy.

"Could you?" said Old North, countering.

"Well, I suppose not. But I'm not a law officer."

"No, you're not. But I'll tell you the reason I can't shoot. A bullet to stop that brain of his—a frightful thing to think of! And what we'd all miss, and what the world would miss! On the other hand, suppose that he's finally slipped into a jail, and held, by some miracle, until his trial. Ah, there would be a sight, Flash—Tom Winter twisting and turning, and pouring water on the fire, and sand on the oil that feeds it. Tom Winter preparing his face every morning, and imposing it on the jury all day long. Tom Winter avoiding this danger and that fear, while I heap up mountains and mountains of evidence until his keen lawyer is staggered and begins to turn gray. Tom convicted, at last, and his ringing speech to the judge, protesting, claiming his innocence. Tom appealing to a higher court. Tom sentenced again. Tom lodged in prison, at last—surely they would not simply hang such a brain as his—and then devoting his talents to writing his memoirs. That would be the temptation to which he would have to succumb. For the weak point of every criminal is his vanity. They're all vain. It's because of vanity and a disdain for the drudging way of ordinary humanity that they become criminals in the first place. So Tom Winter would surely write his memoirs, and then we would have a book worth reading! Then we would have Hindu princes, and Arabian sheiks, and dark kings in Central Africa, and blackbirding in the South Seas, and train robberies, and financial frauds on the biggest, most noble, most Wall Street scale. We should have stories about train holdups, too, and the cracking of big fat safes, and the double-crossing of friends, and the murder of enemies. There would be an encyclopedia of crime laid before the eyes of the world.

"And think of my pleasure, my lad, as I sat in my little cottage, somewhere between a hill and a brook, and watched my cows grazing in the meadow, and turned over on my knee the last pages that had come from his wise pen. That would be a way to sit, and dream, and die. That would be one long taste of happiness to fill up the end of my days!"

The Flash, listening to that murmuring voice, gradually understood. The pursuit of Winter had lasted so long that it had become almost a legend, an appetite with Old North. Probably he would curl up and die.

Winter continued in the same hushed voice: "Twenty years ago, in New York City, I arrested a sneak thief, a pickpocket, in a crowd at a theater entrance. He was young. He looked somewhere between eighteen and twenty-five. I took him to the station. He broke down and cried. At least, he seemed to break down. He told me a terrible story about a starving mother in Brooklyn. I was in doubt. I was a veteran, even then, in the detective department; but I was an unknown. I never had done an important thing in my life. The sergeant at the desk believed young Tom Winter, but he sent me with him across to Brooklyn to investigate. On the way, the boy escaped. It was the only time I ever had him inside the doors of a jail!"

"Too bad that you didn't shoot him down as he ran," said the Flash.

"I had my gun poised to shoot," said Old North. "And in those days I didn't miss very often, at such a distance. However, I'm not sorry that I didn't shoot. He's been my liberal education. I was in grammar school, so to speak. He graduated me from a technical college of crime. I sharpened my wits trailing him, trying to solve the problem he set for me. He began as a mere sneak thief. I began as a stupid ordinary policeman. He became a great criminal, trying to fool me. I became a pretty good detective, trying to solve his crimes. Do you see, Flash?"

The Flash nodded.

He was glad that he had listened to Old North, for now his own affairs seemed of less importance. Even Jacqueline Moore no longer made his heart ache so bitterly. For Old North was speaking of a lapse of twenty years! Twenty years had been poured into this work of his, and yet he could lie there calmly, not a nerve disturbed, while he looked out at the man he had pursued so long.

It made the Flash feel his youth; it made him feel an infant in arms.

Old North sat up.

"You were harsh to that poor girl," said he.

"Harsh?" said the Flash. "What makes you think that?"

"Oh, I could tell by the set of your head on your shoulders. And when you came back here, you were miserable and satisfied, the way a man is when he's spoken too much of his mind."

"I only told her the truth," said the Flash.

"Never tell a woman the truth," said Old North. "Never tell anyone the naked truth, because it's always blinding. I would as soon look at the blaze of the sun at midday as to try to glance at the truth—even the truth about myself. You know, Flash, that no matter what we've done, we always treat ourselves in a very Christian manner. That ought to teach us to treat others after the same plan. And every time you hurt another fellow, you hurt yourself."

As he spoke, he leaned gradually forward, until his face was close to that of the Flash.

Now he whispered: "There's somebody standing behind us, inside of that high brush. He's watching. He's listening and trying to hear what we say."

"I'll have a look at him," murmured the Flash.

"Too late!" answered Old North. "Now he's shifted. He's going away."

"By heaven," said the Flash. "I didn't hear a thing, and I still can't see."

"You've been looking at the lights," said Old North, "and most of the time I've had my eyes closed. Besides, seeing in the dark is a trick that takes practice."

"Who could it have been?" asked the Flash, troubled.

"One of Winter's extra pairs of eyes and ears," said Old North, calmly. "From now on, you're in danger and I'm in danger. Great danger for both of us. Whatever we do, we ought to do quickly."

"There's the sheriff," said the Flash, bitterly. "There's the man who ought to be helping us, but the poor fool is on the other side and doesn't know what he's doing."

"Don't call him a fool," said Old North. "Remember that it's Winter who has been operating on him. That's the thing to keep in mind. Now, my advice is that we both get out of this place as quickly as we can. Do you agree?"

"Get out? Leave the place?" said the Flash, his nostrils quivering with anger. "Not until I've had another chance at Winter or his hired men."

"What chance? What possible chance would you have?" asked Old North. "My idea is that Winter already has his suspicions about you. My lad, the one safe thing for us is to get out of here at once. There are too many against us. And the moment that your identity is known, you'll have no chance for explanations. Every man's hand will be against you!"

"Shift your place," said the Flash. "Move further off. There's a good lying-up cove for you. And I'll go out there and try another turn. It's after eleven, already. It's time for them to expect me, before very long—"

Here he was interrupted by the loud braying of a horn, which reduced all the gathering to silence, and then appeared the announcer, bawling out that Sonia, the dancer, would repeat her dance with her partner—it had been asked for and an encore could not be refused.

The music swung through a few bars. Sonia appeared, looking right and left, smiling and gay. But her partner did not come forth.

"It's a call for me," said the Flash, suddenly, "and I'm going."

"Hush, lad," said Old North. "Going out to dance a dance that you never—"

"I know it by heart," said the Flash carelessly. "I've danced the same one with the same girl before this. And I'll do as well as that gypsy sneak thief."

"Flash," said the old man hurriedly, "you're putting your life on the bare palm of your hands and offering to give it away."

"I'm taking my chance where I find it," said the Flash. "That's all. Shift your place over yonder. I'm gone. Good luck to us both! But if I miss you here?"

"You'll find me later at Moore's house," said Old North.

And the boy stepped out into the broad, irregular ring of the lantern light.

CHAPTER XXXVIII

When he was sighted, two or three of the gypsies spotted him at once and shouted to him to hurry. Their voices were angry. A big puncher—that same hawk-eyed fellow who had danced with Jacqueline some time before—caught the Flash by the arm and gave him a powerful swing toward the central dancing canvas.

The Flash wanted to take the cowboy by the throat, but instead he merely laughed, for that was what his part required. And spinning like a top, as though the original propulsion still mastered him, he spun out onto the canvas, caught the beat of the music, and slid into dancing step with Sonia.

He watched her as he came. He saw her eyes flash down to his feet. Then, bewildered, she looked up and started at so much of his face as was not covered by the mask.

In that instant she knew it was not her usual partner; and the Flash was aware that she understood a substitution had been made. However, she gave the thing no serious meaning. Her eyes gleamed. She seemed to enjoy the jest, and as they spun through the first measure it was only at the last step that she realized who he was and breathed the word: "Flash!"

They parted, he swaying to the right, she to the left, with a bewildering pattern of steps. Already applause was coming to them from the direction of the beer table.

And the Flash, watching her, saw alarm, then terror in her face.

He was confident enough that she intended to betray him, that night, as Old North had first suggested. But he could not help admiring the way she now masked her first fear with a smile.

As they spun together again in a whirl of the music, she was saying to him, smiling upward: "Oh, I've been waitin', Flash—"

166

"To collect fifteen thousand on me," said he.

She almost lost her step. He supported her with a strong hand. People standing near the edge of the canvas were clapping their hands in unison to reinforce the beat of the orchestra and to applaud the dancers at the same time; that noise enabled the Flash to say to Sonia:

"But what do I care, Sonia? I couldn't keep away from you. I haven't slept for thinking of you, you treacherous little gold getter. What do I care, Sonia, now that I have you here, dancing!"

The white disappeared. She was rosy again in a moment. And as they separated again for further flourishes she seemed wholly lost in the spirit of the dance, flirting with him, laughing at him over her shoulder.

He scanned the crowd, for his part, since his work for the instant was to be the proud and disdainful lover. And he marked down the face—the octaroon and the fellow with the patched sleeve—who had been pointed out to him by Old North. And there was Winter as well, smoking his cigarette and waving it a little in rhythm with the dance. There was lovely Jacqueline Moore beside him, trying to smile, but looking very pale indeed while her fascinated eyes followed every move of the Flash. The drum crashed into a roll; once more the two dancers were spinning together and he was saying: "Who wrote out the letter for you, Sonia? Who tempted you, poor youngster?"

"You know the whole thing," said Sonia, no longer in fear.

"You're inside of it all, then?"

"Of course I am," said the Flash. "Where is he now?"

"Back at the wagon, of course," said the girl. "He's waiting inside the wagon, of course, Flash. I wish I'd never set an eye on him. I wish you'd crack his head *wide* open, when you slammed him!"

It was Jim, then?

It could hardly be any other man.

As they separated again—it was supposed to be in the triumph of a mutual love this time—it was not hard for the Flash to dance the part. He could not help laughing, and as he laughed he noticed Winter, the narrow white bandage around his head like a sort of coronet, no longer smiling, but intent, with keen suspicious eyes that stared back at the dancer.

Let him suspect as much as he pleased, then. If only the Flash could have two minutes after the termination of the dance—?

It ended, cymbals clashing, the accordion screaming out a high, snorting note. And the Flash ran off the canvas and

167

took his small hat in his hand and passed it around the edges of the crowd. One continuous glittering shower of silver—even some yellow streaks of gold fell into the hat.

To end all, he poured the little treasure into the lap of Sonia. And as the people clapped and applauded him still more, asking for yet another encore, the Flash was off into the dark green gloom of the trees.

He gave only one glance behind him. They were still gathered around the dancing canvas, clapping, waiting for him to return and Sonia was bowing and waving to the applause. He could see her pretty, bobbing head.

He saw the tall Negro also, but not Winter or the fellow with the patched sleeve.

But he could not wait for a second look. He went away through the trees like a wildcat after a rabbit in the white of the winter, when that meager meal means life or death to the beast of prey.

He knew where Sonia's wagon formerly stood, and there he found it again, a little removed from the main group of the vehicles, with the lantern light of the inner circle breaking through the trees only with a faint ray here and there.

The Flash circled it. His hands were twitching. There was such a passion in him that his eyes grew dim, and he had to set his teeth and tell himself, almost aloud, to be calm.

For in that wagon, secure beneath its canvas top, there was one of Winter's tools, one who had hunted him before and who would hunt him no longer, after this night.

So the Flash swore to himself.

Then he began to work out toward the wagon.

He did not come straight on. He slid, instead, from one cover to another, taking advantage of a rock here, and a stump there, and finally of a patch of brush close beside the wagon.

There were obviously only two ways of getting into the wagon. He could try it from the rear, or from the front.

He listened. There was no sound from within. In the distance, the orchestra struck up a valiant tune, but was drowned out by impatient hand clapping. They had enjoyed his dancing so much that they were insisting upon his return!

He grinned, mirthlessly, and stepped from the brush. He put a foot on the hub of the near forewheel, another on the footboard. Gripping the dash and the iron rail behind the seat, he drew himself up by inches, and less than inches. For he dreaded lest the old wood might give out a sound.

His head was high enough now to look into the jumbled interior of the wagon, and at the same moment the iron rail in the grip of his right hand stirred a little and faintly groaned.

Instantly a muffled voice muttered, inside the canopy of the wagon: "Who's there?"

And the Flash saw the loom of a dim figure rising above the clutter inside.

He raised his lower foot to the footboard and dived at the shadow within as a swimmer dives recklessly into deep water. He heard a grunt, saw a dim gleam of steel before his eyes, and then his shoulder went home against the body of the man.

Over they went with a crash, but the hands of the Flash were busy as they fell. He found the throat of the other; and instantly the crook of his right arm had it in a strangle hold.

They tumbled over, hit the little traveling stove, and brought it down in a jangling ruin.

They rolled again, and over the tailboard of the wagon they dropped heavily to the ground.

Sheer grace of luck made Jim with his bandaged head strike as the underman, with the weight of the Flash above him. He shuddered and lay still. The Flash, kneeling beside him, hushed his own panting and listened. In the near distance he could hear them coming, rapid steps, racing through the underbrush heedlessly. They had heard the noise from the wagon, in spite of the sound of the music, which had commenced again. Or was it that Winter already had guessed what was up and was coming now as fast as he could to the rescue?

The Flash snatched out the gypsy's knife. No man ever had forfeited his life more surely than had this scion of Winter. The left hand of the Flash found the hollow of the man's throat. The right hand raised the knife to strike home. But though the fingers tightened, he could not strike.

Jim groaned and stirred, and the Flash shook him by the hair of the head, then pricked him in the shoulder with the knife point.

"Stand up!" he commanded. "Stand up, and come with me. That's it. Walk fast, and straight ahead. If you stop— if you so much as stumble—I'll ram this knife through your back, Jim."

And Jim, without a murmur of response, walked straight ahead, from the side of the wagon toward the nearest brush.

They had not gained it when the rush of half a dozen men gained the wagon.

The Flash heard the rapid but calm voice of Winter directing.

"There's no noise. It's over, then, and Jim has gone west. Show a light, someone."

A match was scratched. Its feeble glow reached, however,

to the Flash and his captive. But it dazzled the eyes of those who stood nearer to it.

The light disappeared, held inside the back of the wagon.

"Gone?" they heard Winter echoing some remark from the man who held the match. "What the devil can that mean? Dead, you mean. Not gone!"

The Flash heard no more. He and his captive had entered the dark of the woods, and just inside the verge he drew out a piece of cord and lashed Jim's hands firmly behind his back.

He heard the gritting of the man's teeth; but there was no attempt to cry out. A sort of pity came up in the Flash, as he thought of the emotions of Jim, hearing the voices of his friends and with every instant passing farther from the help of their hands.

But the touch of the knife appeared to have been convincing. They moved steadily on through the trees. Presently they could make better speed. They crossed a small clearing, and beyond it they came to the place where the two horses had been left by Old North and the Flash.

But there was no sight of either!

CHAPTER XXXIX

The Flash did not pause.

He turned to the left, keeping back in the brush, and hurried big Jim before him, whispering in his ear: "If you let a twig snap under your feet, I'll drive this knife through your backbone!"

And Jim seemed to understand, for he moved as softly as as ghost.

They had headed back toward the region of the greater lights inside the trees, and out of the distance the stir of the music was busier than ever, and the murmurings of the gay voices. Through the branches above them they could see the stars of a cloudless sky drifting in waves as they moved along.

They passed a little jungle of brush, and through it as through a screen they saw three or four men standing, and with the men were two horses.

The Flash did not pause. He could guess that one of those horses was Rags, and he could guess that the watchers were there for him! It was well that he had not paused to search for the missing mare and so come within the range of those guns!

Yet he felt that there was something clumsy here. They might have left the mare where she was tethered with her companion. They might have opened fire, securely, after he was in the shadow. The only explanation was that where he left the mare was the darkest spot in the grove and accurate shooting would have been difficult.

Nevertheless, he had a distinct sense of conquest and superiority. In this respect, at least, Winter had failed.

The Flash went on.

They came into the open beyond the willows. A number of horses were fastened here to the outermost trees, and the Flash did not hesitate. He untethered two of them and assisted Jim to mount, handicapped as the latter was by his bound hands. Thereby the Flash added horse stealing to his other crimes.

But he was not disturbed. He gambled now for such a prize that he hardly cared what he ventured.

They mounted as several men, aparently leaving the festivities in the grove, came sauntering down the line of the horses.

"Hello," said one, as the Flash turned his nag away. "This is where you tied up yours, Joe, isn't it?"

"That's the place," said another voice. "Who's that riding off there? Hello, you!"

"Gallop," said the Flash to Jim. "But not too fast. Remember that I'm right behind you with a gun. And I'd rather have you dead than not to have you at all!"

Jim, obediently, kicked his heels into the side of the mustang he rode, and away they went at a rattling pace while a loud outcry went up behind them.

The Flash groaned. There were good fighting men back there, no doubt, and not the sort to allow horses to be stolen for nothing. As they galloped he looked back, and he could see through the starlight the dim streaks of several riders running after them.

His own horse was a stiff-shouldered brute without an ounce of pace in him. Jim was better mounted, but he had neither hand free to manage the animal. Straight riding would never save them now! And how the Flash yearned for the supple strength of Rags beneath him!

They entered the mouth of a draw where, for a few days during the period of the melting snows, floods raged and had torn out a wide gully with fifty-foot banks on either hand, as sheer as cliffs of rock.

It angled suddenly to the side and the Flash, as he saw the turn, made up his mind. He caught the reins of Jim's mount, checked it, and forced both horses back under the inner wall of the turn, just where the bluff angled sharply back.

The roar of hoofs entered the lower end of the draw, then swept clear, and around the bend came four riders, cursing their horses, lashing them to get them to a greater speed, crouching low over the pommels to jockey them along.

They took the curve wide, forced outward by their impetus. And with never a head turned they dashed on and were lost beyond the next curve, the echoes flying back behind them.

Through the dust-stained air which that cavalcade left floating in the draw, the Flash and his companion rode down to the level, and turning out from it they cantered steadily towards the north. One adventitious peril had been escaped. More, perhaps, lay before them.

Jim began to curse softly. And when the horses stopped to a walk, climbing a steep, sandy rise, he broke out: "You're a cool youngster, Flash. That was an easy trick, but it took nerve. If there'd been one gent with eyes in his head in that lot, they would have swallowed you alive!"

"Not alive," said the Flash, grimly. "I'll never be swallowed alive, Jim. As for their eyes, you're so used to playing with crooks that you never can realize that honest men are two-thirds blind."

Jim grunted.

"That might be straight," said he. "But I'll tell you a thing, Flash. You're a fool to work against Winter. Step over on his side of the line and he'll fix things for you so that you'll be easy. You're his style. He'd gamble a million on you."

"Tell me about it later," said the Flash. "Now we've got to make time. Here's free hands for you. Jockey that horse, Jim."

A touch with a knife freed Jim's hands, and soon both riders were tearing across the level. It was loose sand and the horses sank into it almost fetlock deep in places, but presently they came to a small hollow, with the triangular roof of a shack appearing above the farther rim of it.

It was black and deserted. When the Flash checked the horses here and dismounted, one could see through the skeleton walls the starlight beyond.

He ordered Jim to the ground also and rebound his hands.

"I dunno what's the scheme in front of you, Flash," said Jim.

"You'll see in a moment," said the Flash.

Inside the shack half of the floor was boarded over; the

172

other half had been torn up, apparently by campers in search of fuel. Half the walls and the fallen roof of the shack had gone the same way. And on the bare ground the Flash kindled quickly a little blaze, a mere handful of flame that wavered and flickered weakly.

"You see that fire, Jim?" said the Flash.

"Yeah," said Jim. "You could boil coffee on that, I guess."

"You couldn't melt steel, though," said the Flash.

"Not by a mile."

"But you could melt the heart out of men with that," suggested the Flash.

Jim was silent.

In the dull firelight, his eyes had grown big as the eyes of a frightened animal.

"I've got some paper with me," said the Flash, "and I've got a stub of indelible pencil. My aim is to have you write out what I ask you to write. My aim is to have you date it and sign it. What do you say to that?"

Jim shuddered so violently that his teeth clashed together.

"Winter would tear me to bits!" said he.

"Otherwise," said the Flash, "I'll feed you into the fire feet first, Jim."

Jim attempted to laugh. The hollow sound ended abruptly.

"You're too straight a boy for that sort of dirty work, Flash," said he.

"You've framed me and double-crossed me," said the Flash. "You laid low for me to murder me this same night. I'll feed you to that fire as willingly as I'd feed a stick of wood. I'm not giving you till I count to ten. I'm asking you now. D'you hear?"

He stepped closer to the big man, and Jim for one instant wavered. Then he broke down with a groan.

"I'm beat," he said. "Turn one hand free and I'll write."

"Take both hands," said the Flash, liberating him again. "Take both hands. It might help you to think the thing out. There's no hurry. There you are. Sit down there where the fire will give you a better light. Here's a board for a desk top. Here's the pencil. Now begin. Tom Winter is alias who?"

"Alias?" said Jim. "Why, I dunno know what alias he might have!"

"You lie," said the Flash, quoting a little from the information which Old North had given to him. "Winter was alias Oliver J. Boles, of Liverpool, when you were with him in Shanghai. Is that wrong?"

Jim looked up, gaping.

"Who are you?" he asked.

"I'm the uncle of the devil," said the Flash. "You ought

to have recognized me long ago. He went to school to me. Write down that and a couple of more aliases, and say why he's wanted by what governments."

"Thomas Winter," wrote Jim, "alias Oliver J. Boles, Samuel Richardson Crawford, Raymond Purchases, William Dixon, etc.—"

He broke off writing.

"Look here, Flash," said he, "you don't think that I know everything about Winter, do you?"

"You know enough to please me," said the Flash. "What did they want him for last in New York City?"

"I don't know," said Jim. "Accused him of smuggling or something like that, and—"

"You're lying again," said the Flash. "He's wanted in New York state for the murder of Josiah Clinton, of Albany, and before that, under the alias of Dixon, he was wanted for the killing of Chester Gray. Write the truth and the whole truth, Jim. Do you think that I'm here to play with you?"

"You *are* the uncle of the devil!" said Jim. "Aside from —one man—I thought there was nobody in the world who could tell these things about Winter. Flash, I'll write what you want."

Five minutes later he asked: "And now what? I've got down some of his pet names and what he's wanted for under 'em."

"Write out how he had the gypsy killed."

"Hank killed him. I was down there with Hank, but Hank killed him, and used the gun that Winter had slicked from you."

"I knew it. But I want to hear it from you and to see it in writing. Go on, Jim. And hurry it a little. Write small. That envelope has two sides, but that's all it has, and I need information on it!"

For a moment Jim studied that young, hard-drawn face. And then he began to write, studiously, seriously. Now and again he stopped and drew in a groaning breath. But he continued afterward, shaking his head, as though he already felt the consequences which would pour out upon his head on account of this narrative.

When he had ended, the Flash took the paper. He already had followed the words over the shoulder of the writer.

"There's a horse outside for you," said he. "Take it and get. You'll need to ride pretty far and fast, Jim, to get away from Winter and his gang."

"Ride?" said Jim, bitterly. "I'm as dead now as though the bullet were already through my brain!"

CHAPTER XL

When Winter reached Moore's house with Jacqueline, he said good night to her with a perfect calm, but when he reached his own room he was in a cold fury. Sammy, his huge body servant, crouched in corners, skulking out of the way of his angry master. And when Hank's head appeared at the window, Winter stepped to him and cursed him softly, steadily.

"You found Jim?" demanded Winter.

"We searched the whole woods for him," said Hank. His appearance was a proof of the anxiety and the haste of that search, for his face was scratched and his clothes were torn by the twigs and the thorns which had whipped against him.

But Winter regarded these things without sympathy.

"The Flash was there!" said he. "The Flash was out there dancing in full sight of everybody. And you've let him go!"

"Dancing in full sight of everybody?" gasped Hank. "Now, look here, Winter, I've got a pretty good pair of eyes in my head, and I didn't see any sign of him."

"He was the second gypsy to dance with the witch of a girl. She sold us to him, and she'll learn to repent of it. Damn him! When I think that I had him here in this room—under the muzzle of my gun—"

He made a turn up and down, controlling his passion.

"He's a gone goose," said Hank, to comfort his master. "He's got the fattest price on his head that I ever heard of. He's as good as cooked!"

"Time fights on the side of the honest man," said Winter. "Every minute fights against us. Every second is telling, one way or another. Even the girl—"

He stopped himself short.

"Is she tumbling?" asked Hank, casually.

His master seemed as though about to strike his subordinate, but he controlled himself again. He was sweating with the effort of that self-control.

"Whatever is done is only to be done quickly," said Winter. "Mind that, Hank. Keep close to the house. Watch this window like a hawk. You've played like a fool tonight. You've let him come and go. What about Jim? What could have become of the fool?"

"The Flash must of taken him away," suggested Hank.

"Would he carry him off, as a hawk carries a pullet?" demanded Winter. "And why the devil would he want to carry him away, instead of braining him?"

"He doesn't kill," said Hank, with a nod of the head, but with wonder in his eyes. "He doesn't kill. Not when he has the upper hand. They all say that. There's no murder chalked up against him, except what you've rung in on him, chief."

"Get out of the window," said Winter brutally. "Stay away, but stay close. This night's not ended. It's only beginning. Keep away, but keep a watch. You may need your guns before morning, Hank. The Flash is loose, and I'll tell you this—I'd rather have any six other men—barring one who is dead—than the Flash against me!"

Hank disappeared and Winter, lighting a cigar, sat down in a corner of his room to unsavory thoughts.

He had been sure that the girl was in his hand, in the beginning of his evening. So strong was his position that he could afford to take his time and his ease in Moore's household, convinced as he was that he had silenced the father for good and all.

But on the way home from the gypsy festival he had noticed a sharp change in Jacqueline. She seemed to shrink from him. She looked steadily before her into the blank face of the night, through which the road wound and twisted and arose like a pale spiral of smoke.

It was then that he cast back into his mind for what could have happened. There was only one moment when she could have been touched. He remembered, then, the peculiar smile of the pseudo-gypsy who had danced with the girl and left her pale, with large, strained eyes of fear. He discarded at once the name she had given him for the fellow. It was someone else. It was someone able to touch her to the soul with a few words. And so, out of his hatred of the man, his guess struck upon the Flash.

He tried her with the name, casually.

"He dances well," said he.

"Who?" she had asked, hardly hearing the remark.

"The Flash, of course," said Winter.

He heard the catch of her breath. The sound went through him with a cold touch of pain and a sense of loss. She was not the first that he had pursued. But suddenly he felt that she would be the last. The words he had spoken to her father no longer seemed a lie but the bitter truth—the time had come for him to end his wild ways and to settle down. Old North was dead, of course. With him, the past of Winter was burnt out like a candle. There only remained that slender youth, the Flash, between Winter and the accomplishment of his new hopes.

"How did you know? How did you guess?" exclaimed the girl. "I don't know how you could have guessed that it was the Flash!"

He did not turn toward her, but gathered in the reins of the span he was driving. He did not want to risk a glance, lest even by starlight he should see the lovely outline of her face and the soft glint of her eyes looking up to him, startled and afraid.

"You know, Jack," said he, "that everyone of us has a little touch of divination in his make-up. I suppose that I simply divined it. Besides, who else would touch you so— with pity for him, poor fellow!"

"You didn't give the alarm," she was saying thoughtfully, as though to herself. "That was grand of you, Tom. That was bighearted and kind all the way through, it seems to me. Oh, they would have swarmed on him like wolves!"

"I knew it," said Winter. "But do you dream that I wish the poor lad any harm? No, no! God alone can tell what miseries lie in front of him, before the end. I don't mean the mere death, but I mean the change in his own character, the hardening, the cruelty, the viciousness that will be sure to rise in him. The same qualities that made him attempt the life of your father, Jack. And that's a thing that I still can hardly understand. But I pity the poor boy with all my heart. I wish I could transport him to another hemisphere, another life, another name. However, that can't be done."

He had talked on, easily, with emotion in his voice.

And to himself he smiled a little, thinking of exactly the hemisphere of fire to which he would have liked to transfer the Flash.

She made no answer to that last speech. And he was troubled by her silence more than by any speech. She spoke no more until they were home, and then as they said good night she looked at him distantly, seeing her own thoughts, he knew, more clearly than his face.

It was that parting look of hers that he held in his mind's eye when he was alone in his room. It haunted him. It thrust him through with a chilly, empty sense of loss.

But Jacqueline, in the meantime, had gone straight up the stairs to her room, where she threw off her hat and the scarf that had been over her head. Then she went to her father's room, for a question was seething in her.

When she knocked, he answered at once in a wide-awake voice, and she entered to find him reading. The table lamp beside his bed threw steep shadows beneath his eyes and outlined a mouth that seemed endlessly set to endure pain.

When he saw her, a pucker appeared between his brows.

She was amazed. It was as though the sight of her were unpleasant to him, a thing to be avoided.

She sat down on the chair nearest the bed and clasped her hands in her lap.

"Father," she said, "I've come to ask you an odd question."

A gust of wind struck the climbing vines at the window and rattled the shutters violently, and sent a breath of outdoor fragrance through the room. And Lawrence Moore looked fixedly at his daughter.

"Ask it, then, Jack," said he. "But I'm in no mood for talking."

"Was it really the Flash who shot you that other day in the barn?"

She saw his lips part, his eyes open.

Then he closed his eyes and held them squinting shut. He shook his head a little.

"Jack," he said, "it's a thing that I don't want to talk about."

She got up from her chair and leaned over him.

"You're the straightest and finest man in the world, dad," she said. "But there's something on your mind. I've seen the Flash. He swears that he didn't draw a gun on you. He swears that the gun that was found there and the gun found by the dead gypsy were both stolen from him. He told me to ask you, and that you would never say that he was there in the barn, that day."

Her father lay motionless, staring up to the ceiling.

"You've got to answer," said his daughter. "It's something more than Flash that depends on it. It's you and I that hang on the same answer. If you won't speak, we'll be an ocean apart as long as we live."

She dropped to her knees and took his hand; but Lawrence Moore looked upward into the softly shifting circles of shadow which the reading lamp cast upon the ceiling, altering as the flame breathed up and down in the chimney.

He said nothing.

Another voice spoke in the room, coming closer from the window.

"He'll speak now," said the voice. "You're too square a fellow not to do me right, Mr. Moore."

The girl jerked her head about and saw the Flash coming into the circle of the lamplight. Moore turned his head, slowly, unwillingly, and saw the same dapper form, brilliant in the gypsy costume, the crimson plume floating like an arm of flame beside his head.

"Now tell her," said the Flash. "Did I ever raise a hand or a gun against you in my life?"

Twice the other tried to speak before the sound would come.

At last he said huskily: "Never in your life, Flash. Never in your life—and God forgive me for a cur and a coward!"

"Steady, steady!" said the Flash. "It's a little too much for her."

He raised Jacqueline from her knees and placed her in a chair.

Her head fell back. Her face was white.

"Oh, Flash, what have we done to you?" she whispered to him.

"Stumbled with me," said the Flash.

Suddenly he was smiling at her.

"You've only stumbled with me," he repeated. "I thought tonight that you'd shaken me off, and that I'd shaken you off. But I find that we're only shaken closer together than ever. Is that right, Jack?"

CHAPTER XLI

Lawrence Moore had placed his hands across his face, as though in the darkness of his own making he wished to see more clearly the probable future which his last speech had laid before them. But his daughter and the Flash hardly looked at him.

The color had come back to Jacqueline. She was all in a breathless haste.

"You only meant a part of what you said to me, Flash?" she entreated.

"I meant none of it. I was hot," said he. "I mean, to think of you against me. It wasn't like you. You used to be only against me when the rest were clapping me down. That was why I was so hot. Forget every word I said."

"Not one," she answered. "Every word was true and right. I'm so ashamed that I'm sick."

"And Winter?" he said.

She shuddered.

"I can't think of him," she said. "I don't want to think of him."

"You don't have to," said the Flash. "I'll deal with him."

She clung to his hands.

"I'll never leave hold on you until you promise that you won't go near him tonight," she begged.

"Not by myself," said the Flash. "I have something better for him. I have the law, Jacqueline. I have it in my pocket, and I can use it, use it like a gun at his head. I'm going now—to the sheriff!"

"Flash!" gasped the girl. "Are you quite mad?"

"Not a bit," said he. "Not a bit mad, Jack. I'm going to the sheriff, and in five minutes I'll have him riding beside me with his best men. My hands will be clean. And the sheriff will be damning himself and all the hard work he's put in to catch me."

"Do you mean it?"

"On my honor. I'm going now."

"You can go down through the house. Winter's in bed by now. He went to his room as soon as we came back. Flash, Flash, you should have gone to the sheriff before you ever came near us!"

"I wanted to," said he. "I tried to. But my horse took me this way, it seemed. I had to see you first. By heaven, Jack, since I raked you over the coals, I've been all broken up. In about another second, I'll being making a fool of myself and telling you that I'm in love. I'm going now."

"Good night," said the girl. "It's more like good morning. I mean, it seems the beginning of everything better and finer. It's like a sun in the sky. I'm so happy I could sing, Flash."

"Good night," said the Flash, and leaned to kiss her forehead, as he had done many a time before.

But he found her lips instead, and they both started back, a little astonished, and blushed like two children.

He was still a little dizzy as he left the room and went down the hall. He found the stairs with a fumbling foot. A well of darkness lay beneath, but he was singing under his breath as he went down that pit of shadow.

As he turned at the landing below, into the main lower hall, he thought that he saw a shadow deeper than the others, and it leaned toward him, as it were, from the wall.

"I'm turning into a fool—afraid of the dark," thought the Flash to himself.

And in the next moment he was caught by the throat, and both of his arms were pinioned behind him in the crook of a vast elbow.

So, stunned by the shock, helpless as a half-filled sack, he was jerked from his feet. A door opened before him. And he saw Thomas Winter standing in the lamplight smoking a thin cigar. He stood in bedroom slippers, a newspaper in his hand. It was as though their first interview in that room was now resumed.

Sammy, for it was he who had throttled the Flash, held him securely until Winter had taken his weapons. Then Sammy placed him in a chair and himself crouched behind it. He half encircled the chair with his two great arms, so that on either of the arms of the chair lay one of his vast hands, covered with close red fur. The Flash would be held by something more secure than chains, and a great deal more frightful.

Winter, in the meantime, carefully folded his newspaper and laid it upon the table. He looked at the Flash with a mild eye.

"It was careless, Flash," said he.

The boy nodded.

"I was a fool," he agreed. "You had a man outside, of course?"

"Yes, of course," said Winter. "So that's that. Have a cigar?"

"I keep to cigarettes," said the Flash.

And he made one.

He saw it was the end; he dared not think of the nearness of eternal night. For, as Jacqueline had said, it seemed that a new and more glorious sun had been rising in the sky.

"Leave him the tobacco," said Winter, "but go through the other pockets, Sammy."

Sammy did not come around before the chair. Without rising from his place, blindly he dipped thumb and forefinger into pocket after pocket. There was nothing except a handkerchief—not the Flash's—and a folded envelope covered with writing.

Winter took it and glanced through the contents. Then he sighed and tossed the paper onto the table.

"A good man, was Jim," said he. "He used to give me a great deal of comfort. Not an extraordinary mind," he explained, "but a really wonderful pair of hands. He had the ear of an owl to hear the tumblers fall inside a combination lock; it was a beautiful thing to see him work. And now Jim is gone where better men have gone before him. You'll barely be ahead to show him the way, Flash. And I dare say you're a better man. A much better and greater man than Jim."

It was odd to hear him talk in this manner; as though big Jim were already securely in his power. It was one of the most extraordinary qualities of this extraordinary man that he had no doubt of himself or of the future.

"Thank you," said the Flash. "That's a compliment I know how to appreciate. But I've an idea that Jim will get away from you. He's traveling fast, just now."

Winter smiled and shook his head.

"No matter how fast he travels, I know where he'll go. One of half a dozen places, Flash. A fellow of real intelligence, a real touch of genius, like yourself, would know how to disappear—how to leave all his old haunts, step into a new sphere of life, as it were. But the lower grade cannot do this.

They must go home. Home is wherever they've enjoyed them-selves before. And so I'll find Jim, in due time. There's no hurry. Who wants to kill the fox at once? No, a good run first. You, for instance, have given us a good run!"

The Flash nodded.

"And beaten you, in a way, Winter," he remarked.

"In what way?" said Winter, his voice suddenly hard and sharp as a knife-edge. "In what way have you beaten?"

The Flash smiled in his turn. He raised a finger, slowly, and pointed up.

Winter started. He made two quick steps and stood above the Flash with his hands gripped hard.

And the Flash looked up at him, studying the change in the face. He felt he was so close to the end of life that it mattered little what preliminary dangers came to him. The insouciance of Winter's usual expression had been stripped away and left a hard, brutal face, glaring down at the boy.

"There you are," said the Flash. "I've been waiting to see you. I'll put my bet that not three men in the world have seen you look like this!"

Winter controlled himself, but slowly, with a manifest effort. Then he stepped back.

"Has she seen that?" he asked, pointing to the paper.

The Flash shook his head.

"Then you've done nothing," said Winter, with a sigh of relief.

"You're wrong," said the Flash. "There's a new sun in her sky. I know that you can cover yourself up in the eyes of the law, for slaughtering me. You'll even collect the re-ward—for your men. But it will be murder in her eyes, Winter."

His surety convinced even the man before him. Winter put back his hand, found the back of a chair, and lowered himself into it. He was breathing hard.

"So," he said finally, "so—and that's the end of it, eh? Well, let it go—let it go!"

He made a slow gesture. By that movement of his hand, he seemed to cast something from his mind and heart.

"History repeats itself," said he, "and I suppose that I may call tonight the end of my youth. Tomorrow I shall be an older man!"

He nodded, confirming himself in the thought.

"Your father did the same thing," said he. "Now who is there who can dodge superstition, and say there's nothing in fate? Your father blocked me in the same way. And he died, Flash, as you shall die."

The Flash shrugged his shoulders.

"Let me tell you the story," said Winter. "Perhaps I ought to polish you off now, Flash. But somehow I linger over the job. I'm reluctant."

"But this was the way of it. Long ago I was in the West working at a job of a good size. Let me call it a banking job—work that had to do with banking, at least—"

The Flash smiled.

"And this task," said Winter, "took several weeks. There were so many people to see, so much to arrange, so many instruments, I might say, to prepare. Like any good general, I had to arrange for both advance and retreat. And I was living not close to the bank but a little distance in the country. It was the end of winter. The country was still black with winter cold when I came there, and I used to drive into town every day past a little house which had a hedge of lilac around it, and a path bordered with big lilac bushes leading up to the front door. Spring came on over the rest of the countryside, and it was flowering, but the lilac bushes remained dark and glistening with the winter varnish over the buds.

"It happened that I had to spend a considerable time in the town, and for day after day I was working hard—at the very bottom of things, as you might say, digging and tunneling to get into the heart of the problem—" he paused and smiled at the Flash, and the Flash smiled back with an almost sympathetic understanding. "So when work was about ended, I drove out into the country, relaxed, the reins hanging over the back of my old gray horse. And as I came up the road, I saw a new thing, a spot of color I had not noticed before. It was the lilacs, Flash. They had bloomed while I was away. They were a glory of pale lavender, and deep tones, too. I drew up near the house, and a thin, chilly wind carried the fragrance about me in waves. I closed my eyes, and breathed of it. And when I looked again, straight down the tunnel of bloom, before the steps of the house, I saw a girl standing, all brilliant in white, with a broad-brimmed hat on her head, the color of lilacs, and the hat was tied under her chin with a ribbon that bent the brim inwards. By the Lord, Flash, if you had seen her, then, glowing with the sunshine and glowing with the light inside her, also, you would have thought you were standing on a path of heaven with one of the most delightful of the common or gardening angels, let us say, standing there to welcome you!"

He paused.

The Flash, however, said nothing, but watched his host puff slowly on a cigar.

"So it went on," said Winter, "until one day your excellent father—that honest man!—stopped by in his turn, and leaned his elbows on the gate, and said six words to my girl of the lilacs. And after that, the path was always empty, when I went by. Except for the shadows of the blossoms on the ground."

He stopped again.

Then, briskly, with a change of tone: "So now to business, Flash. Regretfully, too. Had things been a little different, what a pair you and I could have been together! Had I found you a little younger, a little more ready for the molding, or with just a trace less of the blood of that same honest father of yours—"

He broke off.

"Sammy," said he, angrily, "you didn't latch the door. Close it at once and—"

For the door had sagged slowly, noiselessly open; but now, upon the threshold, appeared the gaunt, lofty form, and the wide shoulders, of Skinny Bill Baldwin, with leveled gun in either hand, and beside him, presenting a riot gun, was Trot Baldwin, and behind them appeared the grim, tense faces of Shorty and Rabbit Joe.

CHAPTER XLII

Sammy crouched like a good dog, ready to spring.

But Winter said, quietly: "Not at all, Sammy. I think too much of you for that. Just back up and be a good boy. Put your hands up, as you see me doing!"

He had risen from his chair as he spoke, making a step toward the table. He raised his hands, and the Flash, staring at him, could not believe this miracle of the calm surrender.

Flash's brothers edged quietly into the room, taking good care not to jostle the gun arms of one another. Shorty was taking command. He spoke in a soft growl.

"Stand here, Skinny. Trot, you get over there in the corner behind the pair of them. Rabbit, you get on the right side of Winter. Mind you, boys. If they so much as wink, just blow them inside out. That's all."

"The clan is up," said Winter.

He had laid aside his cigar in rising. But he seemed to be biting a stray leaf of the tobacco between his teeth. The Flash watched him curiously.

"Help yourself, Flash," said Shorty.

"Thanks," said the Flash, and picked his own weapons from

the table where Sammy had laid them. "Shorty, I don't know that I ever was so glad to see your ugly mug!"

"Leave your damn smart cracks out of this," said Shorty, roughly. "Anyway, there's something in blood, but doggone me if I ain't almost sorry that we came, seein' how sassy you still are. I thought I'd see you three sheets cooler in your color, but I ain't had that luck. Watch these thugs, Flash, I dunno that I need to tell you to do that."

He crossed to the window.

"All right, Blondy and Single-jack," he called, though not loudly. "Bring in that other long drawn-out diluted drink of water, will you?"

"That's Hank," said Winter. "I suppose that's Hank, the poor devil. Was he asleep?"

"Not quite," said Shorty, turning back from the window. "But he's close to takin' a long rest, and so are you, and your monkey man, yonder."

"Tut, tut," said Winter. "I'll have no trouble. If you intend murder in cold blood, you'll swing for it, my dear fellows. No, no, you mustn't talk bigger than your credit allows, even among all the whirligigs of this odd little world."

"You forget Jim's few little words," said the Flash.

And he looked down to the table. To his amazement, he saw that the envelope was gone, and he remembered, then, how Winter, in raising his hands, had first stepped forward, close to the edge of the table.

"I have forgotten," said Winter. He swallowed hard. "You might say," he continued, "that I have every word of it inside me."

The Flash understood. That thin envelope could well have been chewed to bits while Winter stood there, apparently so innocent, with his hands above his head.

"We'll have to have something to hold him," said the Flash. "We'll get him to the jail, and then we'll see—"

"Hold him?" said Shorty. "Oh, we've got enough to hold him, until the hangman starts working. This way, boys."

And through the doorway came Hank, securely pinioned. His face was smudged with blood. Apparently he had made some fight, no matter how brief a one, against great odds.

Behind him walked the last two of the seven Baldwin brothers, and behind them appeared none other than the sheriff, Crusty Bill.

He had his hands on his hips, and he nodded and smiled at Winter.

"Too bad, Winter," said he. "You've made a very good play. You nearly won out. But luck, and a trace of somethin' a bit more than luck has beat you."

185

"You're an amusing fellow, sheriff," said Winter. "I dare say this is all a jolly little practical joke."

"Sure, sure," said the sheriff. "Just a joke. Here's the rest of the joke, to please your eyes!"

And he waved to the doorway, in which appeared the small, bowed form of Old North.

Winter jerked halfway around, exactly as a man does when he has received a heavy blow, and the thrust of a keen blade. There was no trace of his easiness left to him, now. And Sammy, gripping the edge of the table and leaning over it, allowed his lower jaw to drop on his chest, while he gaped in horrified bewilderment at the old man.

North was lighting the butt of one of his cheap cigars. He spoke around the tobacco and through the smoke that issued in small wreaths from his lips.

"Why, hullo, Tommy," said he. "I've got a new suit of clothes, since I saw you last. Kind of a quick fit, but how do you like it?"

Winter said nothing. His eye rolled slowly from side to side.

"It was the kid who did it," went on Old North, in the same matter-of-fact way. "He found me burning up in the sun. He salvaged the old wreck and put him in a half-breed dry dock and sort of patched him up to finish the cruise. So here I am, Winter, and it looks to me like the home port at last."

"It looks like the home port," said Winter, nodding slowly. "It looks like the end of the trail. Well, North, it's been a good run, at least."

"A mighty good twenty-year run," said Old North. "You've stood up fine, Tommy. You've stood up like the best fox of the lot. And you've covered enough country. You won't have to cry, now that it's your time to lie down and rest a bit."

"No," said Winter. "I've had my fun. I suppose you have some irons handy?"

"A set almost specially made for you, partner," said the sheriff.

He took the bright steel from his pocket, but Old North shook his head.

"Not iron bracelets, sheriff," said he. "This little pet of mine, he slips handcuffs like feather chains. A cord is the trick. A good stout piece of twine is what I bet on."

"Damn you!" broke in Hank, snarling at his master. "You've hemmed and hawed until you've landed us all in the brig. You've played the fool about a woman once too often."

"Poor Hank," said Winter. "They've hurt more than your head, it seems. They've broken your spirit, as well as your sconce. Very well, North. No objections if I light a last cigar, is there?"

"Not a bit," said North. "Got a match, one of you boys?"

It was the Flash who saw Winter turn his head just a trifle toward Sammy, for he was watching like a hawk every moment, from the rear. He saw the look, but he attached no importance to it.

Trot Baldwin, stowing his guns, came up from the rear and scratched a match, and all attention, from that instant, was focused on the glow of the match, and the singularly calm face of Winter as he leaned to take the light.

So it was that no one heeded Sammy.

No one saw the vast hands curling tighter about the edges of the table, or the stoop of his monstrous shoulders as he leaned a little forward and down.

But now a great shadow seemed to lurch upward from the floor. It was the whole bulk of that table, wrenched upward by Sammy and held poised.

The Flash had his gun upon the second ready to send a bullet through Sammy's body, but the head and shoulders of Shorty suddenly swayed into his way. It was Old North who fired the first shot, but he, in turn, had to shoot with care because of intervening forms, and the bullet traveled high, ripping through the heavy wooden top of the table.

The next moment, with the unhuman strength of Sammy behind it, that bulky missile was flung straight into the crowding group toward the door.

It struck the sheriff and Old North, bowling them over. The end of it collided with the Flash and knocked him spinning toward the wall.

He put out his hand to fend himself away from it, whirled about with the noise of many shots in his ears, and was in time to hear the lamp crash and leave the room in darkness as two shadowy forms rushed through the doorway.

He fired at them, but knew as he pulled the trigger that they were already out of his shooting angle.

Nevertheless, he was the first to reach the doorway; he was the first down the hall, in time to see the front door slam, ponderously.

He reached it and found the spring had caught. He had to fumble one frightfully long second to get the handle in the darkness and turn it, and then, as he sprang out, he had the empty, blank face of the night before him.

Oh, for silence then, to hear the sound of the retreating footfalls!

But down the hall behind him, as through the tube of a horn, roared a vast outburst of shouts and curses.

Out poured the rest of that eager crowd.

They filled the outer night with a wild babel, but the Flash stood still, trying to think, trying to find the surest course to follow, and finding none.

They might have run straight ahead. They might have run back toward the corrals where the horses were kept.

He turned and fled in that direction. He saw the black of the sheds, the spider weaving of the corral fences, and the huddling shapes of the horses inside.

But there was no sign of the fugitives before him. There was no swirl among the horses as someone strove to get a mount.

Had they been so desperate, then, as to trust to their speed of foot in escaping from a mounted pursuit?

Other men came plunging up beside him, shouting questions.

"Ah, you fools—you blithering idiots!" groaned the Flash. "Keep your faces shut, and try to listen! If I could hear one whisper—"

There was a sudden outbreak of shouting and gunfire from the farther side of the house, and in that direction the Flash and the others rushed.

It developed into nothing. Shorty had seen something in the brush, or thought that he had seen something.

And the gunplay had followed.

And that was where luck took its hand against the men of the law, this night.

For, when lanterns were brought, they saw the place at which the trail of two horses left the corral gate. The gunfire on the farther side of the house had given the pair time to get their mounts and steal away.

CHAPTER XLIII

They hunted Thomas Winter and Sammy as no men ever were hunted up and down the Rio Grande, and over to the Devil Mountains, and the south of the river, too, but all in vain.

That night, the two of them vanished from the ken of man. They might have voyaged out into the desert, where a sandstorm buried all trace of their coming or going, before the morning dawned. None of the towns beyond the desert had a sign of them, to be sure.

But, for a week, the riding back and forth went on, and literally hundreds went forth to find the killers.

They were not found. The nets were flung out in vain, and the hot, tired riders came slowly back.

The Flash was not among them. He had not left to join in the pursuit but remained in Moore's house. Or he was sauntering toward the corral, where Rags would whinny to him. She had been found in the brush outside of the house. It was said that Hank had ridden her to the place.

And Hank himself?

He was the one unlucky dog of the crew. Hank remained in the hands of those who had taken him. Jim was gone, and Winter and Sammy were gone. And so was that puncher with the patch upon his sleeve, and the pale-faced octaroon. But Hank was held.

When he came to trial, money mysteriously appeared; a fine lawyer defended him. There was nothing except coincidence and unwitnessed crimes to be held against Hank, and he was sent up for five years—less good conduct!

That was how the tragedy settled in the end. The law did its best, but money and brains counted against it, as they had counted before, and they will count to the end of time.

The Flash, in the meantime, took his ease in the Moore house.

He had a talk with Lawrence Moore the very next day, and had the painful right to sit still and listen to the complete unbosoming of the unhappy rancher.

In that tale he learned of a robbery, long ago, and the penitence of poor Larry Moore ever since. He learned of many another thing, and finally of the bitter surrender which Moore had made to the power of Winter.

Said the Flash, when the unhappy confession had ended: "Why, Mr. Moore, there's only two things to say. One is that I understand every word of it. I don't blame you, the things done, and there's no apology coming to me. The other thing is that Jack had better stay in the dark, so far as this goes. I think I can understand, but I don't think that a woman ever could—not even about her own father. You know how it is, sir. Children forgive their parents last of all!"

So they let it drop at that.

But the important conference came a week later. It was held among Jacqueline, her father, and the Flash. And Shorty, also, was a member at the talk.

What Shorty had to say was quite amazing.

He offered, on the part of himself and his brothers, to take the Flash back to the ranch, under any conditions that he wanted to name. The Flash need not work. He could remain a guest, and enjoy his full share and profits.

"It ain't all charity," said Shorty, when the Flash thanked

him. "But when we sell our beeves, suppose that a fellow says to us: 'You Baldwins any relation of that fellow Flash Baldwin, that the papers been talkin' about?' 'Sure, he's in our outfit, he's only a brother,' says we. And so we make a quick sale, and good sale, because there ain't any time for making a sale so good as when the other fellow is thinkin' half of something else."

The Flash, however, refused. And Shorty left the conference. He said at the door: "It ain't for you alone that we're thinkin'," said he, "but for poor Skinny. He's made a vow that he'll go where you go, and stick where you stick. And when the trail of Winter is taken again, if it ever is, Skinny, he swears that he's gunna ride at your side."

"The trail of Winter is going to be taken," said the Flash. "But when it's taken, I take it alone. You tell Skinny that he's the salt. But where I go, I go alone. And tell Rabbit and Single-jack and the rest that Baldwin blood is red blood, and there's only one kind in all seven of us. God bless you, Shorty, and so long!"

Shorty departed. And he left a silence behind him.

Said Moore, after a time:

"Do you mean it, Flash? Are you going?"

The Flash looked across at the girl, and Jacqueline looked fixedly back at him.

"I'll not go," said he, "without permission. That's fixed."

Then Jacqueline got up and walked to the window, and she saw outside that the trees flashed, and the garden burned with color, and beyond was the desert mist, that shimmered in the sun. It was not the old sun, but the new one, with a greater joy in it, and now she felt that it brought a greater sorrow also.

She thought of the long trail that lay behind Tom Winter, and of all of the perils with which it must be full. And she thought of the Flash also, his young, handsome, smiling face. And it seemed to her that it was lost under a shadow, and lay still and white and dead and changeless.

"Well, Flash," she said, without turning around, "I don't know what to say."

"Listen, my dear lad," said Moore. And his voice was a mere whisper. "You don't need to mark the words. But listen to the sorrow in that voice, and then give her your answer."

"You know," said the Flash, speaking aloud, "that there's another thing. Suppose I settle down here, as you want me to. A fine sort of a husband I'd make for Jacqueline. What would I be? Just a sort of a loafer and an idler, and nothing else—very much! You know, Mr. Moore, that I'm not a good rancher, or even a good cowpuncher."

"You're yourself, Flash," said Mr. Lawrence Moore. "And that's enough for us."

"Is it?" said the Flash. "Well, I know. My self is enough for Saturday nights, when the work's done. But I wouldn't do so well for blue Mondays."

"And what will you do out there in the world?" asked Lawrence Moore.

"Ah, I don't know," brooded the Flash. "I suppose I'll try to find—"

"Well, there you are! You'll try to find what?" asked Lawrence Moore.

"Myself!" said the Flash.

He looked across the room.

"It's up to you, Jack, after all," he said to the girl. "What do you say, old fellow?"

She swallowed. She tried her vocal chords in silence, and made sure that she could speak.

"Well, we can't leave out another thing," said she.

"What thing? What thing?" asked her father, impatiently.

"His honor—and his father," said the girl.

Now, at those two words, joined together, Lawrence Moore felt a sudden choking in his throat and looked down at the floor. And Jacqueline dared not turn around. She tried to hum a tune; it came quaveringly forth, and looking out through the trees of the garden she saw a cloud shadow sweep across the hollow, and lighter than wings slip up the farther hill, and over its crest, and forever out of her view.